A Nobleman's Nest

Ivan Turgenev

A Nobleman's Nest

The present edition is a reproduction of previous publication of this classic work. Minor typographical errors may have been corrected without note; however, for an authentic reading experience the spelling, punctuation, and capitalization have been retained from the original text.

ISBN: 978-1-63637-848-0

A NOBLEMAN'S NEST

I

The brilliant, spring day was inclining toward the evening, tiny rose-tinted cloudlets hung high in the heavens, and seemed not to be floating past, but retreating into the very depths of the azure.

In front of the open window of a handsome house, in one of the outlying streets of O*** the capital of a Government, sat two women; one fifty years of age, the other seventy years old, and already aged.

The former was named Márya Dmítrievna Kalítin. Her husband, formerly the governmental procurator, well known in his day as an active official—a man of energetic and decided character, splenetic and stubborn—had died ten years previously. He had received a fairly good education, had studied at the university, but, having been born in a poverty-stricken class of society, he had early comprehended the necessity of opening up a way for himself, and of accumulating money. Márya Dmítrievna had married him for love; he was far from uncomely in appearance, he was clever, and, when he chose, he could be very amiable. Márya Dmítrievna (her maiden name had been Péstoff) had lost her parents in early childhood, had spent several years in Moscow, in a government educational institute, and, on returning thence, had lived fifty versts from O***, in her native village, Pokróvskoe, with her aunt and her elder brother. This brother soon removed to Petersburg on service, and kept his sister and his aunt on short commons, until his sudden death put an end to his career. Márya Dmítrievna inherited Pokróvskoe, but did not live there long; during the second year after her marriage to Kalítin, who succeeded in conquering her heart in the course of a few days, Pokróvskoe was exchanged for another estate, much more profitable, but ugly and without a manor-house, and, at the same time, Kalítin acquired a house in the town of O***, and settled down there permanently with his wife. A large garden was attached to the house; on one side, it joined directly on to the open fields, beyond the town. Kalítin,—who greatly disliked the stagnation of the country,—had evidently made up his mind, that there was no reason for dragging out existence on the estate. Márya Dmítrievna, many a time, in her own mind regretted her pretty Pokróvskoe, with its merry little stream, its broad meadows, and

1

verdant groves; but she opposed her husband in nothing, and worshipped his cleverness and knowledge of the world. But when, after fifteen years of married life, he died, leaving a son and two daughters, Márya Dmítrievna had become so wonted to her house, and to town life, that she herself did not wish to leave O***.

In her youth, Márya Dmítrievna had enjoyed the reputation of being a pretty blonde, and at the age of fifty her features were not devoid of attraction, although they had become somewhat swollen and indefinite in outline. She was more sentimental than kind, and even in her mature age she had preserved the habits of her school-days; she indulged herself, was easily irritated, and even wept when her ways were interfered with; on the other hand, she was very affectionate and amiable, when all her wishes were complied with, and when no one contradicted her. Her house was one of the most agreeable in the town. Her fortune was very considerable, not so much her inherited fortune, as that acquired by her husband. Both her daughters lived with her; her son was being educated at one of the best government institutions in Petersburg.

The old woman, who was sitting by the window with Márya Dmítrievna, was that same aunt, her father's sister, with whom she had spent several years, in days gone by, at Pokróvskoe. Her name was Márfa Timoféevna Péstoff. She bore the reputation of being eccentric, had an independent character, told the entire truth to every one, straight in the face, and, with the most scanty resources, bore herself as though she possessed thousands. She had not been able to endure the deceased Kalítin, and as soon as her niece married him, she retired to her tiny estate, where she lived for ten whole years in the hen-house of a peasant. Márya Dmítrievna was afraid of her. Black-haired and brisk-eyed even in her old age, tiny, sharp-nosed Márfa Timoféevna walked quickly, held herself upright, and talked rapidly and intelligibly, in a shrill, ringing voice. She always wore a white cap and a white jacket.

"What art thou doing that for?—" she suddenly inquired of Márya Dmítrievna.—"What art thou sighing about, my mother?"

"Because," said the other.—"What wonderfully beautiful clouds!"

"So, thou art sorry for them, is that it?"

Márya Dmítrievna made no reply.

"Isn't that Gedeónovsky coming yonder?"—said Márfa Timoféevna, briskly moving her knitting-needles (she was knitting a huge, motley-hued scarf). "He might keep thee company in sighing,—or, if not, he might tell us some lie or other."

"How harshly thou always speakest about him! Sergyéi Petróvitch is an—estimable man."

2

"Estimable!" repeated the old woman reproachfully.

"And how devoted he was to my dead husband!" remarked Márya Dmítrievna;—"to this day, I cannot think of it with indifference."

"I should think not! he pulled him out of the mire by his ears,"—growled Márfa Timoféevna, and her knitting-needles moved still more swiftly in her hands.

"He looks like such a meek creature,"—she began again,—"his head is all grey, but no sooner does he open his mouth, than he lies or calumniates. And he's a State Councillor, to boot! Well, he's a priest's son: and there's nothing more to be said!"

"Who is without sin, aunty? Of course, he has that weakness. Sergyéi Petróvitch received no education,—of course he does not speak French; but, say what you will, he is an agreeable man."

"Yes, he's always licking thy hand. He doesn't talk French,—what a calamity! I'm not strong on the French 'dialect' myself. 'T would be better if he did not speak any language at all: then he wouldn't lie. But there he is, by the way—speak of the devil,—" added Márfa Timoféevna, glancing into the street.—"There he strides, thine agreeable man. What a long-legged fellow, just like a stork."

Márya Dmítrievna adjusted her curls. Márfa Timoféevna watched her with a grin.

"Hast thou not a grey hair there, my mother? Thou shouldst scold thy Paláshka. Why doesn't she see it?"

"Oh, aunty, you're always so...." muttered Márya Dmítrievna, with vexation, and drummed on the arm of her chair with her fingers.

"Sergyéi Petróvitch Gedeónovsky!" squeaked a red-cheeked page-lad, springing in through the door.

II

There entered a man of lofty stature, in a neat coat, short trousers, grey chamois-skin gloves, and two neckties—one black, on top, and the other white, underneath. Everything about him exhaled decorum and propriety, beginning with his good-looking face and smoothly brushed temple-curls, and ending with his boots, which had neither heels nor squeak. He bowed first to the mistress of the house, then to Márfa Timoféevna, and slowly drawing off his gloves, took Márya Dmítrievna's hand. After kissing it twice in succession, with respect, he seated himself, without haste, in an arm-chair, and said with a smile, as he rubbed the very tips of his fingers:

"And is Elizavéta Mikhaílovna well?"

"Yes,"—replied Márya Dmítrievna,—"she is in the garden."

"And Eléna Mikhaílovna?"

"Lyénotchka is in the garden also. Is there anything new?"

"How could there fail to be, ma'am, how could there fail to be,"—returned the visitor, slowly blinking his eyes, and protruding his lips. "Hm! ... now, here's a bit of news, if you please, and a very astounding bit: Lavrétzky, Feódor Ivánitch, has arrived."

"Fédya?"—exclaimed Márfa Timoféevna.—"But come now, my father, art not thou inventing that?"

"Not in the least, ma'am, I saw him myself."

"Well, that's no proof."

"He has recovered his health finely,"—went on Gedeónovsky, pretending not to hear Márfa Timoféevna's remark:—"he has grown broader in the shoulders, and the rosy colour covers the whole of his cheeks."

"He has recovered his health,"—ejaculated Márya Dmítrievna, with pauses:—"that means, that he had something to recover from?"

"Yes, ma'am,"—returned Gedeónovsky:—"Any other man, in his place, would have been ashamed to show himself in the world."

"Why so?"—interrupted Márfa Timoféevna;—"what nonsense is this? A man returns to his native place—what would you have him do with himself? And as if he were in any way to blame!"

"The husband is always to blame, madam, I venture to assure you, when the wife behaves badly."

"Thou sayest that, my good sir, because thou hast never been married thyself." Gedeónovsky smiled in a constrained way.

"Permit me to inquire," he asked, after a brief pause,—"for whom is that very pretty scarf destined?"

Márfa Timoféevna cast a swift glance at him.

4

"It is destined"—she retorted,—"for the man who never gossips, nor uses craft, nor lies, if such a man exists in the world. I know Fédya well; his sole fault is, that he was too indulgent to his wife. Well, he married for love, and nothing good ever comes of those love-marriages,"—added the old woman, casting a sidelong glance at Márya Dmítrievna, and rising.—"And now, dear little father, thou mayest whet thy teeth on whomsoever thou wilt, only not on me; I'm going away, I won't interfere."—And Márfa Timoféevna withdrew.

"There, she is always like that,"—said Márya Dmítrievna, following her aunt with her eyes:—"Always!"

"It's her age! There's no help for it, ma'am!" remarked Gedeónovsky.—"There now, she permitted herself to say: 'the man who does not use craft.' But who doesn't use craft nowadays? it's the spirit of the age. One of my friends, a very estimable person, and, I must tell you, a man of no mean rank, was wont to say: that 'nowadays, a hen approaches a grain of corn craftily—she keeps watching her chance to get to it from one side.' But when I look at you, my lady, you have a truly angelic disposition; please to favour me with your snow-white little hand."

Márya Dmítrievna smiled faintly, and extended her plump hand, with the little finger standing out apart, to Gedeónovsky. He applied his lips to it, and she moved her arm-chair closer to him, and bending slightly toward him, she asked in a low tone:

"So, you have seen him? Is he really—all right, well, cheerful?"

"He is cheerful, ma'am; all right, ma'am," returned Gedeónovsky, in a whisper.

"And you have not heard where his wife is now?"

"She has recently been in Paris, ma'am; now, I hear, she has removed to the kingdom of Italy."

"It is dreadful, really,—Fédya's position; I do not know how he can endure it. Accidents do happen, with every one, in fact; but he, one may say, has been advertised all over Europe."

Gedeónovsky sighed.

"Yes, ma'am; yes, ma'am. Why, she, they say, has struck up acquaintance with artists, and pianists, and, as they call it in their fashion, with lions and wild beasts. She has lost her shame, completely...."

"It is very, very sad,"—said Márya Dmítrievna:—"on account of the relationship; for you know, Sergyéi Petróvitch, he's my nephew, once removed."

"Of course, ma'am; of course, ma'am. How could I fail to be aware of everything which relates to your family? Upon my word, ma'am!"

5

"Will he come to see us,—what do you think?"

"We must assume that he will, ma'am; but I hear, that he is going to his country estate."

Márya Dmítrievna cast her eyes heavenward.

"Akh, Sergyéi Petróvitch, when I think of it, how circumspectly we women must behave!"

"There are different sorts of women, Márya Dmítrievna. Unfortunately, there are some of fickle character ... well, and it's a question of age, also; then, again, the rules have not been inculcated in their childhood." (Sergyéi Petróvitch pulled a checked blue handkerchief out of his pocket, and began to unfold it).—"Such women exist, of course," (Sergyéi Petróvitch raised a corner of the handkerchief to his eyes, one after the other),—"but, generally speaking, if we take into consideration, that is.... There is an unusual amount of dust in town," he concluded.

"Maman, maman"—screamed a pretty little girl of eleven, as she rushed into the room:—"Vladímir Nikoláitch is coming to our house on horseback!"

Márya Dmítrievna rose; Sergyéi Petróvitch also rose and bowed:—"Our most humble salute to Eléna Mikhaílovna," he said, and withdrawing into a corner, out of propriety, he began to blow his long and regularly-formed nose.

"What a splendid horse he has!—" went on the little girl.—"He was at the gate just now, and told Liza and me, that he would ride up to the porch."

The trampling of hoofs became audible; and a stately horseman, on a fine brown steed, made his appearance in the street, and halted in front of the open window.

6

III

"Good afternoon, Márya Dmítrievna!"—exclaimed the horseman, in a ringing, agreeable voice.—"How do you like my new purchase?"

Márya Dmítrievna went to the window.

"Good afternoon, Woldemar! Akh, what a magnificent horse! From whom did you buy it?"

"From the remount officer.... He asked a high price, the robber!"

"What is its name?"

"Orlando.... But that's a stupid name; I want to change it.... Eh bien, eh bien, mon garçon.... What a turbulent beast!" The horse snorted, shifted from foot to foot, and tossed his foaming muzzle.

"Pat him, Lénotchka, have no fears...."

The little girl stretched her hand out of the window, but Orlando suddenly reared up, and leaped aside. The rider did not lose control, gripped the horse with his knees, gave him a lash on the neck with his whip, and, despite his opposition, placed him once more in front of the window.

"Prenez garde! prenez garde!"—Márya Dmítrievna kept repeating.

"Pat him, Lyénotchka,"—returned the rider,—"I will not permit him to be wilful."

Again the little girl stretched forth her hand, and timidly touched the quivering nostrils of Orlando, who trembled incessantly and strained at the bit.

"Bravo!"—exclaimed Márya Dmítrievna,—"and now, dismount, and come in."

The horseman turned his steed round adroitly, gave him the spurs, and after dashing along the street at a brisk gallop, rode into the yard. A minute later, he ran in through the door of the anteroom into the drawing-room, flourishing his whip; at the same moment, on the threshold of another door, a tall, graceful, black-haired girl of nineteen—Márya Dmítrievna's eldest daughter, Liza—made her appearance.

7

IV

The young man, with whom we have just made the reader acquainted, was named Vladímir Nikoláitch Pánshin. He served in Petersburg, as an official for special commissions, in the Ministry of the Interior. He had come to the town of O*** to execute a temporary governmental commission, and was under the command of Governor-General Zonnenberg, to whom he was distantly related. Pánshin's father, a staff-captain of cavalry on the retired list, a famous gambler, a man with a crumpled visage and a nervous twitching of the lips, had passed his whole life in the society of people of quality, had frequented the English Clubs in both capitals, and bore the reputation of an adroit, not very trustworthy, but charming and jolly fellow. In spite of his adroitness, he found himself almost constantly on the very verge of indigence, and left behind him to his only son a small and impaired fortune. On the other hand, he had, after his own fashion, taken pains with his education: Vladímir Nikoláitch spoke French capitally, English well, and German badly; but it is permissible to let fall a German word in certain circumstances—chiefly humorous,—"c'est même très chic," as the Petersburg Parisians express themselves. Vladímir Nikoláitch already understood, at the age of fifteen, how to enter any drawing-room whatever without embarrassment, how to move about in it agreeably, and to withdraw at the proper time. Pánshin's father had procured for his son many influential connections; as he shuffled the cards between two rubbers, or after a successful capture of all the tricks, he let slip no opportunity to drop a nice little word about his "Volódka" to some important personage who was fond of social games. On his side, Vladímir Nikoláitch, during his stay in the university, whence he emerged with the rank of actual student, made acquaintance with several young men of quality, and became a frequenter of the best houses. He was received gladly everywhere; he was extremely good-looking, easy in his manners, entertaining, always well and ready for everything; where it was requisite, he was respectful; where it was possible, he was insolent, a capital companion, un charmant garçon. The sacred realm opened out before him. Pánshin speedily grasped the secret of the science of society; he understood how to imbue himself with genuine respect for its decrees; he understood how, with half-bantering gravity, to busy himself with nonsense and assume the appearance of regarding everything serious as trivial; he danced exquisitely, he dressed in English style. In a short time he became renowned as

8

one of the most agreeable and adroit young men in Petersburg. Pánshin was, in reality, very adroit,—no less so than his father: but he was, also, very gifted. He could do everything: he sang prettily, he drew dashingly, he wrote verses, he acted very far from badly on the stage. He had only just passed his twenty-eighth birthday, but he was already Junior Gentleman of the Emperor's bedchamber, and had a very tolerable rank. Pánshin firmly believed in himself, in his brains, in his penetration; he advanced boldly and cheerfully, at full swing; his life flowed along as on oil. He was accustomed to please everybody, old and young, and imagined that he was a judge of people, especially of women: he did know well their everyday weaknesses. As a man not a stranger to art, he felt within him both fervour, and some enthusiasm, and rapture, and in consequence of this he permitted himself various deviations from the rules: he caroused, he picked up acquaintance with persons who did not belong to society, and, in general, maintained a frank and simple demeanour; but in soul he was cold and cunning, and in the midst of the wildest carouse his clever little brown eye was always on guard, and watching; this bold, this free young man could never forget himself and get completely carried away. To his honour it must be said, that he never bragged of his conquests. He had hit upon Márya Dmítrievna's house immediately on his arrival in O***, and had promptly made himself entirely at home there. Márya Dmítrievna fairly adored him.

Pánshin amiably saluted all who were in the room, shook hands with Márya Dmítrievna and Lizavéta Mikhaílovna, lightly tapped Gedeónovsky on the shoulder, and whirling round on his heels, caught Lyénotchka by the head, and kissed her on the brow.

"And you are not afraid to ride such a vicious horse?"—Márya Dmítrievna asked him.

"Good gracious! it is a very peaceable beast; but I'll tell you what I am afraid of: I'm afraid to play preference with Sergyéi Petróvitch; last night, at the Byelenítzyns', he won my last farthing."

Gedeónovsky laughed a shrill and servile laugh: he fawned on the brilliant young official from Petersburg, the pet of the governor. In his conversations with Márya Dmítrievna, he frequently alluded to Pánshin's remarkable capacities. "For why should not I praise him?" he argued. "The young man is making a success in the highest sphere of life, discharges his service in an exemplary manner, and is not the least bit proud." Moreover, even in Petersburg Pánshin was considered an energetic official: he got through an immense amount of work; he alluded to it jestingly, as is befitting a fashionable man who attaches no particular importance to his labours, but he was

9

"an executor." The higher officials love such subordinates; he never had the slightest doubt himself, that, if he so wished, he could become a Minister in course of time.

"You are pleased to say that I beat you at cards,"—remarked Gedeónovsky:—"but who was it that won twelve rubles from me last week? and besides...."

"Villain, villain," Pánshin interrupted him, with a caressing but almost disdainful carelessness, and without paying any further attention to him, he stepped up to Liza.

"I have not been able to find the overture of 'Oberon' here," he began:—"Mme. Byelenítzyn was merely boasting, that she had all the classical music,—as a matter of fact, she has nothing except polkas and waltzes; but I have already written to Moscow, and within a week I shall have that overture. By the way,"—he continued,—"I wrote a new romance yesterday; the words also are my own. Would you like to have me sing it for you? I do not know how it has turned out; Mme. Byelenítzyn thought it extremely charming, but her words signify nothing,—I wish to know your opinion. However, I think it will be better later on...."

"Why later on?"—interposed Márya Dmítrievna:—"Why not now?"

"I obey, ma'am,"—said Pánshin, with a certain bright, sweet smile, which was wont to appear on his face, and suddenly to vanish,—pushed forward a chair with his knee, seated himself at the piano, and after striking several chords, he began to sing, clearly enunciating the words, the following romance:

> The moon floats high above the earth
> Amid the clouds so pale;
> But from the crest of the sea surge moveth
> A magic ray.
> The sea of my soul hath acknowledged thee
> To be its moon,
> And 't is moved,—in joy and in sorrow,—
> By thee alone.
> With the anguish of love, the anguish of dumb aspirations,
> The soul is full;
> I suffer pain.... But thou from agitation art as free
> As that moon.

Pánshin sang the second couplet with peculiar expression and force; the surging of the waves could be heard in the tempestuous accompaniment. After the words: "I suffer pain...." he heaved a slight sigh, dropped his eyes, and lowered his voice,—morendo.

When he had finished, Liza praised the motive, Márya Dmítrievna said: "It is charming;"—while Gedeónovsky even shouted: "Ravishing! both poetry and harmony are equally ravishing!..." Lyénotchka, with childish adoration, gazed at the singer. In a word, the composition of the youthful dilettante pleased all present extremely; but outside of the door of the drawing-room, in the anteroom, stood an elderly man, who had just arrived, to whom, judging by the expression of his downcast face and the movement of his shoulders, Pánshin's romance, charming as it was, afforded no pleasure. After waiting a while, and whisking the dust from his boots with a coarse handkerchief, this man suddenly screwed up his eyes, pressed his lips together grimly, bent his back, which was already sufficiently bowed without that, and slowly entered the drawing-room.

"Ah! Christofór Feódoritch, good afternoon!"—Pánshin was the first of all to exclaim, and sprang hastily from his seat.—"I had no suspicion that you were here,—I could not, on any account, have made up my mind to sing my romance in your presence. I know that you do not care for frivolous music."

"I vas not listening," remarked the newcomer, in imperfect Russian, and having saluted all, he remained awkwardly standing in the middle of the room.

"Have you come, Monsieur Lemm,"—said Márya Dmítrievna,— "to give a music lesson to Liza?"

"No, not to Lisaféta Mikhaílovna, but to Eléna Mikhaílovna."

"Ah! Well,—very good. Lyénotchka, go upstairs with Monsieur Lemm."

The old man was on the point of following the little girl, but Pánshin stopped him.

"Do not go away after the lesson, Christofór Feódoritch,"—he said:—"Lizavéta Mikhaílovna and I will play a Beethoven sonata for four hands."

The old man muttered something, but Pánshin went on in German, pronouncing his words badly:

"Lizavéta Mikhaílovna has shown me the spiritual cantata which you presented to her—'tis a very fine thing! Please do not think that I am incapable of appreciating serious music,—quite the contrary: it is sometimes tiresome, but, on the other hand, it is very beneficial."

The old man crimsoned to his very ears, cast a sidelong glance at Liza, and hastily left the room.

Márya Dmítrievna requested Pánshin to repeat the romance; but he declared, that he did not wish to wound the ears of the learned German, and proposed to Liza that they should occupy

11

themselves with the Beethoven sonata. Then Márya Dmítrievna sighed, and in her turn, proposed to Gedeónovsky that he should take a stroll in the garden with her.—"I wish,"—she said, "to talk and take counsel with you still further, over our poor Fédya." Gedeónovsky grinned, bowed, took up—with two fingers, his hat, and his gloves neatly laid on its brim, and withdrew, in company with Márya Dmítrievna. Pánshin and Liza were left alone in the room; she fetched the sonata, and opened it; both seated themselves, in silence, at the piano.—From above, the faint sounds of scales, played by Lyénotchka's uncertain little fingers, were wafted to them.

V

Christopher-Theodore-Gottlieb Lemm was born in the year , in
the kingdom of Saxony, in the town of Chemnitz, of poor musicians.
His father played the French horn, his mother the harp; he himself,
at the age of five, was already practising on three different
instruments. At eight years of age he became an orphan, and at the
age of ten he began to earn a bit of bread for himself by his art. For a
long time he led a wandering life, played everywhere—in inns, at
fairs, and at peasant weddings and at balls; at last, he got into an
orchestra, and rising ever higher and higher, he attained to the post
of director. He was rather a poor executant; but he possessed a
thorough knowledge of music. At the age of twenty-eight he
removed to Russia. He was imported by a great gentleman, who
himself could not endure music, but maintained an orchestra as a
matter of pride. Lemm lived seven years with him, in the capacity of
musical conductor, and left him with empty hands; the gentleman
was ruined, and wished to give him a note of hand, but afterward
refused him even this,—in a word, did not pay him a farthing.
People advised him to leave the country: but he was not willing to
return home in poverty from Russia, from great Russia, that gold-
mine of artists; he decided to remain, and try his luck. For the space
of twenty years he did try his luck: he sojourned with various gentry,
he lived in Moscow and in the capitals of various governments, he
suffered and endured a great deal, he learned to know want, he
floundered like a fish on the ice; but the idea of returning to his
native land never abandoned him in the midst of all these calamities
to which he was subjected; it alone upheld him. But it did not suit
Fate to render him happy with this last and first joy: at the age of
fifty, ill, prematurely infirm, he got stranded in the town of O***
and there remained for good, having finally lost all hope of quitting
the Russia which he detested, and managing, after a fashion, to
support his scanty existence by giving lessons. Lemm's external
appearance did not predispose one in his favour. He was small of
stature, round-shouldered, with shoulder-blades which projected
crookedly, and a hollow chest, with huge, flat feet, with pale-blue
nails on the stiff, unbending fingers of his sinewy, red hands; he had
a wrinkled face, sunken cheeks, and tightly-compressed lips, that he
was incessantly moving as though chewing, which, added to his
customary taciturnity, produced an almost malevolent impression;
his grey hair hung in elf-locks over his low brow; his tiny,
motionless eyes smouldered like coals which had just been
13

extinguished; he walked heavily, swaying his clumsy body from side to side at every step. Some of his movements were suggestive of the awkward manner in which an owl in a cage plumes itself when it is conscious that it is being watched, though it itself hardly sees anything with its huge, yellow, timorously and dozily blinking eyes. Confirmed, inexorable grief had laid upon the poor musician its ineffaceable seal, had distorted and disfigured his already ill-favoured figure; but for any one who knew enough not to stop at first impressions, something unusual was visible in this half-wrecked being. A worshipper of Bach and Handel, an expert in his profession, gifted with a lively imagination, and with that audacity of thought which is accessible only to the German race, Lemm, in course of time—who knows?—might have entered the ranks of the great composers of his native land, if life had led him differently; but he had not been born under a fortunate star! He had written a great deal in his day—and he had not succeeded in seeing a single one of his compositions published; he had not understood how to set about the matter in the proper way, to cringe opportunely, to bustle at the right moment. Once, long, long ago, one of his admirers and friends, also a German and also poor, had published two of his sonatas at his own expense,—and the whole edition remained in the cellars of the musical shops; they had vanished dully, without leaving a trace, as though some one had flung them into the river by night. At last Lemm gave up in despair; moreover, his years were making themselves felt: he had begun to grow rigid, to stiffen, as his fingers stiffened also. Alone, with an aged cook, whom he had taken from the almshouse (he had never been married), he lived on in O***, in a tiny house, not far from the Kalítin residence; he walked a great deal, read the Bible and collections of Protestant psalms, and Shakespeare in Schlegel's translation. It was long since he had composed anything; but, evidently, Liza, his best pupil, understood how to arouse him: he had written for her the cantata to which Pánshin had alluded. He had taken the words for this cantata from the psalms; several verses he had composed himself; it was to be sung by two choruses,—the chorus of the happy, and the chorus of the unhappy; both became reconciled, in the end, and sang together: "O merciful God, have mercy upon us sinners, and purge out of us by fire all evil thoughts and earthly hopes!"—On the title-page, very carefully written, and even drawn, stood the following: "Only the Just are Right. A Spiritual Cantata. Composed and dedicated to Miss Elizavéta Kalítin, my beloved pupil, by her teacher, C. T. G. Lemm." The words: "Only the Just are Right," and "Elizavéta Kalítin," were

14

surrounded by rays. Below was added: "For you alone,"—"Für Sie allein."—Therefore Lemm had crimsoned and had cast a sidelong glance at Liza; it pained him greatly when Pánshin spoke of his cantata in his presence.

VI

Pánshin struck the opening chords of the sonata loudly, and with decision (he was playing the second hand), but Liza did not begin her part. He stopped, and looked at her. Liza's eyes, fixed straight upon him, expressed displeasure; her lips were not smiling, her whole face was stern, almost sad.

"What is the matter with you?"—he inquired.

"Why did not you keep your word?" said she.—"I showed you Christofór Feódoritch's cantata on condition that you would not mention it to him."

"Pardon me, Lizavéta Mikhaílovna, it was a slip of the tongue."

"You have wounded him—and me also. Now he will not trust me any more."

"What would you have me do, Lizavéta Mikhaílovna! From my earliest childhood, I have never been able to endure the sight of a German: something simply impels me to stir him up."

"Why do you say that, Vladímir Nikoláitch! This German is a poor, solitary, broken man—and you feel no pity for him? You want to stir him up?"

Pánshin was disconcerted.

"You are right, Lizavéta Mikhaílovna,"—he said. "My eternal thoughtlessness is responsible for the whole thing. No, do not say a word; I know myself well. My thoughtlessness has done me many an ill turn. Thanks to it, I have won the reputation of an egoist."

Pánshin paused for a moment. No matter how he began a conversation, he habitually wound up by speaking of himself, and he did it in a charming, soft, confidential, almost involuntary way.

"And here in your house,"—he went on:—"your mother likes me, of course,—she is so kind; you ... however, I do not know your opinion of me; but your aunt, on the contrary, cannot bear me. I must have offended her, also, by some thoughtless, stupid remark. For she does not like me, does she?"

"No," said Liza, with some hesitation:—"you do not please her."

Pánshin swept his fingers swiftly over the keys; a barely perceptible smile flitted across his lips.

"Well, and you?"—he said:—"Do I seem an egoist to you also?"

"I know you very slightly,"—returned Liza:—"but I do not consider you an egoist; on the contrary, I ought to feel grateful to you...."

"I know, I know, what you mean to say,"—Pánshin interrupted her, and again ran his fingers over the keys:—"for the music, for the books which I bring you, for the bad drawings with which I decorate your album, and so forth and so on. I can do all that—and still be an egoist. I venture to think, that you are not bored in my company, and that you do not regard me as a bad man, but still you assume, that I—how in the world shall I express it?—would not spare my own father or friend for the sake of a jest."

"You are heedless and forgetful, like all worldly people,"—said Liza:—"that is all."

Pánshin frowned slightly.

"Listen," he said:—"let us not talk any more about me; let us play our sonata. One thing only I will ask of you,"—he said, as with his hand he smoothed out the leaves of the bound volume which stood on the music-rack:—"think what you will of me, call me an egoist even,—so be it! but do not call me a worldly man: that appellation is intolerable to me.... Anch'io son pittore. I also am an artist,—and I will immediately prove it to you in action. Let us begin."

"We will begin, if you please,"—said Liza.

The first adagio went quite successfully, although Pánshin made more than one mistake. He played his own compositions and those which he had practised very prettily, but he read music badly. On the other hand, the second part of the sonata—a rather brisk allegro—did not go at all: at the twentieth measure, Pánshin, who had got two measures behind, could hold out no longer, and pushed back his chair with a laugh.

"No!"—he exclaimed:—"I cannot play to-day; it is well that Lemm does not hear us: he would fall down in a swoon."

Liza rose, shut the piano, and turned to Pánshin.

"What shall we do now?"—she asked.

"I recognise you in that question! You cannot possibly sit with folded hands. Come, if you like, let us draw, before it has grown completely dark. Perhaps the other muse,—the muse of drawing ... what's her name? I've forgotten ... will be more gracious to me. Where is your album? Do you remember?—my landscape there is not finished."

Liza went into the next room for her album, and Pánshin, when he was left alone, pulled a batiste handkerchief from his pocket, polished his nails, and gazed somewhat askance at his hands. They were very handsome and white; on the thumb of the left hand he wore a spiral gold ring. Liza returned; Pánshin seated himself near the window, and opened the album.

"Aha!"—he exclaimed:—"I see that you have begun to copy my landscape—and that is fine. Very good! Only here—give me a pencil—the shadows are not put on thickly enough.... Look."

17

And Pánshin, with a bold sweep, prolonged several long strokes. He constantly drew one and the same landscape: in the foreground were large, dishevelled trees, in the distance, a meadow, and saw-toothed mountains on the horizon. Liza looked over his shoulder at his work.

"In drawing, and in life in general,"—said Pánshin, bending his head now to the right, now to the left:—"lightness and boldness are the principal thing."

At that moment, Lemm entered the room, and, with a curt inclination, was on the point of departing; but Pánshin flung aside the album and pencil, and barred his way.

"Whither are you going, my dear Christofór Feódoritch? Are not you going to stay and drink tea?"

"I must go home,"—said Lemm in a surly voice:—"my head aches."

"Come, what nonsense!—stay. You and I will have a dispute over Shakespeare."

"My head aches,"—repeated the old man.

"We tried to play a Beethoven sonata without you,"—went on Pánshin, amiably encircling his waist with his arm, and smiling brightly:—"but we couldn't make it go at all. Just imagine, I couldn't play two notes in succession correctly."

"You vould haf done better to sing your romantz,"—retorted Lemm, pushing aside Pánshin's arm, and left the room.

Liza ran after him. She overtook him on the steps.

"Christofór Feódoritch, listen,"—she said to him in German, as she accompanied him to the gate, across the close-cropped green grass of the yard:—"I am to blame toward you—forgive me."

Lemm made no reply.

"I showed your cantata to Vladímir Nikoláitch; I was convinced that he would appreciate it,—and it really did please him greatly."

Lemm halted.

"Zat is nozing,"—he said in Russian, and then added in his native tongue:—"but he cannot understand anything; how is it that you do not perceive that?—he is a dilettante—and that's all there is to it!"

"You are unjust to him,"—returned Liza:—"he understands everything, and can do nearly everything himself."

"Yes, everything is second-class, light-weight, hasty work. That pleases, and he pleases, and he is content with that—well, and bravo! But I am not angry; that cantata and I—we are old fools; I am somewhat ashamed, but that does not matter."

"Forgive me, Christofór Feódoritch,"—said Liza again.

"It does not mattair, it does not mattair," he repeated again in

18

Russian:—"you are a goot girl ... but see yonder, some vun is coming to your house. Good-bye. You are a fery goot girl."

And Lemm, with hasty strides, betook himself toward the gate, through which was entering a gentleman with whom he was not acquainted, clad in a grey coat and a broad-brimmed straw hat. Courteously saluting him (he bowed to all newcomers in the town of O***; he turned away from his acquaintances on the street—that was the rule which he had laid down for himself), Lemm passed him, and disappeared behind the hedge. The stranger looked after him in amazement, and, exchanging a glance with Liza, advanced straight toward her.

VII

"You do not recognise me,"—he said, removing his hat,—"but I recognise you, although eight years have passed since I saw you last. You were a child then. I am Lavrétzky. Is your mother at home? Can I see her?"

"Mamma will be very glad,"—replied Liza:—"she has heard of your arrival."

"Your name is Elizavéta, I believe?"—said Lavrétzky, as he mounted the steps of the porch.

"Yes."

"I remember you well; you had a face, at that time, such as one does not forget; I used to bring you bonbons then."

Liza blushed and thought, "What a strange man he is!" Lavrétzky paused for a minute in the anteroom. Liza entered the drawing-room, where Pánshin's voice and laughter were resounding; he had imparted some gossip of the town to Márya Dmítrievna and Gedeónovsky, who had already returned from the garden, and was himself laughing loudly at what he had narrated. At the name of Lavrétzky, Márya Dmítrievna started in utter trepidation, turned pale, and advanced to meet him.

"How do you do, how do you do, my dear cousin!"—she exclaimed, in a drawling and almost tearful voice:—"how glad I am to see you!"

"How do you do, my kind cousin,"—returned Lavrétzky; and shook her proffered hand in a friendly way:—"how does the Lord show mercy on you?"

"Sit down, sit down, my dear Feódor Ivánitch. Akh, how delighted I am! Permit me, in the first place, to present to you my daughter Liza...."

"I have already introduced myself to Lizavéta Mikhaílovna,"— Lavrétzky interrupted her.

"Monsieur Pánshin.... Sergyéi Petróvitch Gedeónovsky.... But pray sit down! I look at you, and I simply cannot believe my eyes. How is your health?"

"As you see, I am blooming. And you, cousin,—I don't want to cast the evil eye on you—you have not grown thin during these eight years."

"Just think, what a long time it is since we saw each other,"— remarked Márya Dmítrievna, dreamily.—"Whence come you now? Where have you left ... that is, I meant to say"—she hastily caught herself up—"I meant to say, are you to be with us long?"

"I have just come from Berlin,"—returned Lavrétzky,—"and to-morrow I set out for my estate—probably to remain there a long time."

"Of course, you will live at Lavríki?"

"No, not at Lavríki, but I have a tiny village about twenty-five versts from here; I am going there."

"The village which you inherited from Glafíra Petróvna?"

"The same."

"Good gracious, Feódor Ivánitch! You have a splendid house at Lavríki!"

Lavrétzky scowled slightly.

"Yes ... but in that little estate there is a small wing; and, for the present, I need nothing more. That place is the most convenient for me just now."

Márya Dmítrievna again became so perturbed, that she even straightened herself up, and flung her hands apart. Pánshin came to her assistance, and entered into conversation with Lavrétzky. Márya Dmítrievna recovered her composure, leaned back in her chair, and only interjected a word from time to time; but, all the while, she gazed so compassionately at her visitor, she sighed so significantly, and shook her head so mournfully, that the latter, at last, could endure it no longer, and asked her, quite sharply: was she well?

"Thank God, yes,"—replied Márya Dmítrievna,—"why?"

"Because it seemed to me that you were not quite yourself."

Márya Dmítrievna assumed a dignified and somewhat offended aspect.—"If that's the way you take it,"—she said to herself,—"I don't care in the least; evidently, my good man, nothing affects thee any more than water does a goose; any one else would have pined away with grief, but it swells thee up more than ever." Márya Dmítrievna did not stand on ceremony with herself; she expressed herself more elegantly aloud.

As a matter of fact, Lavrétzky did not resemble a victim of fate. His rosy-cheeked, purely-Russian face, with its large, white brow, rather thick nose, and broad, regular lips, fairly overflowed with native health, with strong, durable force. He was magnificently built,—and his blond hair curled all over his head, like a young man's. Only in his eyes, which were blue and prominent and fixed, was there to be discerned something which was not revery, nor yet weariness, and his voice sounded rather too even.

In the meantime, Pánshin had continued to keep up the conversation. He turned it on the profits of sugar-refining, concerning which two French pamphlets had recently made their appearance, and with calm modesty undertook to set forth their contents, but without saying one word about them.

"Why, here's Fédya!" suddenly rang out Márfa Timoféevna's voice in the adjoining room, behind the half-closed door:—"Actually, Fédya!" And the old woman briskly entered the room. Before Lavrétzky could rise from his chair, she clasped him in her embrace.—"Come, show thyself, show thyself,"—she said, moving back from his face.—"Eh! What a splendid fellow thou art! Thou hast grown older, but hast not grown in the least less comely, really! But why art thou kissing my hands,—kiss me myself, if my wrinkled cheeks are not repulsive to thee. Can it be, that thou didst not ask after me: 'Well, tell me, is aunty alive?' Why, thou wert born into my arms, thou rogue! Well, never mind that; why shouldst thou have remembered me? Only, thou art a sensible fellow, to have come. Well, my mother,"—she added, addressing Márya Dmítrievna,—"hast thou given him any refreshments?"

"I want nothing,"—said Lavrétzky, hastily.

"Come, drink some tea, at least, my dear little father. O Lord my God! He has come, no one knows whence, and they don't give him a cup of tea! Go, Liza, and see about it, as quickly as possible. I remember that, as a little fellow, he was a dreadful glutton, and he must be fond of eating even now."

"My respects, Márfa Timoféevna,"—said Pánshin, approaching the angry old woman from one side, and bowing low.

"Excuse me, sir,"—retorted Márfa Timoféevna,—"I did not notice you for joy.—Thou hast grown to resemble thy mother, the darling,"—she went on, turning again to Lavrétzky:—"only, thy nose was and remains like thy father's. Well—and art thou to be long with us?"

"I am going away to-morrow, aunty."

"Whither?"

"Home, to Vasílievskoe."

"To-morrow?"

"Yes."

"Well, if it must be to-morrow, it must. God be with thee,—thou knowest best. Only, see here, thou must come to say farewell."—The old woman tapped him on the cheek.—"I did not think I should live to see thee; and that not because I was preparing to die; no—I am good for another ten years, probably: all we Péstoffs are tenacious of life; thy deceased grandfather used to call us double-lived; but the Lord only knew how much longer thou wouldst ramble about abroad. Well, but thou art a dashing fine fellow, a fine fellow; thou canst still lift ten puds in one hand as of yore, I suppose? Thy deceased father, excuse me, was cranky in some respects, but he did well when he hired a Swiss for thee; thou rememberest, how thou and he had fistfights; that's called gymnastics, isn't it?—But why

22

have I been cackling thus? I have only been keeping Mr. Panshín" (she never called him Pánshin, as she ought) "from arguing. But we had better drink tea; let us go and drink it on the terrace, my dear; our cream—is not like what you get in your Londons and Parises. Let us go, let us go, and do thou, Fédiusha, give me thy arm. O! how thick it is! There's no danger of falling with thee."

All rose and betook themselves to the terrace, with the exception of Gedeónovsky, who quietly departed. During the entire duration of Lavrétzky's conversation with the mistress of the house, Pánshin, and Márfa Timoféevna, he had sat in a corner, attentively blinking, and sticking out his lips, in childish curiosity: he now hastened to carry the news about the new visitor throughout the town.

On that same day, at eleven o'clock in the evening, this is what was going on at Mme. Kalítin's house. Down-stairs, on the threshold of the drawing-room, Vladímir Nikoláitch, having seized a favourable moment, was saying farewell to Liza, and telling her, as he held her hand: "You know who it is that attracts me hither; you know why I am incessantly coming to your house; what is the use of words, when everything is so plain?" Liza made him no reply, and without a smile, and with eyebrows slightly elevated, and blushing, she stared at the floor, but did not withdraw her hand; and up-stairs, in Márfa Timoféevna's chamber, by the light of the shrine-lamp, which hung in front of the dim, ancient holy pictures, Lavrétzky was sitting in an arm-chair, with his elbows on his knees, and his face in his hands; the old woman, standing before him, was silently stroking his hair, from time to time. He spent more than an hour with her, after taking leave of the mistress of the house; he said almost nothing to his kind old friend, and she did not interrogate him.... And what was the use of talking, what was there to interrogate him about? She understood everything as it was, and she sympathised with everything wherewith his heart was full to overflowing.

VIII

Feódor Ivánovitch Lavrétzky (we must ask the reader's permission to break the thread of our narrative for a time) was descended from an ancient family of the nobility. The ancestral founder of the Lavrétzkys had come out of Prussia during the princely reign of Vasíly the Blind, and had been granted two hundred quarters[1] of land, on Byezhétsk Heights. Many of his descendants were members of various branches of the public service, and sat under princes and distinguished personages in distant governorships, but not one of them ever rose above the rank of table-decker at the Court of the Tzars, or acquired any considerable fortune. The most opulent and noteworthy of all the Lavrétzkys had been Feódor Ivánitch's great-grandfather, Andréi, a harsh, insolent, clever, and crafty man. Down to the day of which we are speaking, the fame of his arbitrary violence, of his fiendish disposition, his mad lavishness, and unquenchable thirst had not died out. He had been very stout and lofty of stature, swarthy of visage, and beardless; he lisped, and appeared to be sleepy; but the more softly he spoke, the more did every one around him tremble. He obtained for himself a wife to match. Goggle-eyed, with hawk-like nose, with a round, sallow face, a gipsy by birth, quick-tempered and revengeful, she was not a whit behind her husband, who almost starved her to death, and whom she did not survive, although she was eternally snarling at him.

Andréi's son, Piótr, Feódor's grandfather, did not resemble his father: he was a simple squire of the steppes, decidedly hare-brained, a swashbuckler and dawdler, rough but not malicious, hospitable, and fond of dogs. He was more than thirty years old when he inherited from his father two thousand souls in capital order; but he speedily dispersed them, sold a part of his estate, and spoiled his house-servants. Petty little people, acquaintances and non-acquaintances, crawled from all sides, like black-beetles, to his spacious, warm, and slovenly mansion; all these ate whatever came to hand, but ate their fill, drank themselves drunk, and carried off what they could, lauding and magnifying the amiable host; and the host, when he was not in a good humour, also magnified his guests—as drones and blackguards—but he was bored without them. Piótr Andréitch's wife was a meek person: he took her from a neighbouring family, at his father's choice and command; her name

---

[1] An ancient land-measure, varying in different localities; the average "quarter" being about thirty by forty fathoms.—Translator.

24

was Anna Pávlovna. She never interfered with anything, received visitors cordially, and was fond of going out herself, although powdering her hair, according to her own words, was death to her. They put a felt hood on your head, she was wont to narrate in her old age, combed your hair all up on top, smeared it with tallow, sprinkled on flour, stuck in iron pins,—and you could not wash yourself afterward; but to go visiting without powder was impossible—people would take offence;—torture!—She was fond of driving after trotters, was ready to play cards from morning until night, and always covered up with her hand the few farthings of winnings set down to her when her husband approached the card-table; but she gave her dowry and all her money to him, and required no accounting for its use. She bore him two children: a son, Iván, Feódor's father, and a daughter, Glafíra.

Iván was not brought up at home, but at the house of a wealthy old aunt, Princess Kubenskóy; she had designated him as her heir (had it not been for that, his father would not have let him go); she dressed him like a doll, hired every sort of teacher for him, provided him with a governor, a Frenchman, a former abbé, a disciple of Jean-Jacques Rousseau, a certain M. Courtin de Vaucelles, an adroit and subtle intriguer,—the most fine fleur of the emigration, as she expressed it,—and ended by marrying this "fine-fleur" when she was almost seventy years of age; she transferred to his name her entire fortune, and soon afterward, rouged, scented with amber, à la Richelieu, surrounded by small negroes, slender-legged dogs, and screeching parrots, she died on a crooked little couch of the time of Louis XV, with an enamelled snuff-box, the work of Petitot, in her hands,—and died, deserted by her husband: the sneaking M. Courtin had preferred to retire to Paris with her money.

Iván was only in his twentieth year when this blow (we are speaking of the Princess's marriage, not of her death) descended upon him; he did not wish to remain in his aunt's house, where from a wealthy heir he had suddenly been converted into a parasite; in Petersburg, the society in which he had been reared, was closed to him; to service, beginning with the lowest ranks, difficult and dark, he felt repugnance (all this took place at the very beginning of the reign of the Emperor Alexander). He was compelled, perforce, to return to the country, to his father. Dirty, poor, tattered did his native nest appear to him: the dulness and soot of existence on the steppes offended him at every step; he was tormented with boredom; on the other hand, every one in the house, with the exception of his mother, looked upon him with unfriendly eyes. His father did not like his habits of the capital; his dress-suits, frilled shirts, books, his flute, his cleanliness, in which, not without reason, they scented his fastidiousness; he was constantly complaining and grumbling at his son.—"Nothing here suits him," he was wont to say: "at table he is dainty, he does not eat, he cannot endure the odour of the servants, the stifling atmosphere; the sight of drunken men disturbs him, and you mustn't dare to fight in his presence, either; he will not enter government service: he's frail in health, forsooth; phew, what an effeminate creature! And all because Voltaire sticks in his head!"

The old man cherished a particular dislike for Voltaire, and for the "fanatic" Diderot, although he had never read a single line of their writings: reading was not in his line. Piótr Andréitch was not mistaken: Diderot and Voltaire really were sticking in his son's head, and not they only,—but Rousseau and Raynal and Helvetius, and many other writers of the same sort, were sticking in his head,— but only in his head. Iván Petróvitch's former tutor, the retired abbé and encyclopedist, had contented himself with pouring the whole philosophy of the XVIII century into his pupil in a mass, and the latter went about brimful of it; it gained lodgment within him, without mingling with his blood, without penetrating into his soul, without making itself felt as a firm conviction.... And could convictions be demanded of a young fellow of fifty years ago, when we have not even yet grown up to them? He also embarrassed the visitors to his father's house: he loathed them, and they feared him; and with his sister, Glafíra, who was twelve years older than he, he did not get on at all.

This Glafíra was a strange being; homely, hunchbacked, gaunt, with stern, staring eyes and thin, tightly compressed lips; in face, voice, and quick, angular movements, she recalled her grandmother, the gipsy, the wife of Andréi. Persistent, fond of power, she would not even hear of marriage. The return of Iván Petróvitch did not please her; so long as the Princess Kubenskóy had kept him with her, she had cherished the hope of receiving at least half of the parental estate: she resembled her grandmother in her avarice. Moreover, Glafíra was envious of her brother: he was so cultivated, he spoke French so well, with a Parisian accent, while she was scarcely able to say: "bon jour," and "comment vous portez vous?" To tell the truth, her parents did not understand any French at all,—but that did not render it any the more pleasant for her.

Iván Petróvitch did not know what to do with himself for tedium and melancholy; he spent nearly a year in the country, and it seemed to him like ten years.—Only with his mother did he relieve his heart, and he was wont to sit, by the hour, in her low-ceiled rooms, listening to the simple prattle of the good woman, and gorging himself with preserves. It so happened, that among Anna

26

Pávlovna's maids there was one very pretty girl, with clear, gentle eyes and delicate features, named Malánya, both clever and modest. She pleased Iván Petróvitch at first sight, and he fell in love with her: he fell in love with her timid walk, her shy answers, her soft voice, her gentle smile; with every passing day she seemed to him more charming. And she became attached to Iván Petróvitch with her whole soul, as only Russian girls can become attached—and gave herself to him.

In the country manor-house of a landed proprietor, no secret can be kept long: every one soon knew of the bond between the young master and Malánya; the tidings of this connection at last reached Piótr Andréitch himself. At any other time, he would, in all probability, have paid no heed to such an insignificant matter; but he had long been in a rage with his son, and rejoiced at the opportunity to put to shame the Petersburg philosopher and dandy. Tumult, shrieks, and uproar arose: Malánya was locked up in the lumber-room; Iván Petróvitch was summoned to his parent. Anna Pávlovna also hastened up at the outcry. She made an effort to pacify her husband, but Piótr Andréitch no longer listened to anything. Like a vulture he pounced upon his son, upbraided him with immorality, with impiety, with hypocrisy; incidentally, he vented on him all his accumulated wrath against the Princess Kubenskóy, and overwhelmed him with insulting epithets. At first, Iván Petróvitch held his peace, and stood firm, but when his father took it into his head to threaten him with a disgraceful chastisement, he lost patience. "The fanatic Diderot has come on the stage again," he thought,—"so just wait, I'll put him in action; I'll astonish you all."

Thereupon, in a quiet voice, although trembling in every limb, Iván Petróvitch announced to his father, that there was no necessity for upbraiding him with immorality, that, although he did not intend to justify his fault, yet he was ready to rectify it, and that the more willingly because he felt himself superior to all prejudices—in short, he was ready to marry Malánya. By uttering these words, Iván Petróvitch did, undoubtedly, attain his object: he astounded Piótr Andréitch to such a degree, that the latter stared with all his eyes, and was rendered dumb for a moment; but he immediately recovered himself, and just as he was, clad in a short coat lined with squirrel-skin, and with slippers on his bare feet, he flung himself with clenched fists upon Iván Petróvitch, who that day, as though expressly, had his hair dressed à la Titus, and had donned a new blue English dress-coat, boots with tassels, and dandified chamois trousers, skin-tight. Anna Pávlovna shrieked at the top of her voice, and covered her face with her hands, but her son ran through the whole house, sprang out into the yard, rushed into the vegetable garden, across the garden, flew out upon the highway, and kept running, without looking behind him, until, at last, he ceased to hear behind him the heavy tramp of his father's footsteps, and his violent, broken shouts.... "Stop, rascal!" he roared,—"stop! I'll curse thee!"

Iván Petróvitch hid himself in the house of a neighbouring peasant proprietor, while Piótr Andréitch returned home utterly exhausted and perspiring, and announcing almost before he had recovered his breath, that he would deprive his son of his blessing and his heritage, ordered all his idiotic books to be burned, and the maid Malánya to be sent forthwith to a distant village. Kind people turned up, who sought out Iván Petróvitch and informed him of all. Mortified, enraged, he vowed that he would take revenge on his father; and that very night, lying in wait for the peasant cart in which Malánya was being carried off, he rescued her by force, galloped off with her to the nearest town, and married her. He was supplied with money by a neighbour, an eternally intoxicated and extremely good-natured retired naval officer, a passionate lover of every sort of noble adventure, as he expressed it. On the following day, Iván Petróvitch wrote a caustically-cold and courteous letter to Piótr Andréitch, and betook himself to an estate where dwelt his second cousin, Dmítry Péstoff, and his sister, Márfa Timoféevna, already known to the reader. He told them everything, announced that he intended to go to Petersburg to seek a place, and requested them to give shelter to his wife, for a time at least. At the word "wife" he fell to weeping bitterly, and, despite his city breeding and his philosophy, he prostrated himself humbly, after the fashion of a Russian beggar, before the feet of his relatives, and even beat his brow against the floor. The Péstoffs, kind and compassionate people, gladly acceded to his request; he spent three weeks with them, in secret expectation of a reply from his father; but no reply came,—and none could come. Piótr Andréitch, on learning of his son's marriage, had taken to his bed, and had forbidden the name of Iván Petróvitch to be mentioned in his presence; but his mother, without the knowledge of her husband, borrowed five hundred rubles from the ecclesiastical supervisor of the diocese, and sent them to him, together with a small holy picture for his wife;[2] she was afraid to write, but she gave orders that Iván Petróvitch was to be told, by the lean peasant her envoy, who managed to walk sixty versts in the course of twenty-four hours, that he must not grieve too much, that, God willing, everything would come right, and his

[2] That is to say, she sent her maternal blessing.—Translator.

28

father would convert wrath into mercy; that she, also, would have preferred a different daughter-in-law, but that, evidently, God had so willed it, and she sent her maternal blessing to Malánya Sergyéevna. The lean little peasant received a ruble, requested permission to see his new mistress, to whom he was related as co-sponsor at a baptism, kissed her hand, and hastened off homeward.

And Iván Petróvitch set off for Petersburg with a light heart. The unknown future awaited him; poverty, perhaps, menaced him, but he had bidden farewell to the life in the country which he detested, and, most important of all, he had not betrayed his teachers, he really had "put in action" and justified in fact Rousseau, Diderot, and la déclaration des droits de l'homme. A sense of duty accomplished, of triumph, of pride, filled his soul; and his separation from his wife did not greatly alarm him; the necessity of living uninterruptedly with his wife would have perturbed him more. That affair was ended; he must take up other affairs. In Petersburg, contrary to his own expectation, fortune smiled on him: Princess Kubenskóy—whom Monsieur Courtin had already succeeded in abandoning, but who had not yet succeeded in dying,—by way, in some measure, of repairing the injury which she had done to her nephew, recommended him to the good graces of all her friends, and gave him five thousand rubles,—almost her last farthing,—and a Lepíkovsky watch with his coat of arms in a garland of cupids. Three months had not elapsed, when he had already obtained a place in the Russian mission to London, and he went to sea on the first English ship which sailed (there was no thought of steamers in those days). A few months later, he received a letter from Péstoff. The kind-hearted squire congratulated Iván Petróvitch on the birth of a son, who had made his appearance in the world, in the village of Pokróvskoe, on August 20, 1807, and was named Feódor, in honour of the holy martyr, Feódor the Strategist. Owing to her extreme weakness, Malánya Sergyéevna added only a few lines; but those few lines astonished Iván Petróvitch: he was not aware that Márfa Timoféevna had taught his wife to read and write. However, Iván Petróvitch did not give himself up for long to the sweet agitation of paternal emotions: he was paying court to one of the most famous Phrynes or Laïses of the period (classical appellations were still flourishing at that epoch); the peace of Tilsit had just been concluded, and everybody was making haste to enjoyment, everything was whirling round in a sort of mad whirlwind. He had very little money; but he played luckily at cards, he picked up acquaintances, he took part in all the merrymakings,—in a word, he was dashing along under full sail.

29

IX

It was long before old Lavrétzky could forgive his son for his marriage; if, after the lapse of half a year, Iván Petróvitch had presented himself in contrition, and had flung himself at his feet, he would, probably, have pardoned him, after first scolding him roundly, and administering a few taps with his crutch, by way of inspiring awe; but Iván Petróvitch was living abroad, and, evidently, cared not a rap.—"Hold your tongue! Don't dare!" Piótr Andréitch kept repeating to his wife, as soon as she tried to incline him to mercy: "He ought to pray to God for me forever, the pup, for not having laid my curse upon him; my late father would have slain him with his own hands, the good-for-nothing, and he would have done right." At such terrible speeches, Anna Pávlovna merely crossed herself furtively. As for Iván Petróvitch's wife, Piótr Andréitch, at first, would not allow her to be mentioned, and even in reply to a letter of Péstoff, wherein the latter alluded to his daughter-in-law, he gave orders to say to him, that he knew nothing whatever about any daughter-in-law of his, and that it was prohibited by the laws to harbour runaway maids, on which point he regarded it as his duty to warn him; but later on, when he learned of the birth of a grandson, he softened, gave orders that inquiries should be made on the sly concerning the health of the young mother, and sent her, also as though it did not come from him, a little money. Fédya had not reached his first birthday, when Anna Pávlovna was seized with a fatal illness. A few days before her end, when she could no longer leave her bed, she declared to her husband, in the presence of the priest, that she wished to see and bid farewell to her daughter-in-law, and to bestow her blessing on her grandchild. The afflicted old man soothed her, and immediately sent his own equipage for his daughter-in-law, for the first time calling her Malánya Sergyéevna.[3] She came with her son and with Márfa Timoféevna, who would not let her go alone on any terms, and would not have allowed her to be affronted. Half dead with terror, Malánya entered Piótr Andréitch's study. The nurse carried Fédya after her. Piótr Andréitch gazed at her in silence; she approached to kiss his hand; her quivering lips hardly met in a noiseless kiss.

"Well, new-ground, undried noblewoman,"—he said at last:—"how do you do; let us go to the mistress."

---

[3] Serfs were not addressed with their patronymic by their superiors.—Translator.

He rose and bent over Fédya; the baby smiled, and stretched out his little, white arms. The old man was completely upset.

"Okh," he said,—"thou orphan! Thou hast plead thy father's cause with me; I will not abandon thee, my birdling!"

As soon as Malánya Sergyéevna entered the bedchamber of Anna Pávlovna, she knelt down near the door. Anna Pávlovna beckoned her to the bed, embraced her, blessed her son; then, turning her countenance, ravaged by disease, to her husband, she tried to speak....

"I know, I know what entreaty thou desirest to make,"—said Piótr Andréitch:—"do not worry: she shall stay with us, and I will pardon Vánka for her sake."

Anna Pávlovna, with an effort, grasped her husband's hand, and pressed it to her lips. On that same evening she died.

Piótr Andréitch kept his word. He informed his son, that, for the sake of his mother's dying hour, for the sake of baby Feódor, he restored to him his blessing, and would keep Malánya Sergyéevna in his own house. Two rooms were set apart for her use in the entresol, he introduced her to his most respected visitor, one-eyed Brigadier Skuryókhin, and to his wife; he presented her with two maids and a page-boy for errands. Márfa Timoféevna bade her farewell; she detested Glafíra, and quarrelled with her thrice in the course of one day.

At first the poor woman found her situation painful and awkward; but afterward, she learned to bear things patiently, and became accustomed to her father-in-law. He, also, became accustomed to her, he even grew to love her, although he almost never spoke to her, although in his caresses a certain involuntary disdain toward her was perceptible. Malánya Sergyéevna had most of all to endure from her sister-in-law. Glafíra, already during her mother's lifetime, had succeeded in getting gradually the entire house into her hands: every one, beginning with her father, was subject to her; not a lump of sugar was given out without her permission; she would have consented to die, rather than to share the power with any other mistress of the house! Her brother's marriage had angered her even more than it had Piótr Andréitch: she took it upon herself to teach the upstart a lesson, and from the very first hour Malánya Sergyéevna became her slave.

And how could she contend with the self-willed, arrogant Glafíra, she who was mild, constantly agitated, and terrified, and also weak in health? Not a day passed, that Glafíra did not remind her of her former position, did not praise her for not forgetting her place. Malánya Sergyéevna would gladly have reconciled herself to these reminders and praises, however bitter they might be ... but

31

they took Fédya away from her: that was what broke her heart. Under the pretext that she was not competent to take charge of his education, she was hardly permitted to see him; Glafíra took this matter upon herself; the child passed under her full control. Malánya Sergyéevna began, out of grief, to entreat Iván Petróvitch, in her letters, to come home as speedily as possible; Piótr Andréitch himself wished to see his son; but he merely wrote in reply, thanking his father about his wife, and for the money sent, and promising to come soon,—and did not come. The year ' recalled him, at last, to his fatherland from abroad.

On meeting again, for the first time, after their six years' separation, the father and son exchanged embraces, and did not allude, by so much as a word, to their former dissensions; they were not in the mood for it then: all Russia had risen against the enemy, and both of them felt that Russian blood was flowing in their veins. Piótr Andréitch, at his own expense, clothed an entire regiment of soldiers. But the war came to an end, the danger passed; again Iván Petróvitch began to feel bored, again he longed for far-away places, for the world to which he had grown fast, and where he felt himself at home. Malánya Sergyéevna could not hold him back; she counted for too little with him. Even her hopes had not been realised: her husband, also, deemed it much more fitting that Fédya's education should be entrusted to Glafíra. Iván Petróvitch's poor wife could not withstand this blow, could not endure this second parting: without a murmur, in a few days she expired. During the whole course of her life, she had never been able to offer resistance, and she did not combat her malady. She could no longer speak, the shadows of the tomb had already descended upon her face, but her features, as of old, expressed patient perplexity, and the steadfast gentleness of submission; with the same dumb humility she gazed at Glafíra, and, like Anna Pávlovna on her deathbed, she kissed the hand of Piótr Andréitch, and pressed her lips to Glafíra's hand also, entrusting to her, Glafíra, her only son. Thus ended its earthly career a kind and gentle being, torn, God alone knows why, from its native soil and immediately flung aside, like an uprooted sapling, with its roots to the sun; it faded away, it vanished, without a trace, that being, and no one mentioned it. Those who grieved for Malánya Sergyéevna were her maid and Piótr Andréitch. The old man missed her silent presence. "Forgive—farewell, my patient one!" he whispered, as he made her the parting reverence in church. He wept as he threw a handful of earth into the grave.

He did not long survive her—not more than five years. In the winter of , he died peacefully in Moscow, whither he had removed with Glafíra and his grandson, and left orders in his will, that he should be buried by the side of Anna Pávlovna and "Malásha." Iván Petróvitch was in Paris at the time, for his pleasure; he had resigned from the service soon after . On hearing of his father's death, he decided to return to Russia. It was necessary to consider the organisation of the estate ... and Fédya, according to Glafíra's letter, had reached the age of twelve years, and the time had arrived for occupying himself seriously with the boy's education.

X

Iván Petróvitch returned to Russia an Anglomaniac. His closely-clipped hair, starched neckcloth, long-skirted, yellowish-gray overcoat with a multitude of capes, his sour expression of visage, a certain harshness and also indifference of demeanour, his manner of talking through his teeth, a wooden, abrupt laugh, the absence of smiles, a conversation exclusively political and politico-economical, a passion for bloody roast beef and port wine,—everything about him fairly reeked of Great Britain; he seemed thoroughly imbued with her spirit. But—strange to say! while he had turned into an Anglomaniac, Iván Petróvitch had simultaneously become a patriot; at all events, he called himself a patriot, although he was but badly acquainted with Russia, was not wedded to a single Russian habit, and expressed himself queerly in Russian: in ordinary conversation, his speech was clumsy and pithless, studded all over with Gallicisms; but no sooner did the discussion touch upon important topics, than Iván Petróvitch instantly brought out such expressions as: "to show new proofs of self-zeal,"[4] "that doth not agree with the nature of the circumstances," and so forth. Iván Petróvitch brought with him several manuscript plans touching the organisation and amelioration of the empire; he was extremely dissatisfied with everything he saw,—the absence of system, in particular, stirred up his bile. On meeting his sister, he announced to her, with his very first words, that he intended to introduce radical reforms, that henceforth everything on his estate should proceed upon a new system. Glafíra Petróvna made no reply to Iván Petróvitch, but merely set her teeth, and said to herself: "And what is to become of me?"—But when she reached the country estate, in company with her brother and her nephew, she speedily regained her composure. In the house, several changes actually took place: the female hangers-on and drones were subjected to instant expulsion; among their number two old women suffered, one who was blind and the other crippled with paralysis, also a decrepit Major of the Otchakóff period, who, on account of his truly astonishing voracity, was fed on nothing but black bread and lentils. A decree was also issued, that the former guests were not to be received: they were superseded by a distant neighbour, a fair-haired, scrofulous baron, a very well

---

4 That is to say, he used such fundamentally national words as occur only in the Old Church Slavonic, well-nigh untranslatable here, also employed upon occasions of ceremony.—Translator.

educated and very stupid man. New furniture from Moscow made its appearance; cuspidors, and bells, and wash-stands were introduced and they began to serve the noon breakfast differently; foreign wines took the place of vódka and homemade liqueurs; new liveries were made for the servants; the motto, "in recto virtus," was added to the family coat of arms.... But, in reality, Glafíra's power was not diminished: all the disbursements and purchases depended on her, as before; the imported Alsatian valet made an attempt to vie with her—and lost his place, in spite of the fact that his master took his side. So far as the management, the administration, of the estates was concerned (Glafíra Petróvna entered into all these matters), despite Iván Petróvitch's frequently expressed intention "to infuse new life into this chaos," everything remained as of yore, except that, here and there, the quit-rents were augmented, and the husbandry-service became more oppressive, and the peasants were forbidden to apply directly to Iván Petróvitch. The patriot heartily despised his fellow-citizens. Iván Petróvitch's system was applied, in its full force, to Fédya only: his education actually was subjected to "radical reform"; his father had exclusive charge of it.

35

Up to the time of Iván Petróvitch's return from abroad, Fédya had been, as we have already said, in the hands of Glafíra Petróvna. He was less than eight years of age when his mother died, he had not seen her every day, and he had loved her passionately: the memory of her, of her pale and gentle face, her melancholy glances and timid caresses, had forever imprinted itself upon his heart; but he dimly comprehended her position in the house; he was conscious that between him and her there existed a barrier which she dared not and could not overthrow. He shunned his father, and Iván Petróvitch never petted him; his grandfather occasionally stroked his head, and permitted him to kiss his hand, but he called him and considered him a little fool. After the death of Malánya Sergyéevna, his aunt took him in hand definitively. Fédya feared her,—feared her bright, keen eyes, her sharp voice; he dared not utter a sound in her presence; it sometimes happened that when he had merely fidgeted on his chair, she would scream out: "Where art thou going? sit still!" On Sundays, after the Liturgy, he was permitted to play,—that is to say, he was given a thick book, a mysterious book, the work of a certain Maxímovitch-Ambódik, entitled: "Symbols and Emblems." This book contained about a thousand in part very puzzling pictures, with equally puzzling explanations in five languages. Cupid, with a plump, naked body, played a great part in these pictures. To one of them, labelled "Saffron and Rainbow," was appended the explanation: "The action of this is great ..."; opposite another, which represented "A Heron flying with a violet blossom in his mouth," stood the inscription: "All of them are known unto thee." Cupid and a bear licking its cub was designated as: "Little by little." Fédya contemplated these pictures; he was familiar with the most minute details of them all; some of them—always the same ones—set him to thinking and excited his imagination; he knew no other diversions. When the time came to teach him languages and music, Glafíra Petróvna hired, for a paltry sum, an elderly spinster, a Swede, with frightened, hare-like eyes, who spoke French and German indifferently, played the piano after a fashion, and, in addition, knew how to salt cucumbers in first-class style. In the society of this instructress, of his aunt, and of an old chambermaid, Vasílievna, Fédya passed four whole years. He used to sit in the corner with his "Emblems"—and sit ... and sit ... while the low-ceiled room smelled of geraniums, a solitary tallow candle burned dimly, a cricket chirped monotonously, as though it were bored, the little clock ticked hastily on the wall, a mouse stealthily scratched and gnawed behind the wall-hangings, and the three old maids, like the Parcæ, moved their knitting-needles silently and swiftly to and fro, the shadows cast by their hands now flitted, again quivered strangely in the semi-darkness, and strange thoughts, also half-dark, swarmed in the child's head. No one would have called Fédya an interesting child: he was quite pallid, but fat, awkwardly built, and clumsy,—"a regular peasant," according to Glafíra Petróvna's expression; the pallor would speedily have disappeared from his face if he had been permitted to go out of doors more frequently. He studied tolerably well, although he frequently idled; he never wept; on the other hand, at times a fierce obstinacy came over him; then no one could do anything with him. Fédya loved none of the persons around him.... Woe to the heart which loves not in its youth!

Thus did Iván Petróvitch find him, and without loss of time he set to work to apply his system to him.—"I want to make a man of him first of all, un homme,"—he said to Glafíra Petróvna:—"and not only a man, but a Spartan." Iván Petróvitch began the execution of his intention by dressing his son in Highland garb: the lad of twelve began to go about with bare knees, and with a cock's feather in his crush-cap; the Swede was superseded by a young Swiss man, who had learned gymnastics to perfection; music, as an occupation unworthy of a man, was banished forever; the natural sciences, international law, mathematics, the carpenter's trade after the advice of Jean-Jacques Rousseau, and heraldry, for the maintenance of knightly sentiments—these were the things wherewith the future "man" was to occupy himself; he was waked at four o'clock in the morning, was immediately drenched with cold water, and made to run around a tall pillar, at the end of a rope; he ate once a day, one dish, rode on horseback, practised firing a cross-bow; on every convenient opportunity he exercised his strength of will, after the model of his parent, and every evening he noted down in a special book an account of the past day and his impressions; and Iván Petróvitch, on his side, wrote him precepts in French, in which he called him mon fils, and addressed him as vous. In Russian Fédya called his father "thou," but he dared not sit down in his presence. The "system" bewildered the boy, introduced confusion into his head, squeezed it; but, on the other hand, the new mode of life acted beneficially on his health: at first he caught a fever, but soon recovered, and became a fine, dashing fellow. His father was proud of him, and called him, in his strange jargon: "A son of nature, my product." When Fédya reached the age of sixteen, Iván Petróvitch regarded it as his duty to instil into him betimes scorn for the fair sex,—and the youthful Spartan, with timidity in his soul, with the first down upon his lips, full of vigour, strength, and blood, attempted to appear indifferent, cold, and harsh.

Meanwhile, time passed and passed. Iván Petróvitch spent the greater part of the year at Lavríki (that was the name of his paternal estate), and in the winters he went alone to Moscow, stopped at an inn, diligently frequented the club, orated and set forth his plans in drawing-rooms, and conducted himself more like an Anglomaniac, a grumbler, and a statesman than ever. But the year arrived, and brought with it much woe.[5] Iván Petróvitch's intimate friends and acquaintances were subjected to severe trials. Iván Petróvitch made haste to retreat to his country estate, and locked himself up in his house. Another year elapsed, and Iván Petróvitch suddenly grew feeble, weakened, declined, his health deserted him. A free-thinker—he took to going to church, and to ordering services of prayer; a European—he began to steam himself at the bath, to dine at two o'clock, to go to bed at nine, to fall asleep to the chatter of the aged butler; a statesman—he burned all his plans, all his correspondence, trembled before the governor, and fidgeted in the presence of the rural chief of police; a man with a will of iron—he whimpered and complained when an abscess broke out on him, when he was served with a plate of cold soup. Glafíra Petróvna again reigned over everything in the house; again clerks, village bailiffs, common peasants, began to creep through the back entrance to the "ill-tempered old hag,"—that was what the house-servants called her. The change in Iván Petróvitch gave his son a great shock; he was already in his nineteenth year, and had begun to reason and to free himself from the weight of the hand which oppressed him. He had noticed, even before this, a discrepancy between his father's words and deeds, between his broad and liberal theories and his harsh, petty despotism; but he had not anticipated such a sudden break. The inveterate egoist suddenly revealed himself at full length. Young Lavrétzky was getting ready to go to Moscow, to prepare himself for the university,—when an unforeseen, fresh calamity descended upon the head of Iván Petróvitch: he became blind, and that hopelessly, in one day.

Not trusting in the skill of Russian physicians, he began to take measures to obtain permission to go abroad. It was refused. Then he took his son with him, and for three whole years he roamed over Russia, from one doctor to another, incessantly journeying from town to town and driving the physicians, his son, his servants, to despair by his pusillanimity and impatience. He returned to Lavríki

---

[5] At the accession to the throne of Nicholas I.—Translator.

a perfect rag, a tearful and capricious child. Bitter days ensued, every one endured much at his hands. Iván Petróvitch calmed down only while he was eating his dinner; he had never eaten so greedily, nor so much; all the rest of the time he never gave himself or others any peace. He prayed, grumbled at fate, railed at himself, reviled politics, his system,—reviled everything which he had made his boast and upon which he had prided himself, everything which he had held up as an example for his son; he insisted that he believed in nothing, and then prayed again; he could not bear to be left alone for a single moment, and demanded from the members of his household, that they should sit uninterruptedly, day and night, beside his arm-chair, and amuse him with stories, which he incessantly interrupted with the exclamation: "You are inventing the whole of it—what trash!"

Glafíra Petróvna had a particularly hard time; he positively could not get along without her—and to the end she complied with all the invalid's whims, although sometimes she could not make up her mind on the instant to answer him, lest the sound of her voice should betray her inward wrath. In this manner he lingered on two years, and died in the beginning of May, when he had been carried out upon the balcony, in the sunshine. "Gláshka, Gláshka! the bouillon, the bouillon, you old foo ..." lisped his stiffening tongue, and without finishing the last word, it became silent forever. Glafíra Petróvna, who had just snatched the cup of bouillon from the hands of the butler, stopped short, stared her brother in the face, crossed herself slowly and broadly, and withdrew in silence; and his son, who was present, said nothing, either, but leaned against the railing of the balcony, and gazed for a long time into the garden, all fragrant and verdant, all glittering in the rays of the golden sun of spring. He was twenty-three years old; how terribly, how imperceptibly fast those three and twenty years had sped past!... Life was opening before him.

XII

After having buried his father, and entrusted to the immutable Glafíra Petróvna the management of the farming and the oversight over the clerks, young Lavrétzky betook himself to Moscow, whither he was drawn by an obscure but powerful sentiment. He recognised the defects of his education, and intended to repair omissions, so far as possible. During the last five years, he had read a great deal, and had seen some things; many thoughts had been seething in his brain; any professor might have envied him some of his knowledge, but, at the same time, he did not know much with which every gymnasium lad has long been familiar. The Anglomaniac had played his son an evil trick; his whimsical education had borne its fruits. For long years, he had abased himself before his father without a question; but when, at last, he had divined him, the deed was done, the habits had become rooted. He did not know how to make acquaintance with people: at twenty-three years of age, with an indomitable thirst for love in his shame-stricken heart, he did not dare to look a single woman in the eye. With his clear, solid but somewhat heavy sense, with his inclination to stubbornness, contemplation, and indolence, he ought, from his earliest years, to have been cast into the whirlpool of life, but he had been kept in an artificial isolation.... And now the charmed circle was broken, yet he continued to stand in one spot, locked up, tightly compressed in himself. It was ridiculous, at his age, to don a student's uniform; but he was not afraid of ridicule: his Spartan training had served its turn to this extent at least, that it had developed in him scorn for other people's remarks,—and so, unabashed, he donned the uniform of a student. He entered the physico-mathematical department. Healthy, rosy-cheeked, with a well-grown beard, taciturn, he produced a strange impression upon his comrades; they did not suspect that in this surly man, who punctually drove to the lectures in a roomy country sledge and pair, there was concealed almost a child. He seemed to them some sort of wise pedant; they did not need him and did not seek his society, he avoided them. In the course of the first two years which he spent at the university, he came into close contact with only one student, from whom he took lessons in Latin. This student, Mikhalévitch by name, an enthusiast and a poet, sincerely loved Lavrétzky, and quite innocently became the cause of an important change in his fate.

One day, at the theatre (Motcháloff was then at the height of his fame, and Lavrétzky never missed a performance), he saw a young girl in a box of the bel-étage,—and, although no woman ever passed his surly figure without causing his heart to quiver, it never yet had beaten so violently. With her elbows resting on the velvet of the box, the young girl sat motionless; alert, young life sparkled in every feature of her pretty, round, dark-skinned face; an elegant mind was expressed in the beautiful eyes which gazed attentively and softly from beneath slender brows, in the swift smile of her expressive lips, in the very attitude of her head, her arms, her neck; she was charmingly dressed. Beside her sat a wrinkled, sallow woman, forty-five years of age, with a toothless smile on her constrainedly-anxious and empty countenance, and in the depths of the box an elderly man was visible, wearing an ample coat and a tall neckcloth, with an expression of feeble stateliness and a certain obsequious suspicion in his little eyes, with dyed moustache and side-whiskers, an insignificant, huge forehead, and furrowed cheeks,—a retired General, by all the signs. Lavrétzky could not take his eyes from the young girl who had startled him; all at once, the door of the box opened, and Mikhalévitch entered. The appearance of that man, almost his sole acquaintance in all Moscow,—his appearance in the company of the only young girl who had engrossed his whole attention, seemed to Lavrétzky strange and significant. As he continued to gaze at the box, he noticed that all the persons in it treated Mikhalévitch like an old friend. The performance on the stage ceased to interest Lavrétzky; Motcháloff himself, although that evening he was "in high feather," did not produce upon him the customary impression. In one very pathetic passage, Lavrétzky involuntarily glanced at his beauty: she was bending her whole body forward, her cheeks were aflame; under the influence of his persistent gaze, her eyes, which were riveted on the stage, turned slowly, and rested upon him.... All night long, those eyes flitted before his vision. At last, the artificially erected dam had given way: he trembled and burned, and on the following day he betook himself to Mikhalévitch. From him he learned, that the beauty's name was Varvára Pávlovna Koróbyn; that the old man and woman who had sat with her in the box were her father and mother, and that he himself, Mikhalévitch, had made their acquaintance a year previously, during his stay in the suburbs of Moscow, "on contract service" (as tutor) with Count N. The enthusiast expressed himself in the most laudatory manner concerning Varvára Pávlovna—"My dear fellow," he exclaimed, with the impetuous harmony in his voice which was peculiar to him,—"that young girl is an amazing, a talented being, an artist in the genuine sense of the word, and extremely amiable to boot."—Perceiving from Lavrétzky's question what an impression Varvára Pávlovna had produced upon him, he himself proposed to introduce him to her, adding that he was quite at home in their house; that the General was not at all a proud man, and the mother was so stupid that she all but sucked a rag. Lavrétzky blushed, muttered something unintelligible, and fled. For five whole days he wrestled with his timidity; on the sixth day the young Spartan donned a new uniform, and placed himself at the disposition of Mikhalévitch, who being his own valet, confined himself to brushing his hair,—and the two set out for the Koróbyns'.

XIII

The father of Varvára Pávlovna, Pável Petróvitch Koróbyn, Major-General on the retired list, had spent his whole life in Petersburg, in the service; had borne the reputation, in his youth, of being an accomplished dancer and officer of the line; found himself, owing to poverty, the adjutant of two or three ill-favoured Generals; married the daughter of one of them, receiving twenty-five thousand rubles as her dowry; acquired, in its finest details, the love of drills and reviews; toiled, and toiled hard, for his livelihood, and at last, at the end of twenty years, attained to the rank of General, and received a regiment. It was time for him to rest, and without delay to establish his prosperity on a firm basis; this was what he calculated on doing, but he managed the matter somewhat incautiously: he hit upon a new method of putting the coin of the realm into circulation,—the method proved to be a capital one, but he did not get out in season: a complaint was made against him; a more than unpleasant, an ugly scandal ensued. The General managed to wriggle out of the scandal, after a fashion, but his career was ruined: he was advised to resign. He hung about in Petersburg for a couple of years longer in the hope that some snug little place would get stranded on him: but the place did not strand on him, and his daughter came out of the government school, and his expenses increased every day.... Repressing his wrath, he decided to remove to Moscow for the sake of economy, hired a tiny, low-roofed house on Old Stable Street, with a coat of arms a fathom tall on the roof, and began to live the life of a Moscow General on the retired list, spending   rubles a year. Moscow is a hospitable town, glad to welcome everybody who comes along, and more particularly, Generals; Pável Petróvitch's heavy figure, which yet was not lacking in military mien, speedily began to make its appearance in the best drawing-rooms of Moscow. His bald nape, with tufts of dyed hair, and the dirty ribbon of the order of St. Anna on a neckcloth the hue of the raven's wing, began to be well known to all the easily bored and pallid young men who morosely hovered around the gambling-tables while dancing was in progress. Pável Petróvitch understood how to place himself in society; he talked little, but, by force of old habit, through his nose,—of course, not with individuals belonging to the higher ranks; he played cards cautiously, at home he ate sparingly, but when visiting he ate for six. Concerning his wife, there is hardly anything to say: her name was Kalliópe Kárlovna; a tear oozed from her left eye, by virtue of which Kalliópe Kárlovna (she was, moreover, of German extraction) regarded herself as a woman of sentiment; she lived in constant fear of something, never seemed to have had quite enough to eat, and wore tight velvet gowns, a turban, and dull bracelets of hollow metal. Varvára Pávlovna, the only daughter of Pável Petróvitch and Kalliópe Kárlovna, had just passed her seventeenth birthday when she came out of the*** Institute, where she had been considered, if not the greatest beauty, certainly the cleverest girl and the best musician, and where she had received the chiffre;[6] she was not yet nineteen when Lavrétzky beheld her for the first time.

---

[6] In the Government Institutes for girls, the chief prize is the Empress's initial, in jewels.—Translator.

XIV

The legs of the Spartan gave way beneath him when Mikhalévitch conducted him into the rather shabbily furnished drawing-room of the Koróbyns, and presented him to the master and mistress of the house. But the feeling of timidity which had taken possession of him promptly disappeared: in the General the kindliness of nature innate in all Russians was greatly increased by that special sort of courtesy which is peculiar to all besmirched people; the Generaless soon disappeared, somehow; as for Varvára Pávlovna, she was so calm and self-possessedly amiable, that any one would immediately have felt himself at home in her presence; moreover, from the whole of her enchanting person, from her smiling eyes, from her innocently-sloping shoulders and faintly-rosy hands, from her light and, at the same time, rather languid gait, from the very sound of her voice, which was low and sweet,—there breathed forth an insinuating charm, as intangible as a delicate perfume, a soft and as yet modest intoxication, something which it is difficult to express in words, but which touched and excited,— and, of course, excited something which was not timidity. Lavrétzky turned the conversation on the theatre, on the performance of the preceding evening; she immediately began, herself, to speak of Motcháloff, and did not confine herself merely to exclamations and sighs, but uttered several just and femininely-penetrating remarks concerning his acting. Mikhalévitch alluded to music; without any affectation she seated herself at the piano, and played with precision several mazurkas by Chopin, which had only just come into fashion. The dinner-hour arrived; Lavrétzky made a motion to depart, but they kept him; at table, the General treated him to good claret, for which the General's lackey had galloped in a cab to Depré's. Late at night, Lavrétzky returned home, and sat for a long time, without undressing, his eyes covered with his hand, in dumb enchantment. It seemed to him, that only now had he come to understand why life was worth living; all his hypotheses, his intentions, all that nonsense and rubbish, vanished instantaneously; his whole soul was merged in one sentiment, in one desire, in the desire for happiness, possession, love, the sweet love of woman. From that day forth, he began to go often to the Koróbyns'. Six months later, he declared himself to Varvára Pávlovna, and offered her his hand. His proposal was accepted; the General had long since, almost on the eve of his first visit, inquired of Mikhalévitch how many serfs he, Lavrétzky, had; and Varvára Pávlovna also, who, during the whole period of the young man's courtship and even at the moment of his declaration, had preserved her habitual tranquillity and clearness of soul,—Varvára Pávlovna also was well aware that her lover was rich; and Kalliópe Kárlovna said to herself: "Meine Tochter macht eine schöne Partie"—and bought herself a new turban.

XV

So his proposal was accepted, but on certain conditions. In the first place, Lavrétzky must immediately leave the university: who marries a student? and what a dreadful idea,—for a landed proprietor, rich, and twenty-six years old, to take lessons like a school-boy! In the second place, Varvára Pávlovna took upon herself the labour of ordering and purchasing the trousseau, even of choosing the bridegroom's gifts. She had a great deal of practical sense, much taste, much love for comfort, and a great knack for securing for herself that comfort. This knack particularly astonished Lavrétzky when, immediately after the wedding, he and his wife set out in a commodious carriage, which she had bought, for Lavríki. How everything which surrounded him had been planned, foreseen, provided for by Varvára Pávlovna! What charming travelling requisites, what fascinating toilet-boxes and coffeepots, made their appearance in divers snug nooks, and how prettily Varvára Pávlovna herself boiled the coffee in the mornings! But Lavrétzky was not then in a mood for observation: he was in a beatific state, he was intoxicating himself with happiness; he gave himself up to it like a child.... And he was as innocent as a child, that young Alcides. Not in vain did witchery exhale from the whole being of his young wife; not in vain did she promise to the senses the secret luxury of unknown delights; she fulfilled more than she had promised. On arriving at Lavríki, in the very hottest part of the summer, she found the house dirty and dark, the servants ridiculous and antiquated, but she did not find it necessary even to hint at this to her husband. If she had been making preparations to settle down at Lavríki, she would have made over everything about it, beginning, of course, with the house; but the idea of remaining in that God-forsaken corner of the steppes never entered her mind for one moment; she lived in it, as though camping out, gently enduring all the inconveniences and making amusing jests over them. Márfa Timoféevna came to see her nursling; Varvára Pávlovna took a great liking for her, but she did not take a liking for Varvára Pávlovna. Neither did the new mistress of the house get on well with Glafíra Petróvna; she would have left her in peace, but old Koróbyn wanted to feather his nest from his son-in-law's affairs; "it was no shame, even for a General," said he, "to manage the estate of so near a relative." It must be assumed that Pável Petróvitch would not have disdained to busy himself with the estate of an entire stranger. Varvára Pávlovna conducted her attack in a very artful manner:

without thrusting herself forward, and still, to all appearances, wholly absorbed in the felicity of the honeymoon, in quiet country life, in music and reading, she little by little drove Glafíra Petróvna to such a state, that one morning the latter rushed like a madwoman into Lavrétzky's study, and, hurling her bunch of keys on the table, announced that it was beyond her power to occupy herself with the housekeeping, and that she did not wish to remain in the country. Having been properly prepared in advance, Lavrétzky immediately consented to her departure.—Glafíra Petróvna had not expected this. "Very well," said she, and her eyes grew dark,—"I see that I am not wanted here! I know who it is that is driving me hence—from my native nest. But do thou remember my words, nephew: thou shalt never be able to build thyself a nest anywhere, thou must wander all thy life. That is my legacy to thee."—That very day she departed to her own little estate, and a week later General Koróbyn arrived, and with agreeable melancholy in his gaze and movements, took the management of the entire estate into his hands.

In September, Varvára Petróvna carried her husband off to Petersburg. She spent two winters in Petersburg (they removed to Tzárskoe Seló for the summer), in a beautiful, light, elegantly furnished apartment; they made many acquaintances in middle-class and even in the higher circles of society, they went out and received a great deal, and gave most charming musical and dancing parties. Varvára Pávlovna attracted guests as a flame attracts moths. Such a dissipated life did not altogether please Feódor Ivánitch. His wife advised him to enter the service; owing to his father's old memories, and his own conceptions, he would not serve, but to please his wife he remained in Petersburg. But he speedily divined that no one prevented his isolating himself, that it was not for nothing that he had the quietest and most comfortable study in all Petersburg, that his solicitous wife was even ready to help him to isolate himself,—and from that time forth all went splendidly. Once more he took up his own education, which, in his opinion, was unfinished, once more he began to read, he even began to study the English language. It was strange to see his mighty, broad-shouldered figure, eternally bent over his writing-table, his full, hairy, ruddy face half concealed by the pages of a dictionary or an exercise-book. Every morning he spent in work, dined capitally (Varvára Pávlovna was an excellent housewife), and in the evening he entered an enchanting, fragrant, brilliant world, all populated with young, merry faces,—and the central point of that world was also the zealous hostess, his wife. She gladdened him with the birth of a son, but the poor boy did not live long: he died in the spring, and in the summer, by the advice of the physicians, Lavrétzky took his wife abroad, to the baths. Diversion was indispensable to her, after such a bereavement, and her health required a warm climate. They spent the summer and autumn in Germany and Switzerland, and in the winter, as might have been expected, they went to Paris. In Paris Varvára Pávlovna blossomed out like a rose, and managed to build a little nest for herself as promptly and as adroitly as in Petersburg. She found an extremely pretty apartment, in one of the quiet but fashionable Paris streets; she made her husband such a dressing-gown as he had never owned before; she hired a trim maid, a capital cook, a smart footman; she got an enchanting carriage, a charming little piano. A week had not passed before she crossed a street, wore her shawl, opened her parasol, and put on her gloves in a style equal to that of the purest-blooded Parisienne. And she soon provided herself with acquaintances. At first, only Russians went to her house, then Frenchmen began to make their appearance, very amiable, courteous, unmarried, with beautiful manners and euphonious family names; they all talked fast and much, bowed with easy grace, and screwed up their eyes in a pleasing way; all of them had white teeth which gleamed beneath rosy lips,—and how they did understand the art of smiling! Every one of them brought his friends, and "la belle Madame de Lavretzki" soon became known from the Chaussée d'Antin to the Rue de Lille. In those days (this took place in 1836), that tribe of feuilleton and chronicle writers, which now swarm everywhere, like ants in an ant-hill which has been cut open, had not multiplied; but even then, a certain M——r Jules presented himself in Varvára Pávlovna's salon, a gentleman of insignificant appearance, with a scandalous reputation, insolent and base, like all duellists and beaten men. This M—r Jules was extremely repulsive to Varvára Pávlovna, but she received him because he scribbled for various journals, and incessantly alluded to her, calling her now "Mme. de L*** tzki," now "Mme. de*** cette grande dame Russe si distinguée, qui demeure rue de P."; narrating to all the world, that is to say, to a few hundred subscribers, who cared nothing whatever about "Mme. de L*** tzki," how that pretty and charming lady was a real Frenchwoman in mind (une vraie française par l'esprit),—there is no higher encomium for the French,—what a remarkable musician she was, and how wonderfully she waltzed (Varvára Pávlovna, in reality, did waltz in such a manner as to draw all hearts after the hem of her light, fluttering gown) ... in a word, he spread her fame throughout the world,—and assuredly that is agreeable, say what you will. Mlle. Mars had already left the stage, and Mlle. Rachel had not yet made her appearance; nevertheless, Varvára Pávlovna diligently frequented the theatres. She went into ecstasies over Italian music, and laughed at the ruins of Odra, yawned decorously at the Comédie Française, and wept at the acting of Mme. Dorval in some ultra-romantic melodrama or other; but, chief of all, Liszt played a couple of times at her house, and was so nice, so simple—it was delightful! In such pleasant sensations passed a winter, at the end of which Varvára Pávlovna was even presented at Court. Feódor Ivánitch, on his side, was not bored, although life, at times, weighed heavily on his shoulders,—heavily, because it was empty. He read the newspapers, he listened to lectures at the Sorbonne and the Collège de France, he kept track of the debates in parliament, he undertook the translation of a well-known scientific work on irrigation. "I am not wasting time,"—he said to himself,—"all this is useful; but next winter I must, without fail, return to Russia and set to work." It is difficult to say, whether he was clearly conscious in what that work consisted, and God knows whether he would have succeeded in returning to Russia for the winter,—in the meantime, he went with his wife to Baden-Baden.... An unexpected event destroyed all his plans.

XVI

One day, on entering Varvára Pávlovna's boudoir in her absence, Lavrétzky beheld on the floor a tiny, carefully-folded scrap of paper. He mechanically picked it up, mechanically unfolded it, and read the following, written in French:

"Dear angel Betsy! (I cannot possibly bring myself to call thee Barbe or Varvára). I waited in vain for thee at the corner of the Boulevard; come to-morrow, at half-past one, to our little apartment. Thy good fatty (ton gros bonhomme de mari) generally buries himself in his books at that hour; again we will sing the song of your poet Puskin (de votre poète Pouskine) which thou hast taught me: 'Old husband, menacing husband!'—A thousand kisses on thy hands and feet! I await thee."

"Ernest."

Lavrétzky did not, on the instant, understand what sort of thing it was he had read; he perused it a second time—and his head reeled, the floor swayed beneath his feet, like the deck of a steamer when it is pitching—he cried out, and sobbed and wept simultaneously.

He lost his senses. He had so blindly trusted his wife, that the possibility of deception, of treachery, had never presented itself to his mind. That Ernest, that lover of his wife's was a fair-haired, good-looking boy of three and twenty, with a small snub nose and thin moustache, almost the most insignificant of all her admirers. Several minutes passed, half an hour passed; Lavrétzky still stood, crushing the fatal missive in his hand and staring senselessly at the floor; through a sort of dark whirlwind, visions of pale faces flitted before him; his heart sank within him, in anguish; it seemed to him that he was falling, falling, falling ... and that there was no end to it. The light, familiar rustle of a silken robe aroused him from his state of stupefaction; Varvára Pávlovna, in bonnet and shawl, had hastily returned from her stroll. Lavrétzky trembled all over, and rushed out of the room; he felt that at that moment he was capable of tearing her to pieces, of beating her until she was half dead, in peasant fashion, of strangling her with his hands. The astonished Varvára Pávlovna tried to stop him; he could only whisper: "Betsy"—and fled from the house.

Lavrétzky took a carriage, and ordered the man to drive him

51

out of town. The entire remainder of the day, and the whole night long until the morning, he roamed about, incessantly halting and wringing his hands: now he raged, again it seemed rather ridiculous to him, even rather amusing. In the morning he was chilled through, and entered a wretched suburban inn, asked for a room, and seated himself on a chair by the window. A convulsive yawning seized hold upon him. He could hardly stand on his feet, his body was exhausted,—but he was conscious of no fatigue,—yet fatigue claimed its rights: he sat and stared, and understood nothing; he did not understand what had happened to him, why he found himself alone, with benumbed limbs, with a bitterness in his mouth, with a stone on his breast, in a bare, strange room; he did not understand what had made her, Várya, give herself to that Frenchman, and how she had been able, knowing herself to be unfaithful, to be as calm, amiable, and confiding toward him as before! "I understand nothing!" whispered his parched lips. "Who will guarantee me now, that in Petersburg...." And he did not finish the question, and yawned again, quivering and writhing all over. The bright and the dark memories tormented him equally; it suddenly occurred to him, that a few days previously, in his presence and in that of Ernest, she had seated herself at the piano and had sung: "Old husband, menacing husband!" He recalled the expression of her face, the strange glitter of her eyes, and the flush on her cheeks,—and he rose from his chair; he wanted to go and to say to them: "You have made a mistake in trifling with me; my great-grandfather used to hang the peasants up by the ribs, and my grandfather himself was a peasant"—and kill them both. Then, all of a sudden, it seemed to him, that everything which was taking place with him was a dream, and not even a dream, but merely some nonsense or other: that all he had to do was to shake himself, to look about him.... He did look about him, and as the hawk buries his claws in the bird he has captured, anguish pierced more and more deeply into his heart. To crown all, Lavrétzky was hoping at the end of a few months to become a father.... The past, the future, his whole life was poisoned. He returned, at last, to Paris, put up at a hotel, and sent Varvára Pávlovna the note of M—r Ernest, with the following letter:

"The accompanying document will explain everything to you. I will say to you, by the way, that I did not recognise you: you, always such a precise person, to drop such an important paper!" (This phrase poor Lavrétzky had prepared and cherished for the space of several hours.) "I

52

can see you no more; I assume that you, also, cannot wish to meet me. I have assigned fifteen thousand francs a year to you; I cannot give more. Send your address to the office of the estate. Do what you will, live where you please. I wish you happiness. No answer is necessary."

Lavrétzky wrote to his wife, that no answer was necessary ... but he waited, he thirsted for an answer, an explanation of this incomprehensible, this incredible affair. Varvára Pávlovna, that very day, sent him a long letter in French. It made an end of him; his last doubts vanished,—and he felt ashamed that he had still cherished doubts. Varvára Pávlovna did not defend herself: she merely wished to see him, she entreated him not to condemn her irrevocably. The letter was cold and constrained, although the traces of tears were visible here and there. Lavrétzky uttered a bitter laugh, and bade the messenger say that it was all very good. Three days later, he had quitted Paris: but he went, not to Russia, but to Italy. He himself did not know why he had chosen Italy, in particular; in reality, it made no difference to him whither he went,—provided it were not home. He sent instructions to his peasant-steward in regard to his wife's pension, ordered him, at the same time, to take all matters pertaining to the estate instantly out of the hands of General Koróbyn, without awaiting the surrender of the accounts, and to make arrangements for the departure of His Excellency from Lavríki; he formed a vivid picture to himself, of the consternation, the fruitless haughtiness of the ejected General, and, with all his grief, he felt a certain malicious satisfaction. Then he invited Glafíra Petróvna, in a letter also, to return to Lavríki, and sent her a power of attorney. Glafíra Petróvna did not return to Lavríki, and herself published in the newspapers that she had destroyed the power of attorney, which was quite superfluous. Hiding himself in a small Italian town, it was a long time still before Lavrétzky could force himself not to watch his wife. He learned from the newspapers, that she had quitted Paris, as it was supposed, for Baden-Baden: her name soon made its appearance in an article written by that same M'sieu Jules. In this article, a sort of friendly condolence pierced through the customary playfulness; Feódor Ivánitch's soul was in a very ugly state when he read that article. Later on, he learned that a daughter had been born to him; at the end of a couple of months, he was informed by his peasant-steward, that Varvára Pávlovna had demanded the first third of her allowance. Then more and more evil reports began to arrive; at last, a tragicomic tale made the rounds—creating a sensation—of the newspapers, wherein his wife played an unenviable part. All was at an end: Varvára Pávlovna had become "a celebrity."

Lavrétzky ceased to follow her career; but he was not able speedily to conquer himself. At times, he was seized with such a longing for his wife, that it seemed to him, he would give everything—he would even, if necessary ... forgive her—if only he might again hear her caressing voice, again feel her hand in his hand. But time went on, and not in vain. He was not born to be a martyr; his healthy nature asserted its rights. Much became clear to him; the very blow which had assailed him, no longer seemed to him unforeseen; he understood his wife,—one understands a person who is near to one, when parted from him. Again he was able to occupy himself, to work, although with far less zeal than of yore: scepticism, for which the way had been prepared by the experiences of life, by his education, definitively took possession of his soul. He became extremely indifferent to everything. Four years elapsed, and he felt himself strong enough to return to his native land, to meet his own people. Without halting either in Petersburg or Moscow, he arrived in the town of O*** where we took leave of him, and whither we now beg the indulgent reader to return with us.

XVII

On the morning following the day which we have described, at nine o'clock, Lavrétzky ascended the porch of the Kalítin house. Liza emerged to meet him, in hat and gloves.

"Where are you going?" he asked her.

"To church. To-day is Sunday."

"And do you really care to go to the Liturgy?"

Liza said nothing, but gazed at him in amazement.

"Pardon me, please,"—said Lavrétzky,—"I ... I did not mean to say that. I came to say good-bye to you: I am going to my country place an hour hence."

"It is not far from here, is it?"—inquired Liza.

"Twenty-five versts."

Lyénotchka made her appearance on the threshold of the door, accompanied by a maid.

"See that you do not forget us,"—said Liza, and descended the steps.

"And do not you forget me. And see here,"—he added,—"you are going to church: pray for me also, by the way."

Liza paused and turned toward him.

"Certainly,"—she said, looking him straight in the face:—"I will pray for you. Come along, Lyénotchka."

Lavrétzky found Márya Dmítrievna alone in the drawing-room. An odour of eau de cologne and mint emanated from her. She had a headache, according to her own account, and she had passed a restless night. She welcomed him with her customary languid amiability, and gradually got to talking.

"What an agreeable young man Vladímir Nikoláitch is," she inquired:—"is he not?"

"What Vladímir Nikoláitch?"

"Why, Pánshin, you know,—the one who was here yesterday evening. He took an immense liking to you; I will tell you, as a secret, mon cher cousin, he is simply beside himself over my Liza. What do you think of that? He comes of a good family, he discharges his service splendidly, he is clever, well, and a Junior Gentleman of the Bedchamber, and if it be God's will.... I, on my side, as a mother, shall be very glad. It is a great responsibility, of course: up to the present time, whether it be for good or evil, you see, I am always, everywhere, entirely alone: I have reared my children, I have taught them, I have done everything ... and now I have ordered a governess from Mme. Bolius...."

55

Márya Dmítrievna launched out into a description of her toils, her efforts, and her maternal feelings. Lavrétzky listened to her in silence, and twirled his hat in his hands. His cold, heavy gaze disconcerted the loquacious lady.

"And how do you like Liza?"—she asked.

"Lizavéta Mikhaílovna is an extremely beautiful girl,"—replied Lavrétzky, rose, bowed, and went to Márfa Timoféevna. Márya Dmítrievna gazed after him with displeasure, and said to herself: "What a dolt, what a peasant! Well, now I understand why his wife could not remain faithful to him."

Márfa Timoféevna was sitting in her own room, surrounded by her suite. It consisted of five beings, almost equally near to her heart: a fat-jowled trained bullfinch, which she loved because he had ceased to whistle and draw water; a tiny, very timorous and peaceable dog, Róska; an angry cat Matrós (Sailor); a black-visaged nimble little girl of nine, with huge eyes and a sharp little nose, who was named Schúrotchka; and an elderly woman, fifty years of age, in a white cap, and a light brown, bob-tailed jacket over a dark gown, by name Nastásya Kárpovna Ogárkoff. Schúrotchka was of the petty burgher class, a full orphan. Márfa Timoféevna had taken charge of her out of pity, as she had of Róska: she had picked up both the dog and the girl in the street; both were thin and hungry, both were being drenched by the autumnal rain, no one had hunted up Róska, and Schúrotchka's uncle, a drunken shoemaker, who had not enough to eat himself, and who did not feed his niece, though he beat her over the head with his last, gladly surrendered her to Márfa Timoféevna. With Nastásya Kárpovna, Márfa Timoféevna had made acquaintance on a pilgrimage, in a monastery; she herself had gone up to her in church (Márfa Timoféevna liked her because, to use her own words, "she prayed tastily"), had herself begun the conversation, and had invited her to come to her for a cup of tea. From that day forth, she had never parted with her. Nastásya Kárpovna was a woman of the merriest and gentlest disposition, a childless widow, member of a poverty-stricken family of the petty nobility; she had a round, grey head, soft white hands, a soft face, with large, kindly features, and a rather ridiculous snub nose; she fairly worshipped Márfa Timoféevna, and the latter loved her greatly, although she jeered at her tender heart: Nastásya Kárpovna felt a weakness for all young people, and involuntarily blushed like a girl at the most innocent jest. Her entire capital consisted of twelve hundred paper rubles; she lived at the expense of Márfa Timoféevna, but on equal terms with her: Márfa Timoféevna would not have tolerated servility.

"Ah, Fédya!" she began, as soon as she caught sight of him:—

"last night, thou didst not see my family: admire it. We are all assembled for tea; this is our second, feast-day tea. Thou mayest pet all: only Schúrotchka will not allow thee, and the cat scratches. Art thou going away to-day?"

"Yes,"—Lavrétzky seated himself on a narrow little chair.—"I have already said farewell to Márya Dmítrievna. I have also seen Lizavéta Mikhaílovna."

"Call her Liza, my father,—why should she be Mikhaílovna to thee! And sit still, or thou wilt break Schúrotchka's chair."

"She has gone to church,"—pursued Lavrétzky. "Is she pious?"

"Yes, Fédya,—very. More than thou and I, Fédya."

"But are not you pious?"—remarked Nastásya Kárpovna, in a whisper. "And to-day: you did not get to the early Liturgy, but you will go to the later one."

"Not a bit of it—thou wilt go alone: I am lazy, my mother,"—retorted Márfa Timoféevna,—"I am pampering myself greatly with my tea."—She called Nastásya thou, although she lived on equal terms with her,—she was not a Péstoff for nothing: three Péstoffs are recorded with distinction in the Book of Remembrance of Iván Vasílievitch, the Terrible;[7] Márfa Timoféevna knew it.

"Tell me, please,"—began Lavrétzky again:—"Márya Dmítrievna has just been talking about that ... what's his name ... Pánshin. What sort of a person is he?"

"What a chatterbox, the Lord forgive her!"—grumbled Márfa Timoféevna:—"I suppose she imparted to you, as a secret, what a fine suitor has turned up. She might do her whispering with her priest's son; but no, that is not enough for her. But there's nothing in it, as yet, and thank God for that! but she's babbling already."

"Why 'thank God'?"—asked Lavrétzky.

"Why, because the young fellow does not please me; and what is there to rejoice about?"

"He does not please you?"

"Yes, he cannot fascinate everybody. It's enough that Nastásya Kárpovna here should be in love with him."

The poor widow was thoroughly startled.

"What makes you say that, Márfa Timoféevna? You do not fear God!"—she exclaimed, and a blush instantly suffused her face and neck.

"And he certainly knows the rogue,"—Márfa Timoféevna

---

[7] Ivan the Terrible left a long record of his distinguished victims, for the repose of whose souls he ordered prayers to be said in perpetuity. "Book of Remembrance" contains the names of persons who are to be prayed for at the general requiem services, and so forth.—Translator.

interrupted her:—"he knows how to captivate her: he presented her with a snuff-box. Fédya, ask her to give thee a pinch of snuff; thou wilt see what a splendid snuff-box it is: on the lid is depicted a hussar on horseback. Thou hadst better not defend thyself, my mother."

Nastásya Kárpovna merely repelled the suggestion with a wave of her hands.

"Well,"—inquired Lavrétzky,—"and is Liza not indifferent to him?"

"Apparently, she likes him,—however, the Lord only knows. Another man's soul, thou knowest, is a dark forest, much more the soul of a young girl. Now, there's Schúrotchka's soul—try to dissect that! Why has she been hiding herself, and yet does not go away, ever since thou camest?"

Schúrotchka snorted with suppressed laughter and ran out of the room, and Lavrétzky rose from his seat.

"Yes,"—he said slowly:—"a maiden's soul is not to be divined."

He began to take leave.

"Well? Shall we see thee again soon?"—asked Márfa Timoféevna.

"That's as it may happen, aunty; it is not far off."

"Yes, but thou art going to Vasílievskoe. Thou wilt not live at Lavríki:—well, that is thy affair; only, go and salute the tomb of thy mother, and the tomb of thy grandmother too, by the bye. Thou hast acquired all sorts of learning yonder abroad, and who knows, perchance they will feel it in their graves that thou hast come to them. And don't forget, Fédya, to have a requiem service celebrated for Glafíra Petróvna also; here's a silver ruble for thee. Take it, take it, I want to pay for having a requiem service for her. During her lifetime I did not like her, but there's no denying it, the woman had plenty of character. She was a clever creature; and she did not wrong thee, either. And now go, with God's blessing, or thou wilt grow weary of me."

And Márfa Timoféevna embraced her nephew.

"And Liza shall not marry Pánshin,—don't worry about that; that's not the sort of husband she deserves."

"Why, I am not worrying in the least," replied Lavrétzky, and withdrew.

XVIII

Four hours later, he was driving homeward. His tarantás rolled swiftly along the soft country road. There had been a drought for a fortnight; a thin milky cloud was diffused through the air, and veiled the distant forests; it reeked with the odour of burning. A multitude of small, dark cloudlets, with indistinctly delineated edges, were creeping across the pale-blue sky; a fairly strong wind was whisking along in a dry, uninterrupted stream, without dispelling the sultriness. Leaning his head against a cushion, and folding his arms on his breast, Lavrétzky gazed at the strips of ploughed land, in fan-shape, which flew past, at the willow-trees slowly flitting by, at the stupid crows and daws gazing with dull suspicion askance at the passing equipage, at the long strips of turf between the cultivated sections, overgrown with artemisia, wormwood, and wild tansy; he gazed ... and that fresh, fertile nakedness and wildness of the steppe, that verdure, those long hillocks, the ravines with stubby oak bushes, the grey hamlets, the flexible birch-trees,—this whole Russian picture, which he had not seen for a long time, wafted into his soul sweet and, at the same time, painful sensations, weighed on his breast with a certain agreeable oppression. His thoughts slowly roved about; their outlines were as indistinct and confused as the outlines of those lofty cloudlets, which, also, seemed to be roving. He recalled his childhood, his mother; he remembered how she died, how they had carried him to her, and how she, pressing his head to her bosom, had begun to sing feebly over him, but had cast a glance at Glafíra Petróvna—and had relapsed into silence. He recalled his father, at first alert, dissatisfied with every one, and with a brazen voice,—then blind, tearful, and with a dirty grey beard; he recalled how, one day, at table, after drinking an extra glass of wine, and spilling the sauce over his napkin, he had suddenly burst out laughing, and had begun, winking his sightless eyes and flushing crimson, to tell stories of his conquests; he recalled Varvára Pávlovna,—and involuntarily screwed up his eyes, as a man does from momentary inward pain, and shook his head. Then his thoughts came to a pause on Liza.

"Here," he thought, "is a new being, who is only just entering upon life. A splendid young girl, what will become of her? She is comely. A pale, fresh face, such serious eyes and lips, and an honest and innocent gaze. It is a pity that she seems to be somewhat enthusiastic. A splendid figure, and she walks so lightly, and her voice is soft. I greatly like to see her pause suddenly, listen

59

attentively, without a smile, and then meditate, and toss back her hair. Really, it strikes me that Pánshin is not worthy of her. But what is there wrong about him? She will traverse the road which all traverse. I had better take a nap." And Lavrétzky closed his eyes.

He could not get to sleep, but plunged into the dreamy stupor of the road. Images of the past, as before, arose in leisurely fashion, floated through his soul, mingling and entangling themselves with other scenes. Lavrétzky, God knows why, began to think about Robert Peel ... about French history ... about how he would win a battle if he were a general; he thought he heard shots and shrieks.... His head sank to one side, he opened his eyes.... The same fields, the same views of the steppe; the polished shoes of the trace-horse flashed in turn through the billowing dust; the shirt of the postilion, yellow, with red gussets at the armpits, puffed out in the wind.... "A pretty way to return to my native land"—flashed through Lavrétzky's head; and he shouted: "Faster!" wrapped himself up in his cloak, and leaned back harder against his pillow. The tarantás gave a jolt: Lavrétzky sat upright, and opened his eyes wide. Before him, on a hillock, a tiny hamlet lay outspread; a little to the right, a small, ancient manor-house was to be seen, with closed shutters and a crooked porch; all over the spacious yard, from the very gates, grew nettles, green and thick as hemp; there, also, stood a small oaken store-house, still sound. This was Vasílievskoe.

The postilion turned up to the gate, and brought the horses to a standstill; Lavrétzky's footman rose on the box, and, as though preparing to spring down, shouted: "Hey!" A hoarse, dull barking rang out, but not even the dog showed himself; the lackey again prepared to leap down, and again shouted: "Hey!" The decrepit barking was renewed, and, a moment later, a man ran out into the yard, no one could tell whence,—a man in a nankeen kaftan, with a head as white as snow; shielding his eyes with his hand, he stared at the tarantás, suddenly slapped himself on both thighs, at first danced about a little on one spot, then ran to open the gate. The tarantás drove into the yard, the wheels rustling against the nettles, and halted in front of the porch. The white-headed man, very nimble, to all appearances, was already standing, with his feet planted very wide apart and very crooked, on the last step; and having unbuttoned the apron, convulsively held up the leather and aided the master to descend to the earth, and then kissed his hand.

"Good-day, good-day, brother,"—said Lavrétzky,—"I think thy name is Antón? Thou art still alive?"

The old man bowed in silence, and ran to fetch the keys. While he was gone, the postilion sat motionless, bending sideways and gazing at the locked door; but Lavrétzky's lackey remained standing as he had sprung down, in a picturesque pose, with one hand resting on the box. The old man brought the keys, and quite unnecessarily writhing like a serpent, raising his elbows on high, he unlocked the door, stepped aside, and again bowed to his girdle.

"Here I am at home, here I have got back,"—said Lavrétzky to himself, as he entered the tiny anteroom, while the shutters were opened, one after the other, with a bang and a squeak, and the daylight penetrated into the deserted rooms.

The tiny house where Lavrétzky had arrived, and where, two
years previously, Glafíra Petróvna had breathed her last, had been
built in the previous century, out of sturdy pine lumber; in
appearance it was decrepit, but was capable of standing another
fifty years or more. Lavrétzky made the round of all the rooms, and,
to the great discomfiture of the aged, languid flies, with white dust
on their backs, who were sitting motionless under the lintels of the
doors, he ordered all the windows to be opened; no one had opened
them since the death of Glafíra Petróvna. Everything in the house
remained as it had been: the small, spindle-legged couches in the
drawing-room, covered with glossy grey material, worn through and
flattened down, vividly recalled the days of Katherine II; in the
drawing-room, also, stood the mistress's favourite chair, with a tall,
straight back, against which, even in her old age, she had not
leaned. On the principal wall hung an ancient portrait of Feódor's
great-grandfather, Andréi Lavrétzky; the dark, sallow face was
barely discernible against the warped and blackened background;
the small, vicious eyes gazed surlily from beneath pendent, swollen
lids; the black hair, devoid of powder, rose in a brush over the
heavy, deeply-seamed brow. On the corner of the portrait hung a
wreath of dusty immortelles. "Glafíra Petróvna herself was pleased
to weave it," announced Antón. In the bedchamber rose a narrow
bed, under a tester of ancient, striped material, of very excellent
quality; a mountain of faded pillows, and a thin quilted coverlet, lay
on the bed, and by the head of the bed hung an image of the
Presentation in the Temple of the All-Holy Birthgiver of God, the
very same image to which the old spinster, as she lay dying alone
and forgotten by every one, had pressed for the last time, her lips
which were already growing cold. The toilet-table, of inlaid wood
with brass trimmings and a crooked mirror with tarnished gilding,
stood by the window. Alongside the bedroom was the room for the
holy pictures, a tiny chamber, with bare walls and a heavy shrine of
images in the corner; on the floor lay a small, threadbare rug,
spotted with wax; Glafíra Petróvna had been wont to make her
prostrations upon it. Antón went off with Lavrétzky's lackey to open
the stable and carriage-house; in his stead, there presented herself
an old woman, almost of the same age as he, with a kerchief bound
round her head, down to her very brows; her head trembled, and
her eyes gazed dully, but expressed zeal, and a long-established
habit of serving with assiduity, and, at the same time, a certain

respectful commiseration. She kissed Lavrétzky's hand, and paused at the door, in anticipation of orders. He positively was unable to recall her name; he could not even remember whether he had ever seen her. It turned out that her name was Apraxyéya; forty years before, that same Glafíra Petróvna had banished her from the manor-house service, and had ordered her to attend to the fowls; however, she said little,—as though she had outlived her mind,—and only looked on cringingly. In addition to these two old people, and three potbellied brats in long shirts, Antón's great-grandchildren, there dwelt in the service-rooms of the manor a one-armed little old peasant, who was exempt from compulsory service; he made a drumming noise like a woodcock when he spoke, and was not capable of doing anything. Not much more useful than he was the decrepit dog, who had welcomed Lavrétzky's home-coming with his bark: it had already been fastened up for ten years with a heavy chain, bought by order of Glafíra Petróvna, and was barely in a condition to move and drag its burden. After inspecting the house, Lavrétzky went out into the park, and was satisfied with it. It was all overgrown with tall grass, burdock, and gooseberry and raspberry bushes; but there was much shade in it: there were many old linden-trees, which surprised the beholder by their huge size and the strange arrangement of their branches; they had been too closely planted, and at some time or other—a hundred years before—had been pollarded. The park ended in a small, clear pond, with a rim of tall, reddish reeds. The traces of human life fade away very quickly: Glafíra Petróvna's farm had not succeeded in running wild, but it already seemed plunged in that tranquil dream wherewith everything on earth doth dream, where the restless infection of people does not exist. Feódor Ivánitch also strolled through the village; the women stared at him from the thresholds of their cottages, each with her cheek propped on one hand; the peasant men saluted him from afar; the children ran away; the dogs barked indifferently. At last he felt hungry, but he did not expect his servants and cook until toward evening; the cart with provisions from Lavríki had not yet arrived,—he was compelled to appeal to Antón. Antón immediately arranged matters: he caught an old hen, cut its throat, and plucked it; Apraxyéya rubbed and scrubbed it for a long time, and washed it, like linen, before she placed it in the stew-pan; when, at last, it was cooked, Antón put on the table-cloth and set the table, placed in front of the plate a blackened salt-cellar of plated ware on three feet, and a small faceted carafe with a round glass stopper and a narrow neck; then he announced to Lavrétzky, in a chanting voice, that the meal was ready,—and took up his post behind his chair, having wound a napkin around his right fist, and disseminating some strong, ancient odour, which resembled the odour of cypress wood. Lavrétzky tasted the soup, and came upon the hen; its skin was all covered with big pimples, a thick tendon ran down each leg, its flesh had a flavour of charcoal and lye. When he had finished his dinner, Lavrétzky said that he would like some tea, if.... "This very moment, sir, I will serve it, sir,"—interrupted the old man,—and he kept his promise. A pinch of tea was hunted up, wrapped in a scrap of red paper, a small but very mettlesome and noisy samovár was searched out, also sugar, in very tiny bits, that seemed to have been melted around the edges. Lavrétzky drank his tea out of a large cup; he remembered that cup in his childhood: playing-cards were depicted on it, only visitors drank out of it,—and he now drank out of it, like a visitor. Toward evening, his servants arrived; Lavrétzky did not wish to sleep in his aunt's bed; he gave orders that a bed should be made up for him in the dining-room. Extinguishing the candle, he stared about him for a long time, and meditated on cheerless thoughts; he experienced the sensation familiar to every man who chances to pass the night, for the first time, in a place which has long been uninhabited; it seemed to him that the darkness which surrounded him on all sides could not accustom itself to the new inhabitant, that the very walls of the house were waxing indignant. At last he sighed, drew the coverlet up over him, and fell asleep. Antón remained afoot longer than the rest; for a long time he whispered with Apraxyéya, groaned in a low tone, and crossed himself a couple of times. Neither of them expected that the master would settle down among them at Vasílievskoe, when, near at hand, he owned such a magnificent estate, with a capitally-organised manor-house; they did not even suspect that it was precisely that manor-house which was repugnant to Lavrétzky: it evoked in him oppressive memories. After having whispered his fill, Antón took his staff, and beat upon the board at the store-house which had long been hanging silent,[8] and immediately lay down for a nap in the yard, without covering up his grey head with anything. The May night was tranquil and caressing—and the old man slumbered sweetly.

---

[8] It is the duty of the night-watchman to beat upon the board at regular intervals, to show that he is vigilant.—Translator.

XX

The next morning Lavrétzky rose quite early, had a talk with the overseer, visited the threshing-floor, ordered the chain to be removed from the watch-dog, who only barked a little, but did not even move away from his kennel;—and on his return home, sank into a sort of peaceful torpor, from which he did not emerge all day. "I have sunk down to the very bottom of the river now," he said to himself more than once. He sat by the window, made no movement, and seemed to be listening to the current of tranquil life which surrounded him, to the infrequent noises of the country solitudes. Yonder, somewhere beyond the nettles, some one began to sing, in the shrillest of voices; a gnat seemed to be chiming in with the voice. Now it ceased, but the gnat still squeaked on; athwart the energetic, insistently-plaintive buzzing of the flies resounded the booming of a fat bumble-bee, which kept bumping its head against the ceiling; a cock on the road began to crow, hoarsely prolonging the last note; a peasant cart rumbled past; the gate toward the village creaked. "Well?" suddenly quavered a woman's voice.—"Okh, thou my dear little sweetheart," said Antón to a little girl of two years, whom he was dandling in his arms. "Fetch some kvas," repeats the same female voice,—and all at once a deathlike silence ensues; nothing makes any noise, nothing stirs; the breeze does not flutter a leaf; the swallows dart along near the ground, one after the other, without a cry, and sadness descends upon the soul from their silent flight.— "Here I am, sunk down to the bottom of the river," Lavrétzky says to himself again.—"And life is at all times tranquil, leisurely here," he thinks:—"whoever enters its circle must become submissive: here there is nothing to agitate one's self about, nothing to disturb; here success awaits only him who lays out his path without haste, as the husbandman lays the furrow with his plough." And what strength there is all around, what health there is in this inactive calm! Yonder now, under the window, a sturdy burdock is making its way out from among the thick grass; above it, the lovage is stretching forth its succulent stalk, the Virgin's-tears[9] toss still higher their rosy tendrils; and yonder, further away, in the fields, the rye is gleaming, and the oats are beginning to shoot up their stalks, and every leaf on every tree, every blade of grass on its stalk, spreads itself out to its fullest extent. "My best years have been spent on the love of a woman," Lavrétzky pursued his meditations:—"may the

---

9 This plant bears round seed-pods of mottled-grey, which are often used to make very pretty rosaries.—Translator.

irksomeness here sober me, may it soothe me, prepare me so that I may understand how to do my work without haste"; and again he began to lend an ear to the silence, expecting nothing,—and, at the same time, as it were incessantly expecting something: the silence enfolds him on all sides, the sun glides quietly across the calm blue sky, a cloud floats gently in its wake; it seems as though they know whither and why they are floating. At that same moment, in other spots on earth, life was seething, bustling, roaring; here the same life was flowing on inaudibly, like water amid marsh-grass; and until the very evening, Lavrétzky could not tear himself from the contemplation of that life fleeting, flowing onward; grief for the past melted in his soul like snows of springtime,—and, strange to say!— never had the feeling of his native land been so deep and strong within him.

XXI

In the course of a fortnight, Feódor Ivánitch brought Glafíra Petróvna's little house into order; cleaned up the yard, the garden; comfortable furniture was brought to him from Lavríki, wine, books, newspapers from the town; horses made their appearance in the stables; in a word, Feódor Ivánitch provided himself with everything that was necessary and began to live—not exactly like a country squire, nor yet exactly like a recluse. His days passed monotonously, but he was not bored, although he saw no one; he occupied himself diligently and attentively with the farming operations, he rode about the neighbourhood on horseback, he read. He read but little, however: it was more agreeable for him to listen to the tales of old Antón. As a rule, Lavrétzky would seat himself with a pipe of tobacco and a cup of cold tea near the window; Antón would stand near the door, with his hands clasped behind him, and begin his leisurely stories of olden times,—of those fabulous times—when the oats and barley were sold not by measures but by huge sacks, at two or three kopéks the sack; when in all directions, even close to the town, stretched impenetrable forests, untouched steppes. "And now," wailed the old man, who was already over eighty years of age:—"they have felled and ploughed up everything until there is no place to drive through." Antón, also, related many things concerning his mistress Glafíra Petróvna: how sagacious and economical she had been; how a certain gentleman, a youthful neighbour, had attempted to gain her good-will, had taken to calling frequently,—and how she had been pleased, for his benefit, even to don her cap with rose-purple ribbons, and her yellow gown of tru-tru levantine; but how, later on, having flown into a rage with her neighbour, on account of the unseemly question: "What might your capital amount to, madam?" she had given orders that he should not be admitted, and how she had then commanded, that everything, down to the very smallest scrap, should be given to Feódor Ivánitch after her death. And, in fact, Lavrétzky found all his aunt's effects intact, not excepting the festival cap, with the rose-purple ribbons, and the gown of yellow tru-tru levantine. The ancient papers and curious documents, which Lavrétzky had counted upon, proved not to exist, with the exception of one tattered little old book, in which his grandfather, Piótr Andréitch, had jotted down, now—"Celebration in the city of Saint Petersburg of the peace concluded with the Turkish Empire by his Illustriousness Prince Alexánder Alexándrovitch Prozoróvsky"; now a recipe for a decoction for the chest, with the comment: "This instruction was given to Generaless Praskóvya Feódorovna Saltykóff, by Feódor Avkséntievitch, Archpriest of the Church of the Life-giving Trinity"; again, some item of political news, like the following: "In the 'Moscow News,' it is announced that Premier-Major Mikhaíl Petróvitch Kolýtcheff has died. Was not he the son of Piótr Vasílievitch Kolýtcheff?" Lavrétzky also found several ancient calendars and dream-books, and the mystical works of Mr. Ambódik; many memories were awakened in him by the long-forgotten but familiar "Symbols and Emblems." In Glafíra Petróvna's toilet-table Lavrétzky found a small packet, tied with black ribbon, and sealed with black wax, thrust into the remotest recesses of the drawer. In the packet, face to face, lay a pastel portrait of his father in his youth, with soft curls tumbling over his brow, with long, languid eyes, and mouth half opened,—and the almost effaced portrait of a pale woman in a white gown, with a white rose in her hand,—his mother. Glafíra Petróvna had never permitted her own portrait to be made.—"Dear little father Feódor Ivánitch,"—Antón was wont to say to Lavrétzky:—"although I did not then have my residence in the manor-house of the masters, yet I remember your great-grandfather, Andréi Afanásievitch,—that I do; I was eighteen years of age when he died. Once I met him in the garden,—my very hamstrings shook; but he did nothing, only inquired my name,—and sent me to his chamber for a pocket-handkerchief. He was a real gentleman, there's no gainsaying that,—and he recognised no superior over him. For I must inform you, that your great-grandfather had a wonderful amulet,—a monk from Mount Athos gave him that amulet. And that monk said to him: 'I give thee this for thine affability, Boyárin; wear it—and fear not fate.' Well, and of course, dear little father, you know, what sort of times those were; what the master took a notion to do, that he did. Once in a while, some one, even one of the gentry, would take it into his head to thwart him; but no sooner did he look at him, than he would say: 'You're sailing in shoal water'—that was his favourite expression. And he lived, your great-grandfather of blessed memory, in a tiny wooden mansion; but what property he left behind him, what silver, and all sorts of supplies,—all the cellars were filled to the brim! He was a master. That little carafe, which you were pleased to praise,—belonged to him: he drank vódka from it. And then your grandfather, Piótr Ivánitch, built himself a stone mansion; but he acquired no property; with him everything went at sixes and sevens; and he lived worse than his papa, and got no pleasure for himself,—but wasted all the money, and there was none to pay for requiems for his soul; he left not even a silver spoon behind him, so it was lucky that Glafíra Petróvna brought things into order."

"And is it true,"—Lavrétzky interrupted him,—"that she was called an ill-tempered old hag?"

"Why, surely, some did call her that!"—returned Antón, in displeasure.

"Well, little father,"—the old man one day summoned the courage to ask;—"and how about our young mistress; where is she pleased to have her residence?"

"I have separated from my wife,"—said Lavrétzky, with an effort:—"please do not inquire about her."

"I obey, sir,"—replied the old man, sadly.

After the lapse of three weeks, Lavrétzky rode into O*** on horseback, to the Kalítins', and passed the evening with them. Lemm was there; Lavrétzky conceived a great liking for him. Although, thanks to his father, he did not play on any instrument, yet he was passionately fond of music,—intelligent, classical music. Pánshin was not at the Kalítins' that evening. The Governor had sent him off somewhere, out of town. Liza played alone, and with great precision; Lemm grew animated, excited, rolled a piece of paper into a baton, and beat time. Márya Dmítrievna laughed, at first, as she watched him, and then went off to bed; as she said, Beethoven was too agitating for her nerves. At midnight, Lavrétzky escorted Lemm to his lodgings, and sat with him until three o'clock in the morning. Lemm talked a great deal; his bent shoulders straightened up, his eyes opened widely and sparkled; his very hair stood upright above his brow. It was such a very long time since any one had taken an interest in him, but Lavrétzky evidently did take an interest, and interrogated him solicitously and attentively. This touched the old man; he ended by showing his visitor his music, he even played and sang to him, with his ghost of a voice, several selections from his compositions,—among others, the whole of Schiller's ballad "Fridolin," which he had set to music. Lavrétzky lauded it, made him repeat portions of it, and invited him to visit him for a few days. Lemm, who was escorting him to the street, immediately accepted, and shook his hand warmly; but when he was left alone, in the cool, damp air of the day which was just beginning to dawn, he glanced around him, screwed up his eyes, writhed, and went softly to his tiny chamber, like a guilty creature: "Ich bin wohl nicht klug" (I'm not in my right mind),—he muttered, as he lay down on his hard, short bed. He tried to assert that he was ill when, a few days later, Lavrétzky came for him in a calash; but Feódor Ivánitch went to him, in his room, and persuaded him. The circumstance which operated most powerfully of all on Lemm was, that Lavrétzky had ordered a piano to be sent to his country-house from the town: a piano for his—Lemm's—use. Together they went to the Kalítins', and spent the evening, but not so agreeably as on the former occasion. Pánshin was there, had a great deal to narrate about his journey, and very amusingly mimicked and illustrated in action the country squires he had seen; Lavrétzky laughed, but Lemm did not emerge from his corner, maintained silence, quietly quivered all over like a spider, looked glum and dull, and grew animated only when Lavrétzky began to take his leave. Even when he was seated in the calash, the old man continued to be shy and to fidget; but the quiet, warm air, the light breeze, the delicate shadows, the perfume of the grass, of the birch buds, the peaceful gleam of the starry, moonless heaven, the energetic hoof-beats and snorting of the horses, all the charms of the road, of spring, of night,—descended into the heart of the poor German, and he himself was the first to address Lavrétzky.

XXII

He began to talk of music, of Liza, then again of music. He seemed, somehow, to utter his words more slowly when he spoke of Liza. Lavrétzky turned the conversation on his compositions, and, half in jest, proposed to write a libretto for him.

"H'm, a libretto!"—rejoined Lemm:—"no, that is beyond me: I have not that animation, that play of fancy, which is indispensable for an opera; I have already lost my powers.... But if I could still do something,—I would be satisfied with a romance; of course, I should like some good words...."

He relapsed into silence, and sat for a long time motionless, with his eyes raised heavenward.

"For example," he said at last:—"something of this sort: 'Ye stars, O ye pure stars'?"...

Lavrétzky turned his face slightly toward him and began to stare at him.

"'Ye stars, ye pure stars,'"—repeated Lemm.... "'Ye gaze alike upon the just and upon the guilty ... but only the innocent of heart,'—or something of that sort ... 'understand you,' that is to say, no,—'love you.' However, I am not a poet ... how should I be! But something in that style, something lofty."

Lemm pushed his hat back on the nape of his neck; in the delicate gloom of the light night, his face seemed whiter and more youthful.

"'And ye also,'"—he went on, with a voice which gradually grew quieter:—"'ye know who loves, who knows how to love, for ye are pure, ye, alone, can comfort.'... No, that's not right yet! I am not a poet,"—he said:—"but something of that sort...."

"I regret that I am not a poet,"—remarked Lavrétzky.

"Empty visions!" retorted Lemm, and huddled in the corner of the calash. He closed his eyes, as though preparing to go to sleep. Several moments elapsed.... Lavrétzky listened.... "'Stars, pure stars, love,'"—the old man was whispering.

"Love,"—Lavrétzky repeated to himself, became thoughtful, and his soul grew heavy within him.

"You have written some very beautiful music for 'Fridolin,' Christofór Feódoritch,"—he said aloud:—"and what think you; did that Fridolin, after the Count had led him to his wife, become her lover—hey?"

"That is what you think,"—returned Lemm: "because, probably, experience...." He suddenly fell silent, and turned away in confusion. Lavrétzky laughed in a constrained way, turned away also, and began to stare along the road.

The stars had already begun to pale, and the sky was grey, when the calash rolled up to the porch of the little house at Vasílievskoe. Lavrétzky conducted his guest to the chamber which had been assigned to him, returned to his study, and sat down by the window. In the park, a nightingale was singing its last lay before the dawn. Lavrétzky remembered that a nightingale had been singing in the Kalítins' garden also; he recalled, too, the tranquil movement of Liza's eyes when, at the first sounds of it, they had turned toward the dark window. He began to think of her, and his heart grew calm within him. "Pure little star,"—he said to himself, in a low tone:— "pure stars,"—he added, with a smile, and calmly lay down to sleep.

But Lemm sat, for a long time, on his bed, with a book of music-paper on his knees. It seemed as though a strange, sweet melody were about to visit him: he was already burning and growing agitated, he already felt the lassitude and sweetness of its approach ... but it did not come.

"I am not a poet, and not a musician!"—he whispered at last....

And his weary head sank back heavily on the pillow.

XXIII

On the following morning, host and guest drank tea in the garden, under an ancient linden-tree.

"Maestro!"—said Lavrétzky, among other things:—"you will soon have to compose a triumphal cantata."

"On what occasion?"

"On the occasion of the marriage of Mr. Pánshin to Liza. Did you notice how he was paying court to her last evening? It seems as though everything were going smoothly with them."

"That shall not be!" exclaimed Lemm.

"Why not?"

"Because it is impossible. However,"—he added, after a pause:—"everything is possible in this world. Especially here, with you, in Russia."

"Let us leave Russia out of the question for the present; but what evil do you see in that marriage?"

"All is evil, all. Lizavéta Mikhaílovna is an upright, serious maiden, with exalted sentiments,—but he ... he is a di-let-tante, in one word."

"But surely she loves him?"

Lemm rose from the bench.

"No, she does not love him, that is to say, she is very pure in heart, and does not know herself what 'love' means. Madam von Kalítin tells her, that he is a nice young man, and she listens to Madam von Kalítin, because she is still a perfect child, although she is nineteen years of age: she says her prayers in the morning, she says her prayers in the evening,—and that is very praiseworthy; but she does not love him. She can love only the fine, but he is not fine; that is, his soul is not fine."

Lemm uttered this whole speech coherently and with fervour, pacing back and forth, with short strides, in front of the tea-table, and with his eyes flitting over the ground.

"My dearest Maestro!"—exclaimed Lavrétzky all at once:—"it strikes me, that you are in love with my cousin yourself."

Lemm came to a sudden halt.

"Please,"—he began in an uncertain voice:—"do not jest thus with me. I am not a lunatic."

Lavrétzky felt sorry for the old man; he entreated his forgiveness. After tea, Lemm played him his cantata, and at dinner, being instigated thereto by Lavrétzky himself, he again began to talk about Liza. Lavrétzky listened to him with attention and curiosity.

"What think you, Christofór Feódoritch,"—he said at last—"everything appears to be in order with us now, the garden is in full bloom.... Shall not we invite her here for the day, together with her mother and my old aunt,—hey? Would that be agreeable to you?"

Lemm bent his head over his plate.

"Invite her,"—he said, almost inaudibly.

"And Pánshin need not be asked?"

"He need not,"—replied the old man, with a half-childlike smile.

Two days later, Feódor Ivánitch set out for the town, to the Kalítins.

74

XXIV

He found them all at home, but he did not immediately announce to them his intention: he wished, first, to have a talk alone with Liza. Chance aided him: they were left alone together in the drawing-room. They fell into conversation: she had succeeded in getting used to him,—and, in general, she was not shy of any one. He listened to her, looked her straight in the face, and mentally repeated Lemm's words, and agreed with him. It sometimes happens, that two persons who are already acquainted, but not intimate, suddenly and swiftly draw near to each other in the course of a few minutes,—and the consciousness of this approach is immediately reflected in their glances, in their friendly, quiet smiles, in their very movements. Precisely this is what took place with Lavrétzky and Liza. "So that's what he is like," she thought, gazing caressingly at him; "so that's what thou art like," he said to himself also. And therefore, he was not greatly surprised when she, not without a slight hesitation, however, announced to him, that she had long had it in her heart to say something to him, but had been afraid of annoying him.

"Have no fear; speak out,"—he said, and halted in front of her.

Liza raised her clear eyes to his.

"You are so kind,"—she began, and, at the same time, she said to herself:—"'yes, he really is kind' ... you will pardon me, but I ought not to speak of this to you ... but how could you ... why did you separate from your wife?"

Lavrétzky shuddered, glanced at Liza, and seated himself beside her.

"My child," he began,—"please do not touch that wound; your hands are tender, but nevertheless I shall suffer pain."

"I know,"—went on Liza, as though she had not heard him:—"she is culpable toward you, I do not wish to defend her; but how is it possible to put asunder that which God has joined together?"

"Our convictions on that point are too dissimilar, Lizavéta Mikhaílovna,"—said Lavrétzky, rather sharply;—"we shall not understand each other."

Liza turned pale; her whole body quivered slightly; but she did not hold her peace.

"You ought to forgive,"—she said softly:—"if you wish to be forgiven."

"Forgive!"—Lavrétzky caught her up:—"Ought not you first to know for whom you are pleading? Forgive that woman, take her back into my house,—her,—that empty, heartless creature! And who has told you, that she wishes to return to me? Good heavens, she is entirely satisfied with her position.... But what is the use of talking about it! Her name ought not to be uttered by you. You are too pure, you are not even in a position to understand what sort of a being she is."

"Why vilify her?"—said Liza, with an effort. The trembling of her hands became visible. "It was you yourself who abandoned her, Feódor Ivánitch."

"But I tell you,"—retorted Lavrétzky, with an involuntary outburst of impatience:—"that you do not know what sort of a creature she is!"

"Then why did you marry her?"—whispered Liza, and dropped her eyes.

Lavrétzky sprang up hastily from his seat.

"Why did I marry? I was young and inexperienced then; I was deceived, I was carried away by a beautiful exterior. I did not know women, I did not know anything. God grant that you may make a happier marriage! But, believe me, it is impossible to vouch for anything."

"And I may be just as unhappy,"—said Liza (her voice began to break): "but, in that case, I must submit; I do not know how to talk, but if we do not submit...."

Lavrétzky clenched his fists and stamped his foot.

"Be not angry; forgive me!"—ejaculated Liza, hastily.

At that moment, Márya Dmítrievna entered. Liza rose, and started to leave the room.

"Stop!"—Lavrétzky unexpectedly called after her. "I have a great favour to ask of your mother and of you: make me a visit to celebrate my new home. You know, I have set up a piano; Lemm is staying with me; the lilacs are now in bloom; you will get a breath of the country air, and can return the same day,—do you accept?"

Liza glanced at her mother, and Márya Dmítrievna assumed an air of suffering, but Lavrétzky, without giving her a chance to open her mouth, instantly kissed both her hands. Márya Dmítrievna, who was always susceptible to endearments, and had not expected such amiability from "the dolt," was touched to the soul, and consented. While she was considering what day to appoint, Lavrétzky approached Liza, and, still greatly agitated, furtively whispered to her: "Thank you, you are a good girl, I am to blame.".... And her pale face flushed crimson with a cheerful—bashful smile; her eyes also smiled,—up to that moment, she had been afraid that she had offended him.

"May Vladímir Nikoláitch go with us?"—asked Márya Dmítrievna.

"Certainly,"—responded Lavrétzky:—"but would it not be better if we confined ourselves to our own family circle?"

"Yes, certainly, but you see...." Márya Dmítrievna began. "However, as you like," she added.

It was decided to take Lyénotchka and Schúrotchka. Márfa Timoféevna declined to make the journey.

"It is too hard for me, my dear,"—she said,—"my old bones ache: and I am sure there is no place at your house where I can spend the night; and I cannot sleep in a strange bed. Let these young people do the gallivanting."

Lavrétzky did not succeed in being alone again with Liza; but he looked at her in such a way, that she felt at ease, and rather ashamed, and sorry for him. On taking leave of her, he pressed her hand warmly; when she was left alone, she fell into thought.

XXV

When Lavrétzky reached home, he was met on the threshold of the drawing-room by a tall, thin man, in a threadbare blue coat, with frowzy grey side-whiskers, a long, straight nose, and small, inflamed eyes. This was Mikhalévitch, his former comrade at the university. Lavrétzky did not recognise him at first, but embraced him warmly as soon as he mentioned his name. They had not seen each other since the Moscow days. There was a shower of exclamations, of questions; long-smothered memories came forth into the light of day. Hurriedly smoking pipe after pipe, drinking down tea in gulps, and flourishing his long arms, Mikhalévitch narrated his adventures to Lavrétzky; there was nothing very cheerful about them, he could not boast of success in his enterprises,—but he laughed incessantly, with a hoarse, nervous laugh. A month previously, he had obtained a situation in the private counting-house of a wealthy distiller, about three hundred versts from the town of O*** , and, on learning of Lavrétzky's return from abroad, he had turned aside from his road, in order to see his old friend. Mikhalévitch talked as abruptly as in his younger days, was as noisy and effervescent as ever. Lavrétzky was about to allude to his circumstances, but Mikhalévitch interrupted him, hastily muttering: "I've heard, brother, I've heard about it,—who could have anticipated it?"—and immediately turned the conversation into the region of general comments.

"I, brother,"—he said:—"must leave thee to-morrow; to-day, thou must excuse me—we will go to bed late—I positively must find out what are thy opinions, convictions, what sort of a person thou hast become, what life has taught thee." (Mikhalévitch still retained the phraseology of the 30's.) "So far as I myself am concerned, I have changed in many respects, brother: the billows of life have fallen upon my breast,—who the dickens was it that said that?— although, in important, essential points, I have not changed; I believe, as of yore, in the good, in the truth; but I not only believe,— I am now a believer, yes—I am a believer, a religious believer. Hearken, thou knowest that I write verses; there is no poetry in them, but there is truth. I will recite to thee my last piece: in it I have given expression to my most sincere convictions. Listen."— Mikhalévitch began to recite a poem; it was rather long, and wound up with the following lines:

"To new feeling I have surrendered myself with all my heart,
I have become like a child in soul:

And I have burned all that I worshipped.
I have worshipped all that I burned."

As he declaimed these last two lines, Mikhalévitch was on the verge of tears; slight convulsive twitchings, the signs of deep feeling—flitted across his broad lips, his ugly face lighted up. Lavrétzky listened and listened to him; the spirit of contradiction began to stir within him: the ever-ready, incessantly-seething enthusiasm of the Moscow student irritated him. A quarter of an hour had not elapsed, before a dispute flared up between them, one of those interminable disputes, of which only Russians are capable. After a separation of many years' duration, spent in two widely-different spheres, understanding clearly neither other people's thoughts nor their own,—cavilling at words and retorting with mere words, they argued about the most abstract subjects,—and argued as though it were a matter of life and death to both of them: they shouted and yelled so, that all the people in the house took fright, and poor Lemm, who, from the moment of Mikhalévitch's arrival, had locked himself up in his room, became bewildered, and began, in a confused way, to be afraid.

"But what art thou after this? disillusioned?"—shouted Mikhalévitch at one o'clock in the morning.

"Are there any such disillusioned people?"—retorted Lavrétzky:—"they are all poor and ill,—and I'll pick thee up with one hand, shall I?"

"Well, if not a disillusioned man, then a sceptuik, and that is still worse." (Mikhalévitch's pronunciation still smacked of his native Little Russia.) "And what right hast thou to be a sceptic? Thou hast had bad luck in life, granted; that was no fault of thine: thou wert born with a passionate, loving soul, and thou wert forcibly kept away from women: the first woman that came in thy way was bound to deceive thee."

"And she did deceive me,"—remarked Lavrétzky, gloomily.

"Granted, granted; I was the instrument of fate there,—but what nonsense am I talking?—there's no fate about it; it's merely an old habit of expressing myself inaccurately. But what does that prove?"

"It proves, that they dislocated me in my childhood."

"But set thy joints! to that end thou art a human being, a man; thou hast no need to borrow energy! But, at any rate, is it possible, is it permissible, to erect a private fact, so to speak, into a general law, into an immutable law?"

"Where is the rule?"—interrupted Lavrétzky,—"I do not admit...."

"Yes, it is thy rule, thy rule," Mikhalévitch interrupted him in his turn....

"Thou art an egoist, that's what thou art!"—he thundered, an hour later:—"thou hast desired thine own personal enjoyment, thou hast desired happiness in life, thou hast desired to live for thyself alone...."

"What dost thou mean by personal enjoyment?"

"And everything has deceived thee; everything has crumbled away beneath thy feet."

"What is personal enjoyment,—I ask thee?"

"And it was bound to crumble. For thou hast sought support where it was not to be found, for thou hast built thy house on a quicksand...."

"Speak more plainly, without metaphors, because I do not understand thee."

"Because,—laugh if it pleases thee,—because there is no faith in thee, no warmth of heart; mind, merely a farthing mind; thou art simply a pitiful, lagging Voltairian—that's what thou art!"

"Who—I am a Voltairian?"

"Yes, just the same sort as thy father was, and dost not suspect it thyself."

"After that,"—cried Lavrétzky,—"I have a right to say that thou art a fanatic!"

"Alas!"—returned Mikhalévitch, with contrition:—"unhappily, as yet I have in no way earned so lofty an appellation...."

"Now I have discovered what to call thee,"—shouted this same Mikhalévitch, at three o'clock in the morning;—"thou art not a sceptic, not a disillusioned man, not a Voltairian,—thou art a trifler, and thou art an evil-minded trifler, a conscious trifler, not an ingenuous trifler. Ingenuous triflers lie around on the oven and do nothing, because they do not know how to do anything; and they think of nothing. But thou art a thinking man,—and thou liest around; thou mightest do something—and thou dost nothing; thou liest with thy well-fed belly upward and sayest: 'It is proper to lie thus, because everything that men do is nonsense, and twaddle which leads to nothing.'"

"But what makes thee think that I trifle,"—insisted Lavrétzky:—"why dost thou assume such thoughts on my part?"

"And more than that, all of you, all the people of your sort,"—pursued the obstreperous Mikhalévitch:—"are erudite triflers. You know on what foot the German limps, you know what is bad about the English and the French,—and your knowledge comes to your assistance, justifies your shameful laziness, your disgusting inactivity. Some men will even pride themselves, and say, 'What a clever fellow I am!—I lie around, but the others, the fools, bustle about.' Yes!—And there are such gentlemen among us,—I am not saying this with reference to thee, however,—who pass their whole lives in a sort of stupor of tedium, grow accustomed to it, sit in it like ... like a mushroom in sour cream," Mikhalévitch caught himself up, and burst out laughing at his own comparison.—"Oh, that stupor of tedium is the ruin of the Russians! The repulsive trifler, all his life long, is getting ready to work...."

"Come, what art thou calling names for?"—roared Lavrétzky, in his turn.—"Work ... act ... Tell me, rather, what to do, but don't call names, you Poltáva Demosthenes!"

"Just see what a freak he has taken! I'll not tell thee that, brother; every one must know that himself," retorted Demosthenes, ironically.—"A landed proprietor, a nobleman—and he doesn't know what to do! Thou hast no faith, or thou wouldst know; thou hast no faith—and there is no revelation."

"Give me a rest, at any rate, you devil: give me a chance to look around me,"—entreated Lavrétzky.

"Not a minute, not a second of respite!"—retorted Mikhalévitch, with an imperious gesture of the hand.—"Not one second!—Death does not wait, and life ought not to wait.".．.

"And when, where did men get the idea of becoming triflers?"—he shouted, at four o'clock in the morning, but his voice had now begun to be rather hoarse: "among us! now! in Russia! when on every separate individual a duty, a great obligation is incumbent toward God, toward the nation, toward himself! We are sleeping, but time is passing on; we are sleeping...."

"Permit me to observe to thee,"—said Lavrétzky,—"that we are not sleeping at all, now, but are, rather, preventing others from sleeping. We are cracking our throats like cocks. Hark, isn't that the third cock-crow?"

This sally disconcerted and calmed down Mikhalévitch. "Farewell until to-morrow,"—he said, with a smile,—and thrust his pipe into his tobacco-pouch. "Farewell until to-morrow," repeated Lavrétzky. But the friends conversed for an hour longer. However, their voices were no longer raised, and their speeches were quiet, sad, and kind.

Mikhalévitch departed on the following day, in spite of all Lavrétzky's efforts to detain him. Feódor Ivánitch did not succeed in persuading him to remain; but he talked with him to his heart's content. It came out, that Mikhalévitch had not a penny in the world. Already, on the preceding evening, Lavrétzky, with compassion, had observed in him all the signs and habits of confirmed poverty; his boots were broken, a button was missing from the back of his coat, his hands were guiltless of gloves, down was visible in his hair; on his arrival, it had not occurred to him to ask for washing materials, and at supper he ate like a shark, tearing the meat apart with his hands, and cracking the bones noisily with his strong, black teeth. It appeared, also, that the service had been of no benefit to him, that he had staked all his hopes on the revenue-farmer, who had engaged him simply with the object of having in his counting-house "an educated man." In spite of all this, Mikhalévitch was not dejected, and lived on as a cynic, an idealist, a poet, sincerely rejoicing and grieving over the lot of mankind, over his own calling,—and troubled himself very little as to how he was to keep himself from dying with hunger. Mikhalévitch had not married, but had been in love times without number, and wrote verses about all his lady-loves; with especial fervour did he sing the praises of one mysterious "panna"[10] with black and curling locks.... Rumours were in circulation, it is true, to the effect that the "panna" in question was a plain Jewess, well known to many cavalry officers ... but, when you come to think of it,—does that make any difference?

Mikhalévitch did not get on well with Lemm: his vociferous speeches, his harsh manners, frightened the German, who was not used to such things.... An unfortunate wretch always scents another unfortunate wretch from afar, but rarely makes up to him in old age,—and this is not in the least to be wondered at: he has nothing to share with him,—not even hopes.

Before his departure, Mikhalévitch had another long talk with Lavrétzky, prophesied perdition to him, if he did not come to a sense of his errors, entreated him to occupy himself seriously with the existence of his peasants, set himself up as an example, saying, that he had been purified in the furnace of affliction,—and immediately thereafter, several times mentioned himself as a happy man, compared himself to the birds of heaven, the lilies of the field....

"A black lily, at any rate,"—remarked Lavrétzky.

"Eh, brother, don't put on any of your aristocratic airs,"—retorted Mikhalévitch, good-naturedly:—"but thank God, rather, that in thy veins flows honest, plebeian blood. But I perceive, that thou art now in need of some pure, unearthly being, who shall wrest thee from this apathy of thine."

"Thanks, brother,"—said Lavrétzky:—"I have had enough of those unearthly beings."

"Shut up, cuiniuk!"—exclaimed Mikhalévitch.

---

[10] Polish for "gentlewoman."—Translator.

"Cynic,"—Lavrétzky corrected him.

"Just so, cuinuik,"—repeated Mikhalévitch, in no wise disconcerted.

Even as he took his seat in the tarantás, to which his flat, yellow, strangely light trunk was carried forth, he continued to talk; wrapped up in some sort of a Spanish cloak with a rusty collar, and lion's paws in place of clasps, he still went on setting forth his views as to the fate of Russia, and waving his swarthy hand through the air, as though he were sowing the seeds of its future welfare. At last the horses started.... "Bear in mind my last three words,"—he shouted, thrusting his whole body out of the tarantás, and balancing himself:—"religion, progress, humanity!... Farewell!" His head, with its cap pulled down to the very eyes, vanished. Lavrétzky remained standing alone on the porch and staring down the road until the tarantás disappeared from his sight. "But I think he probably is right,"—he said to himself, as he reentered the house:—"probably I am a trifler." Many of Mikhalévitch's words had sunk indelibly into his soul, although he had disputed and had not agreed with him. If only a man be kindly, no one can repulse him.

XXVI

Two days later, Márya Dmítrievna arrived with all her young people at Vasílievskoe, in accordance with her promise. The little girls immediately ran out into the garden, while Márya Dmítrievna languidly traversed the rooms, and languidly praised everything. Her visit to Lavrétzky she regarded as a token of great condescension, almost in the light of a good deed. She smiled affably when Antón and Apraxyéya, after the ancient custom of house-serfs, came to kiss her hand,—and in an enervated voice, through her nose, she asked them to give her some tea. To the great vexation of Antón, who had donned white knitted gloves, the newly-arrived lady was served with tea not by him, but by Lavrétzky's hired valet, who, according to the assertion of the old man, knew nothing whatever about proper forms. On the other hand, Antón reasserted his rights at dinner: firm as a post he stood behind Márya Dmítrievna's chair—and yielded his place to no one. The long-unprecedented arrival of visitors at Vasílievskoe both agitated and rejoiced the old man: it pleased him to see, that his master knew nice people. However, he was not the only one who was excited on that day: Lemm, also, was excited. He put on a short, snuff-coloured frock-coat, with a sharp-pointed collar, bound his neckerchief tightly, and incessantly coughed and stepped aside, with an agreeable and courteous mien. Lavrétzky noted, with satisfaction, that the close relations between himself and Liza still continued: no sooner did she enter, than she offered him her hand, in friendly wise. After dinner, Lemm drew forth, from the back pocket of his coat, into which he had been constantly thrusting his hand, a small roll of music, and pursing up his lips, he silently laid it on the piano. It was a romance, which he had composed on the preceding day to old-fashioned German words, in which the stars were alluded to. Liza immediately seated herself at the piano and began to decipher the romance.... Alas, the music turned out to be complicated, and disagreeably strained; it was obvious that the composer had attempted to express some passionate, profound sentiment, but nothing had come of it: so the attempt remained merely an attempt. Lavrétzky and Liza both felt this,—and Lemm understood it: he said not a word, put his romance back in his pocket, and in reply to Liza's proposal to play it over again, he merely said significantly, with a shake of his head: "Enough—for the present!"—bent his shoulders, shrank together, and left the room.

Toward evening, they all went fishing together. The pond

beyond the garden contained a quantity of carp and loach. They placed Márya Dmítrievna in an arm-chair near the bank, in the shade, spread a rug under her feet, and gave her the best hook; Antón, in the quality of an old and expert fisherman, offered his services. He assiduously spitted worms on the hook, slapped them down with his hand, spat on them, and even himself flung the line and hook, bending forward with his whole body. That same day, Márya Dmítrievna expressed herself to Feódor Ivánitch, with regard to him, in the following phrase, in the French language of girls' institutes: "Il n'y a plus maintenant de ces gens comme ça comme autrefois." Lemm, with the two little girls, went further away, to the dam; Lavrétzky placed himself beside Liza. The fish bit incessantly, the carp which were caught were constantly flashing their sides, now gold, now silver, in the air; the joyous exclamations of the little girls were unceasing; Márya Dmítrievna herself gave vent to a couple of shrill, feminine shrieks. Lavrétzky and Liza caught fewer than the others; this, probably, resulted from the fact that they paid less attention than the rest to their fishing, and allowed their floats to drift close inshore. The tall, reddish reeds rustled softly around them, in front of them the motionless water gleamed softly, and their conversation was soft also. Liza stood on a small raft; Lavrétzky sat on the inclined trunk of a willow; Liza wore a white gown, girt about the waist with a broad ribbon, also white in hue; her straw hat was hanging from one hand, with the other, she supported, with some effort, the curved fishing-rod. Lavrétzky gazed at the pure, rather severe profile, at her hair tucked behind her ears, at her soft cheeks, which were as sunburned as those of a child,—and said to himself: "O how charmingly thou standest on my pond!" Liza did not turn toward him, but stared at the water,—and half smiled, half screwed up her eyes. The shadow of a linden-tree near at hand fell upon both of them.

"Do you know,"—began Lavrétzky:—"I have been thinking a great deal about my last conversation with you, and have come to the conclusion, that you are extraordinarily kind."

"I did not mean it in that way at all ..." Liza began,—and was overcome with shame.

"You are kind,"—repeated Lavrétzky. "I am a rough man, but I feel that every one must love you. There's Lemm now, for example: he is simply in love with you."

Liza's brows quivered, rather than contracted; this always happened with her when she heard something disagreeable.

"I felt very sorry for him to-day,"—Lavrétzky resumed:—"with his unsuccessful romance. To be young, and be able to do a thing—

85

that can be borne; but to grow old, and not have the power—is painful. And the offensive thing about it is, that you are not conscious when your powers begin to wane. It is difficult for an old man to endure these shocks!... Look out, the fish are biting at your hook.... They say,"—added Lavrétzky, after a brief pause,—"that Vladímir Nikoláitch has written a very pretty romance."

"Yes,"—replied Liza;—"it is a trifle, but it is not bad."

"And what is your opinion,"—asked Lavrétzky:—"is he a good musician?"

"It seems to me that he has great talent for music; but up to the present time he has not cultivated it as he should."

"Exactly. And is he a nice man?"

Liza laughed, and cast a quick glance at Feódor Ivánitch.

"What a strange question!"—she exclaimed, drawing up her hook, and flinging it far out again.

"Why is it strange?—I am asking you about him as a man who has recently come hither, as your relative."

"As a relative?"

"Yes. I believe I am a sort of uncle to you."

"Vladímir Nikoláitch has a kind heart,"—said Liza:—"he is clever; mamma is very fond of him."

"And do you like him?"

"He is a nice man: why should not I like him?"

"Ah!"—said Lavrétzky, and relapsed into silence. A half-mournful, half-sneering expression flitted across his face. His tenacious gaze discomfited Liza, but she continued to smile. "Well, God grant them happiness!"—he muttered, at last, as though to himself, and turned away his head.

Liza blushed.

"You are mistaken, Feódor Ivánitch,"—she said:—"there is no cause for your thinking.... But do not you like Vladímir Nikoláitch?"

"I do not."

"Why?"

"It seems to me, that he has no heart."

The smile vanished from Liza's face.

"You have become accustomed to judge people harshly,"—she said, after a long silence.

"I think not. What right have I to judge others harshly, when I myself stand in need of indulgence? Or have you forgotten that a lazy man is the only one who does not laugh at me?... Well,"—he added:—"and have you kept your promise?"

"What promise?"

"Have you prayed for me?"

86

"Yes, I have prayed, and I do pray for you every day. But please do not speak lightly of that."

Lavrétzky began to assure Liza, that such a thing had never entered his head, that he entertained a profound respect for all convictions; then he entered upon a discussion of religion, its significance in the history of mankind, the significance of Christianity....

"One must be a Christian,"—said Liza, not without a certain effort:—"not in order to understand heavenly things ... yonder ... earthly things, but because every man must die."

Lavrétzky, with involuntary surprise, raised his eyes to Liza's, and encountered her glance.

"What a word you have uttered!"—said he.

"The word is not mine,"—she replied.

"It is not yours.... But why do you speak of death?"

"I do not know. I often think about it."

"Often?"

"Yes."

"One would not say so, to look at you now: you have such a merry, bright face, you are smiling...."

"Yes, I am very merry now,"—returned Liza ingenuously.

Lavrétzky felt like seizing both her hands, and clasping them tightly.

"Liza, Liza!"—called Márya Dmítrievna,—"come hither, look! What a carp I have caught!"

"Immediately, maman,"—replied Liza, and went to her, but Lavrétzky remained on his willow-tree.

"I talk with her as though I were not a man whose life is finished," he said to himself. As she departed, Liza had hung her hat on a bough; with a strange, almost tender sentiment, Lavrétzky gazed at the hat, at its long, rather crumpled ribbons. Liza speedily returned to him, and again took up her stand on the raft.

"Why do you think that Vladímir Nikoláitch has no heart?"—she inquired, a few moments later.

"I have already told you, that I may be mistaken; however, time will show."

Liza became thoughtful. Lavrétzky began to talk about his manner of life at Vasílievskoe, about Mikhalévitch, about Antón; he felt impelled to talk to Liza, to communicate to her everything that occurred to his soul: she was so charming, she listened to him so attentively; her infrequent comments and replies seemed to him so simple and wise. He even told her so.

Liza was amazed.

"Really?"—she said;—"why, I have always thought that I, like my maid Nástya, had no words of my own. One day she said to her betrothed: 'Thou must find it tiresome with me; thou always sayest such fine things to me, but I have no words of my own.'"

"And thank God for that!" thought Lavrétzky.

XXVII

In the meantime, evening drew on, and Márya Dmítrievna expressed a desire to return home. The little girls were, with difficulty, torn away from the pond, and made ready. Lavrétzky announced his intention to escort his guests half way, and ordered his horse to be saddled. As he seated Márya Dmítrievna in the carriage, he remembered Lemm; but the old man was nowhere to be found. He had disappeared as soon as the angling was over. Antón slammed to the carriage door, with a strength remarkable for his years, and grimly shouted: "Drive on, coachman!" The carriage rolled off. On the back seat sat Márya Dmítrievna and Liza; on the front seat, the little girls and the maid. The evening was warm and still, and the windows were lowered on both sides. Lavrétzky rode at a trot by Liza's side of the carriage, with his hand resting on the door,—he had dropped the reins on the neck of his steed, which was trotting smoothly,—and from time to time exchanged a few words with the young girl. The sunset glow vanished; night descended, and the air grew even warmer. Márya Dmítrievna soon fell into a doze; the little girls and the maid also dropped off to sleep. The carriage rolled swiftly and smoothly onward; Liza leaned forward; the moon, which had just risen, shone on her face, the fragrant night breeze blew on her cheeks and neck. She felt at ease. Her hand lay on the door of the carriage, alongside of Lavrétzky's hand. And he, also, felt at ease: he was being borne along through the tranquil nocturnal warmth, never taking his eyes from the kind young face, listening to the youthful voice, which was ringing even in a whisper, saying simple, kindly things; he did not even notice that he had passed the half-way point. He did not wish to awaken Márya Dmítrievna, pressed Liza's hand lightly, and said:—"We are friends, now, are we not?" She nodded, he drew up his horse. The carriage rolled on, gently swaying and lurching: Lavrétzky proceeded homeward at a footpace. The witchery of the summer night took possession of him; everything around him seemed so unexpectedly strange, and, at the same time, so long, so sweetly familiar; far and near,—and things were visible at a long distance, although the eye did not comprehend much of what it beheld,—everything was at rest; young, blossoming life made itself felt in that very repose. Lavrétzky's horse walked briskly, swaying regularly to right and left; its huge black shadow kept pace alongside; there was something mysteriously pleasant in the tramp of its hoofs, something cheerful and wondrous in the resounding call of the quail. The stars were hidden in a sort of brilliant smoke; the moon, not yet at the full, shone with a steady gleam; its light flooded the blue sky in streams, and fell like a stain of smoky gold upon the thin cloudlets which floated past; the crispness of the air called forth a slight moisture in the eyes, caressingly enveloped all the limbs, poured in an abundant flood into the breast. Lavrétzky enjoyed himself, and rejoiced at his enjoyment. "Come, life is still before us," he thought:—"it has not been completely ruined yet by...." He did not finish his sentence, and say who or what had ruined it.... Then he began to think of Liza, that it was hardly likely that she loved Pánshin; that had he met her under different circumstances,—God knows what might have come of it; that he understood Lemm, although she had no "words of her own." Yes, but that was not true: she had words of her own.... "Do not speak lightly of that," recurred to Lavrétzky's memory. He rode for a long time, with drooping head, then he straightened himself up, and slowly recited:

> "And I have burned all that I worshipped,
> I have worshipped all that I burned...."

but immediately gave his horse a cut with the whip, and rode at a gallop all the rest of the way home.

As he alighted from his horse, he cast a last glance around him, with an involuntary, grateful smile. Night, the speechless, caressing night, lay upon the hills and in the valleys; from afar, from its fragrant depths, God knows whence,—whether from heaven or earth,—emanated a soft, quiet warmth. Lavrétzky wafted a last salutation to Liza, and ran up the steps.

The following day passed rather languidly. Rain fell from early morning; Lemm cast furtive glances from beneath his eyebrows, and pursed up his lips more and more tightly, as though he had vowed to himself never to open them again. On lying down to sleep, Lavrétzky had taken to bed with him a whole pile of French newspapers, which had already been lying on his table for two weeks, with their wrappers unbroken. He set to work idly to strip off the wrappers, and glance through the columns of the papers, which, however, contained nothing new. He was on the point of throwing them aside,—when, all of a sudden, he sprang out of bed as though he had been stung. In the feuilleton of one of the papers, M'sieu Jules, already known to us, imparted to his readers "a sad bit of news": "The charming, bewitching native of Moscow," he wrote, "one of the queens of fashion, the ornament of Parisian salons, Madame de Lavretzki, had died almost instantaneously,—and this news, unhappily only too true, had only just reached him, M. Jules. He was,"—he continued,—"he might say, a friend of the deceased...."

Lavrétzky dressed himself, went out into the garden, and until morning dawned, he paced back and forth in one and the same alley.

XXVIII

On the following morning, at tea, Lemm requested Lavrétzky to furnish him with horses, that he might return to town. "It is time that I should set about my work,—that is to say, my lessons," remarked the old man:—"but here I am only wasting time in vain." Lavrétzky did not immediately reply to him: he seemed preoccupied. "Very well,"—he said at last;—"I will accompany you myself."—Without any aid from the servants, grunting and fuming, Lemm packed his small trunk, and tore up and burned several sheets of music-paper. The horses were brought round. As he emerged from his study, Lavrétzky thrust into his pocket the newspaper of the day before. During the entire journey, Lemm and Lavrétzky had very little to say to each other: each of them was engrossed with his own thoughts, and each was delighted that the other did not disturb him. And they parted rather coldly,—which, by the way, frequently happens between friends in Russia. Lavrétzky drove the old man to his tiny house: the latter alighted, got out his trunk, and without offering his hand to his friend (he held his trunk in front of his chest with both hands), without even looking at him,—he said in Russian: "Good-bye, sir!"—"Good-bye,"—repeated Lavrétzky, and ordered his coachman to drive him to his own lodgings. (He had hired a lodging in the town of O*** in case he might require it.) After writing several letters and dining in haste, Lavrétzky took his way to the Kalítins. In their drawing-room he found no one but Pánshin, who informed him that Márya Dmítrievna would be down directly, and immediately entered into conversation with him, with the most cordial amiability. Up to that day, Pánshin had treated Lavrétzky, not exactly in a patronizing way, yet condescendingly; but Liza, in telling Pánshin about her jaunt of the day before, had expressed herself to the effect that Lavrétzky was a very fine and clever man; that was enough: the "very fine" man must be captivated. Pánshin began with compliments to Lavrétzky, with descriptions of the raptures with which, according to his statement, Márya Dmítrievna's whole family had expressed themselves about Vasílievskoe, and then, according to his wont, passing adroitly to himself, he began to talk about his own occupations, his views of life, of the world, of the government service;—he said a couple of words about the future of Russia, about the proper way of keeping the governors in hand; thereupon, merrily jeered at himself, and added, that, among other things, he had been commissioned in Petersburg—"de populariser l'idée du cadastre." He talked for quite a long time, with careless self-confidence solving all difficulties, and juggling with the most weighty administrative and political questions, as a sleight-of-hand performer juggles with his balls. The expressions: "This is what I would do, if I were the government"; "You, as a clever man, will immediately agree with me"—were never absent from his tongue. Lavrétzky listened coldly to Pánshin's idle chatter: he did not like this handsome, clever, and unconstrainedly elegant man, with his brilliant smile, courteous voice, and searching eyes. Pánshin speedily divined, with the swift comprehension of other people's sentiments which was peculiar to him, that he was not affording his interlocutor any particular pleasure, and made his escape, under a plausible pretext, deciding in his own mind that Lavrétzky might be a very fine man, but that he was not sympathetic, was "aigri," and, "en somme," rather ridiculous.—Márya Dmítrievna made her appearance accompanied by Gedeónovsky; then Márfa Timoféevna entered with Liza; after them followed the other members of the household; then came that lover of music, Mme. Byelenítzyn, a small, thin lady, with an almost childish, fatigued and handsome little face, in a rustling black gown, with a motley-hued fan, and heavy gold bracelets; her husband also came, a rosy-cheeked, plump man, with huge feet and hands, with white eyelashes, and an impassive smile on his thick lips; in company his wife never spoke to him, but at home, in moments of tenderness, she was wont to call him "her little pig"; Pánshin returned: the rooms became very full of people and very noisy. Such a throng of people was not to Lavrétzky's liking; Mme. Byelenítzyn particularly enraged him by constantly staring at him through her lorgnette. He would have withdrawn at once, had it not been for Liza: he wished to say two words to her in private, but for a long time he was not able to seize a convenient moment, and contented himself with watching her in secret joy; never had her face seemed to him more noble and charming. She appeared to great advantage from the proximity of Mme. Byelenítzyn. The latter was incessantly fidgeting about on her chair, shrugging her narrow little shoulders, laughing, in an enervated way, and screwing up her eyes, then suddenly opening them very wide. Liza sat quietly, her gaze was direct, and she did not laugh at all. The hostess sat down to play cards with Márfa Timoféevna, Mme. Byelenítzyn, and Gedeónovsky, who played very slowly, was constantly making mistakes, blinking his eyes, and mopping his face with his handkerchief. Pánshin assumed a melancholy mien, expressed himself with brevity, with great significance and mournfulness,—for all the world like an artist who

93

has not had his say,—but despite the entreaties of Mme. Byelenítzyn, who was having a violent flirtation with him, he would not consent to sing his romance: Lavrétzky embarrassed him. Feódor Ivánitch also said little; the peculiar expression of his face had startled Liza, as soon as he entered the room: she immediately felt that he had something to communicate to her, but, without herself knowing why, she was afraid to interrogate him. At last, as she passed into the hall[11] to pour tea, she involuntarily turned her head in his direction. He immediately followed her.

"What is the matter with you?"—she said, as she placed the teapot on the samovár.

"Have you noticed it?"

"You are not the same to-day as I have seen you heretofore."

Lavrétzky bent over the table.

"I wanted,"—he began,—"to tell you a certain piece of news, but now it is not possible.—However, read what is marked with pencil in this feuilleton,"—he added, giving her the copy of the newspaper which he had brought with him.—"I beg that you will keep this secret; I will call on you to-morrow morning."

Liza was surprised.... Pánshin made his appearance on the threshold of the door: she put the newspaper in her pocket.

"Have you read Obermann, Lizavéta Mikhaílovna?"—Pánshin asked her meditatively.

Liza gave him a superficial answer, left the hall, and went up-stairs. Lavrétzky returned to the drawing-room, and approached the card-table. Márfa Timoféevna, with her cap-ribbons untied, and red in the face, began to complain to him about her partner, Gedeónovsky, who, according to her, did not know how to lead.

"Evidently,"—she said,—"playing cards is quite a different thing from inventing fibs."

Her partner continued to blink and mop his face. Liza entered the drawing-room, and seated herself in a corner; Lavrétzky looked at her, she looked at him,—and something like dread fell upon them both. He read surprise and a sort of secret reproach in her face. Long as he might to talk to her, he could not do it; to remain in the same room with her, a guest among strangers, was painful to him: he decided to go away. As he took leave of her, he managed to repeat that he would come on the morrow, and he added that he trusted in her friendship.

"Come,"—she replied, with the same amazement on her face.

Pánshin brightened up after Lavrétzky's departure; he began to

---

[11] A combination of music-room, ball-room, play-room, also used for all sorts of purposes, in all well-to-do Russian houses.—Translator.

give advice to Gedeónovsky, banteringly paid court to Mme. Byelenítzyn, and, at last, sang his romance. But he talked with Liza and gazed at her as before: significantly and rather sadly.

And again, Lavrétzky did not sleep all night long. He did not feel sad, he was not excited, he had grown altogether calm; but he could not sleep. He did not even recall the past; he simply gazed at his life: his heart beat strongly and evenly, the hours flew past, but he did not even think of sleeping. At times, only, did the thought come to the surface in his mind: "But that is not true, it is all nonsense,"—and he paused, lowered his head, and began again to gaze at his life.

XXIX

Márya Dmítrievna did not receive Lavrétzky with any excess of cordiality, when he presented himself on the following day. "Well, you are making yourself pretty free of the house,"—she said to herself. Personally, he did not greatly please her, and, in addition, Pánshin, under whose influence she was, had sung his praises in a very sly and careless manner on the preceding evening. As she did not look upon him in the light of a guest, and did not consider it necessary to trouble herself about a relative almost a member of the family, half an hour had not elapsed before he was strolling down an alley in the garden with Liza. Lyénotchka and Schúrotchka were frolicking a short distance away, among the flower-beds.

Liza was composed, as usual, but paler than usual. She took from her pocket and handed to Lavrétzky the sheet of newspaper, folded small.

"This is dreadful!"—said she.

Lavrétzky made no reply.

"But perhaps it is not yet true,"—added Liza.

"That is why I asked you not to mention it to any one."

Liza walked on a little way.

"Tell me,"—she began:—"you are not grieved? Not in the least?"

"I do not know myself what my feelings are,"—replied Lavrétzky.

"But, assuredly, you used to love her?"

"Yes, I did."

"Very much?"

"Very much."

"And you are not grieved by her death?"

"It is not now that she has died to me."

"What you say is sinful.... Do not be angry with me. You call me your friend: a friend may say anything. To tell the truth, I feel terrified.... Your face was so malign yesterday.... Do you remember, how you were complaining of her, not long ago?—and perhaps, already, at that very time, she was no longer alive. This is terrible. It is exactly as though it had been sent to you as a chastisement."

Lavrétzky laughed bitterly.

"Do you think so?... At all events, I am free now."

Liza gave a slight start.

"Stop, do not talk like that. Of what use to you is your freedom? You must not think about that now, but about forgiveness...."

"I forgave her long ago,"—interrupted Lavrétzky, with a wave of the hand.

"No, not that,"—returned Liza, and blushed. "You did not understand me rightly. You must take means to obtain forgiveness...."

"Who is there to forgive me?"

"Who?—God. Who else but God can forgive us?"

Lavrétzky caught her hand.

"Akh, Lizavéta Mikhaílovna, believe me,"—he exclaimed:—"I have been sufficiently punished as it is. I have already atoned for everything, believe me."

"You cannot know that,"—said Liza in a low voice. "You have forgotten;—not very long ago,—when you were talking to me,—you were not willing to forgive her...."

The two walked silently down the alley.

"And how about your daughter?"—Liza suddenly inquired, and halted.

Lavrétzky started.

"Oh, do not worry yourself! I have already despatched letters to all the proper places. The future of my daughter, as you call ... as you say ... is assured. Do not disquiet yourself."

Liza smiled sadly.

"But you are right,"—went on Lavrétzky:—"what can I do with my freedom? Of what use is it to me?"

"When did you receive that newspaper?"—said Liza, making no reply to his question.

"The day after your visit."

"And is it possible ... is it possible that you did not even weep?"

"No. I was stunned; but where were the tears to come from? Weep over the past,—but, you see, it is entirely extirpated in my case!... Her behaviour itself did not destroy my happiness, but merely proved to me that it had never existed. What was there to cry about? But, who knows?—perhaps I should have been more grieved if I had received this news two weeks earlier...."

"Two weeks?"—returned Liza. "But what has happened in those two weeks?"

Lavrétzky made no answer, and Liza suddenly blushed more furiously than before.

"Yes, yes, you have guessed it,"—interposed Lavrétzky:—"in the course of those two weeks I have learned what a pure woman's soul is like, and my past has retreated still further from me."

Liza became confused, and softly walked toward the flower-garden, to Lyénotchka and Schúrotchka.

"And I am glad that I have shown you this newspaper,"—said Lavrétzky, as he followed her:—"I have already contracted the habit of concealing nothing from you, and I hope that you will repay me with the same confidence."

"Do you think so?"—said Liza, and stopped short. "In that case, I ought to ... but no! That is impossible."

"What is it? Speak, speak!"

"Really, it seems to me that I ought not.... However," added Liza, and turned to Lavrétzky with a smile:—"what is half-frankness worth?—Do you know? I received a letter to-day."

"From Pánshin?"

"Yes, from him.... How did you know?"

"He asks your hand?"

"Yes,"—uttered Liza, and looked seriously in Lavrétzky's eyes. Lavrétzky, in his turn, gazed seriously at Liza.

"Well, and what reply have you made to him?"—he said at last.

"I do not know what reply to make,"—replied Liza, and dropped her clasped hands.

"What? Surely, you like him?"

"Yes, he pleases me; he seems to be a nice man...."

"You said the same thing to me, in those very same words, three days ago. What I want to know is, whether you love him with that strong, passionate feeling which we are accustomed to call love?"

"As you understand it,—no."

"You are not in love with him?"

"No. But is that necessary?"

"Of course it is!"

"Mamma likes him,"—pursued Liza:—"he is amiable; I have nothing against him."

"Still, you are wavering?"

"Yes ... and perhaps,—your words may be the cause of it. Do you remember what you said day before yesterday? But that weakness...."

"Oh, my child!"—suddenly exclaimed Lavrétzky—and his voice trembled:—"do not argue artfully, do not designate as weakness the cry of your heart, which does not wish to surrender itself without love. Do not take upon yourself that terrible responsibility toward a man whom you do not love and to whom you do not wish to belong...."

"I am listening,—I am taking nothing upon myself ..." Liza was beginning.

"Listen to your heart; it alone will tell you the truth,"— Lavrétzky interrupted her.... "Experience, reasoning—all that is stuff and nonsense! Do not deprive yourself of the best, the only happiness on earth."

"Is it you, Feódor Ivánitch, who are speaking thus? You, yourself, married for love—and were you happy?"

Lavrétzky wrung his hands.

"Akh, do not talk to me of that! You cannot even understand all that a young, untried, absurdly educated lad can mistake for love!... Yes, and in short, why calumniate one's self? I just told you, that I had not known happiness ... no! I was happy!"

"It seems to me, Feódor Ivánitch,"—said Liza, lowering her voice (when she did not agree with her interlocutor, she always lowered her voice; and, at the same time, she became greatly agitated):—"happiness on earth does not depend upon us...."

"It does, it does depend upon us, believe me," (he seized both her hands; Liza turned pale, and gazed at him almost in terror, but with attention):—"if only we have not ruined our own lives. For some people, a love-marriage may prove unhappy; but not for you, with your calm temperament, with your clear soul! I entreat you, do not marry without love, from a sense of duty, of renunciation, or anything else.... That, also, is want of faith, that is calculation,—and even worse. Believe me,—I have a right to speak thus: I have paid dearly for that right. And if your God...."

At that moment, Lavrétzky noticed that Lyénotchka and Schúrotchka were standing beside Liza, and staring at him with dumb amazement. He released Liza's hands, said hastily: "Pray pardon me,"—and walked toward the house.

"I have only one request to make of you,"—he said, returning to Liza:—"do not decide instantly, wait, think over what I have said to you. Even if you have not believed me, if you have made up your mind to a marriage of reason,—even in that case, you ought not to marry Mr. Pánshin: he cannot be your husband.... Promise me, will you not, not to be in a hurry?"

Liza tried to answer Lavrétzky, but did not utter a word,—not because she had made up her mind "to be in a hurry"; but because her heart was beating too violently, and a sensation resembling fear had stopped her breath.

XXX

As he was leaving the Kalítins' house, Lavrétzky encountered Pánshin; they saluted each other coldly. Lavrétzky went home to his apartment, and locked himself in. He experienced a sensation such as he had, in all probability, never experienced before. Had he remained long in that state of "peaceful numbness"? had he long continued to feel, as he had expressed it, "at the bottom of the river"? What had altered his position? what had brought him out, to the surface? the most ordinary, inevitable though always unexpected of events;—death? Yes: but he did not think so much about the death of his wife, about his freedom, as,—what sort of answer would Liza give to Pánshin? He was conscious that, in the course of the last three days, he had come to look upon her with different eyes; he recalled how, on returning home, and thinking about her in the silence of the night, he had said to himself: "If...." That "if," wherein he had alluded to the past, to the impossible, had come to pass, although not in the way he had anticipated,—but this was little in itself. "She will obey her mother," he thought, "she will marry Pánshin; but even if she refuses him,—is it not all the same to me?" As he passed in front of the mirror, he cast a cursory glance at his face, and shrugged his shoulders.

The day sped swiftly by in these reflections; evening arrived. Lavrétzky wended his way to the Kalítins. He walked briskly, but approached their house with lingering steps. In front of the steps stood Pánshin's drozhky. "Come,"—thought Lavrétzky,—"I will not be an egoist," and entered the house. Inside he met no one, and all was still in the drawing-room; he opened the door, and beheld Márya Dmítrievna, playing picquet with Pánshin. Pánshin bowed to him in silence, and the mistress of the house uttered a little scream:—"How unexpected!"—and frowned slightly. Lavrétzky took a seat by her side, and began to look over her cards.

"Do you know how to play picquet?"—she asked him, with a certain dissembled vexation, and immediately announced that she discarded.

Pánshin reckoned up ninety, and politely and calmly began to gather up the tricks, with a severe and dignified expression on his countenance. That is the way in which diplomats should play; probably, that is the way in which he was wont to play in Petersburg, with some powerful dignitary, whom he desired to impress with a favourable opinion as to his solidity and maturity. "One hundred and one, one hundred and two, hearts; one hundred

100

and three,"—rang out his measured tone, and Lavrétzky could not understand what note resounded in it: reproach or self-conceit.

"Is Márfa Timoféevna to be seen?"—he asked, observing that Pánshin, still with great dignity, was beginning to shuffle the cards. Not a trace of the artist was, as yet, to be observed in him.

"Yes, I think so. She is in her own apartments, up-stairs,"—replied Márya Dmítrievna:—"you had better inquire."

Lavrétzky went up-stairs, and found Márfa Timoféevna at cards also: she was playing duratchkí (fools) with Nastásya Kárpovna. Róska barked at him; but both the old ladies welcomed him cordially, and Márfa Timoféevna, in particular, seemed to be in high spirits.

"Ah! Fédya! Pray come in,"—she said:—"sit down, my dear little father. We shall be through our game directly. Wouldst thou like some preserves? Schúrotchka, get him a jar of strawberries. Thou dost not want it? Well, then sit as thou art; but as for smoking—thou must not: I cannot bear thy tobacco, and, moreover, it makes Matrós sneeze."

Lavrétzky made haste to assert that he did not care to smoke.

"Hast thou been down-stairs?"—went on the old woman:—"whom didst thou see there? Is Pánshin still on hand, as usual? And didst thou see Liza? No? She intended to come hither.... Yes, there she is; speak of an angel...."

Liza entered the room and, on perceiving Lavrétzky, she blushed.

"I have run in to see you for a minute, Márfa Timoféevna," she began....

"Why for a minute?"—returned the old woman. "What makes all you young girls such restless creatures? Thou seest, that I have a visitor: chatter to him, entertain him."

Liza seated herself on the edge of a chair, raised her eyes to Lavrétzky,—and felt that it was impossible not to give him to understand how her interview with Pánshin had ended. But how was that to be done? She felt both ashamed and awkward. She had not been acquainted with him long, with that man who both went rarely to church and bore with so much indifference the death of his wife,—and here she was already imparting her secrets to him.... He took an interest in her, it is true; she, herself, trusted him, and felt attracted to him; but, nevertheless, she felt ashamed, as though a stranger had entered her pure, virgin chamber.

Márfa Timoféevna came to her assistance.

"If thou wilt not entertain him,"—she began, "who will entertain him, poor fellow? I am too old for him, he is too clever for me, and for Nastásya Kárpovna he is too old, you must give her nothing but very young men."

"How can I entertain Feódor Ivánitch?"—said Liza.—"If he likes, I will play something for him on the piano,"—she added, irresolutely.

"Very good indeed: that's my clever girl,"—replied Márfa Timoféevna,—"Go down-stairs, my dear people; when you are through, come back; for I have been left the 'fool,' and I feel insulted, and want to win back."

Liza rose: Lavrétzky followed her. As they were descending the staircase, Liza halted.

"They tell the truth,"—she began:—"when they say that the hearts of men are full of contradictions. Your example ought to frighten me, to render me distrustful of marriage for love, but I...."

"You have refused him?"—interrupted Lavrétzky.

"No; but I have not accepted him. I told him everything, everything that I felt, and asked him to wait. Are you satisfied?"—she added, with a swift smile,—and lightly touching the railing with her hand, she ran down the stairs.

"What shall I play for you?"—she asked, as she raised the lid of the piano.

"Whatever you like,"—replied Lavrétzky, and seated himself in such a position that he could watch her.

Liza began to play, and, for a long time, never took her eyes from her fingers. At last, she glanced at Lavrétzky, and stopped short: so wonderful and strange did his face appear to her.

"What is the matter with you?"—she asked.

"Nothing,"—he replied:—"all is very well with me; I am glad for you, I am glad to look at you,—go on."

"It seems to me,"—said Liza, a few moments later:—"that if he really loved me, he would not have written that letter; he ought to have felt that I could not answer him now."

"That is of no importance,"—said Lavrétzky:—"the important point is, that you do not love him."

"Stop,—what sort of a conversation is this! I keep having visions of your dead wife, and you are terrible to me!"

"My Lizéta plays charmingly, does she not, Valdemar?"—Márya Dmítrievna was saying to Pánshin at the same moment.

"Yes,"—replied Pánshin;—"very charmingly."

Márya Dmítrievna gazed tenderly at her young partner; but the latter assumed a still more important and careworn aspect, and announced fourteen kings.

102

XXXI

Lavrétzky was not a young man; he could not long deceive himself as to the sentiments with which Liza had inspired him; he became definitively convinced, on that day, that he had fallen in love with her. This conviction brought no great joy to him. "Is it possible," he thought, "that at the age of five and thirty I have nothing better to do than to put my soul again into the hands of a woman? But Liza is not like that one; she would not require from me shameful sacrifices; she would not draw me away from my occupations; she herself would encourage me to honourable, severe toil, and we would advance together toward a fine goal. Yes," he wound up his meditations:—"all that is good, but the bad thing is, that she will not in the least wish to marry me. It was not for nothing that she told me, that I am terrible to her. On the other hand, she does not love that Pánshin either.... A poor consolation!"

Lavrétzky rode out to Vasílievskoe; but he did not remain four days,—it seemed so irksome to him there. He was tortured, also, by expectancy: the information imparted by M—r. Jules required confirmation, and he had received no letters. He returned to the town, and sat out the evening at the Kalítins'. It was easy for him to see, that Márya Dmítrievna had risen in revolt against him; but he succeeded in appeasing her somewhat by losing fifteen rubles to her at picquet,—and he spent about half an hour alone with Liza, in spite of the fact that her mother, no longer ago than the day before, had advised her not to be too familiar with a man "qui a un si grand ridicule." He found a change in her: she seemed, somehow, to have become more thoughtful, she upbraided him for his absence, and asked him—would he not go to church on the following morning (the next day was Sunday)?

"Go,"—she said to him, before he had succeeded in replying:—"we will pray together for the repose of her soul."—Then she added, that she did not know what she ought to do,—she did not know whether she had the right to make Pánshin wait any longer for her decision.

"Why?"—asked Lavrétzky.

"Because,"—said she: "I am already beginning to suspect what that decision will be."

She declared that her head ached, and went off to her own room up-stairs, irresolutely offering Lavrétzky the tips of her fingers.

The next day, Lavrétzky went to the morning service. Liza was already in the church when he arrived. She observed him, although she did not turn toward him. She prayed devoutly; her eyes sparkled softly, her head bent and rose softly. He felt that she was praying for him also,—and a wonderful emotion filled his soul. He felt happy, and somewhat conscience-stricken. The decorously-standing congregation, the familiar faces, the melodious chanting, the odour of the incense, the long, slanting rays of light from the windows, the very gloom of the walls and vaulted roof,—all spoke to his ear. He had not been in a church for a long time, he had not appealed to God for a long time: and even now, he did not utter any words of prayer,—he did not even pray without words, but for a moment, at least, if not in body, certainly with all his mind, he prostrated himself and bowed humbly to the very earth. He recalled how, in his childhood, he had prayed in church on every occasion until he became conscious of some one's cool touch on his brow; "this," he had been accustomed to say to himself at that time, "is my guardian-angel accepting me, laying upon me the seal of the chosen." He cast a glance at Liza.... "Thou hast brought me hither," he thought:—"do thou also touch me, touch my soul." She continued to pray in the same calm manner as before; her face seemed to him joyful, and he was profoundly moved once more; he entreated for that other soul—peace, for his own—pardon....

They met in the porch; she greeted him with cheerful and amiable dignity. The sun brilliantly illuminated the young grass in the churchyard, and the motley-hued gowns and kerchiefs of the women; the bells of the neighbouring churches were booming aloft; the sparrows were chirping in the hedgerows. Lavrétzky stood with head uncovered, and smiled; a light breeze lifted his hair, and the tips of the ribbons on Liza's hat. He put Liza into her carriage, distributed all his small change to the poor, and softly wended his way homeward.

XXXII

Difficult days arrived for Feódor Ivánitch. He found himself in a constant fever. Every morning he went to the post-office, with excitement broke the seals of his letters and newspapers,—and nowhere did he find anything which might have confirmed or refuted the fateful rumour. Sometimes he became repulsive even to himself: "Why am I thus waiting,"—he said to himself, "like a crow for blood, for the sure news of my wife's death?" He went to the Kalítins' every day; but even there he was no more at his ease: the mistress of the house openly sulked at him, received him with condescension; Pánshin treated him with exaggerated courtesy; Lemm had become misanthropic, and hardly even bowed to him,—and, chief of all, Liza seemed to avoid him. But when she chanced to be left alone with him, in place of her previous trustfulness, confusion manifested itself in her: she did not know what to say to him, and he himself felt agitation. In the course of a few days, Liza had become quite different from herself as he had previously known her: in her movements, her voice, in her very laugh, a secret trepidation was perceptible, an unevenness which had not heretofore existed. Márya Dmítrievna, like the genuine egoist she was, suspected nothing; but Márfa Timoféevna began to watch her favourite. Lavrétzky more than once reproached himself with having shown to Liza the copy of the newspaper which he had received: he could not fail to recognise the fact, that in his spiritual condition there was an element which was perturbing to pure feeling. He also assumed that the change in Liza had been brought about by her conflict with herself, by her doubts: what answer should she give to Pánshin? One day she brought him a book, one of Walter Scott's novels, which she herself had asked of him.

"Have you read this book?"—he asked.

"No; I do not feel in a mood for books now,"—she replied, and turned to go.

"Wait a minute: I have not been alone with you for a long time. You seem to be afraid of me."

"Yes."

"Why so, pray?"

"I do not know."

Lavrétzky said nothing for a while.

"Tell me,"—he began:—"you have not yet made up your mind?"

"What do you mean by that?"—she said, without raising her eyes.

"You understand me...."

Liza suddenly flushed up.

"Ask me no questions about anything,"—she ejaculated, with vivacity:—"I know nothing, I do not even know myself...." And she immediately beat a retreat.

On the following day, Lavrétzky arrived at the Kalítins' after dinner, and found all preparations made to have the All-Night Vigil service held there.[12] In one corner of the dining-room, on a square table, covered with a clean cloth, small holy pictures in gold settings, with tiny, dull brilliants in their halos, were already placed, leaning against the wall. An old man-servant, in a grey frock-coat and slippers, walked the whole length of the room in a deliberate manner, and without making any noise with his heels, and placed two wax tapers in slender candlesticks in front of the holy images, crossed himself, made a reverence, and softly withdrew. The unlighted drawing-room was deserted. Lavrétzky walked down the dining-room, and inquired—was it not some one's Name-day? He was answered, in a whisper, that it was not, but that the Vigil service had been ordered at the desire of Lizavéta Mikhaílovna and Márfa Timoféevna; that the intention had been to bring thither the wonder-working ikóna, but it had gone to a sick person, thirty versts distant. There soon arrived, also, in company with the chanters, the priest, a man no longer young, with a small bald spot, who coughed loudly in the anteroom; the ladies all immediately trooped in single file from the boudoir, and approached to receive his blessing; Lavrétzky saluted him in silence; and he returned the salute in silence. The priest stood still for a short time, then cleared his throat again, and asked in a low tone, with a bass voice:

"Do you command me to proceed?"

"Proceed, bátiushka,"—replied Márya Dmítrievna.

He began to vest himself; the chanter obsequiously asked for a live coal; the incense began to diffuse its fragrance. The maids and lackeys emerged from the anteroom and halted in a dense throng close to the door. Róska, who never came down-stairs, suddenly made his appearance in the dining-room: they began to drive him out, and he became confused, turned around and sat down; a footman picked him up and carried him away. The Vigil service began. Lavrétzky pressed himself into a corner; his sensations were strange, almost melancholy; he himself was not able clearly to make

---

[12] This service, consisting (generally) of Vespers and Matins, can be read in private houses, and even by laymen: whereas, the Liturgy, or Mass, must be celebrated at a duly consecrated altar, by a duly ordained priest.— Translator.

out what he felt. Márya Dmítrievna stood in front of them all, before an arm-chair; she crossed herself with enervated carelessness, in regular lordly fashion,—now glancing around her, again suddenly casting her eyes upward: she was bored. Márfa Timoféevna seemed troubled; Nastásya Kárpovna kept prostrating herself, and rising with a sort of modest, soft rustle; Liza took up her stand, and never stirred from her place, never moved; from the concentrated expression of her countenance, it was possible to divine that she was praying assiduously and fervently. When she kissed the cross, at the end of the service, she also kissed the priest's large, red hand. Márya Dmítrievna invited him to drink tea; he took off his stole, assumed a rather secular air, and passed into the drawing-room with the ladies. A not over animated conversation began. The priest drank four cups of tea, incessantly mopping his bald spot with his handkerchief, and narrated, among other things, that merchant Avóshnikoff had contributed seven hundred rubles to gild the "cupola" of the church, and he also imparted a sure cure for freckles. Lavrétzky tried to seat himself beside Liza, but she maintained a severe, almost harsh demeanour, and never once glanced at him; she appeared to be deliberately refraining from noticing him; a certain cold, dignified rapture had descended upon her. For some reason or other, Lavrétzky felt inclined to smile uninterruptedly, and say something amusing; but there was confusion in his heart, and he went away at last, secretly perplexed.... He felt that there was something in Liza into which he could not penetrate.

On another occasion, Lavrétzky, as he sat in the drawing-room, and listened to the insinuating but heavy chatter of Gedeónovsky, suddenly turned round, without himself knowing why he did so, and caught a deep, attentive, questioning gaze in Liza's eyes.... It was riveted on him, that puzzling gaze, afterward. Lavrétzky thought about it all night long. He had not fallen in love in boyish fashion, it did not suit him to sigh and languish, neither did Liza arouse that sort of sentiment; but love has its sufferings at every age,—and he underwent them to the full.

XXXIII

One day, according to his custom, Lavrétzky was sitting at the Kalítins'. A fatiguingly-hot day had been followed by so fine an evening, that Márya Dmítrievna, despite her aversion to the fresh air, had ordered all the windows and doors into the garden to be opened, and had announced that she would not play cards, that it was a sin to play cards in such weather, and one must enjoy nature. Pánshin was the only visitor. Tuned up by the evening, and unwilling to sing before Lavrétzky, yet conscious of an influx of artistic emotions, he turned to poetry: he recited well, but with too much self-consciousness, and with unnecessary subtleties, several of Lérmontoff's poems (at that time, Púshkin had not yet become fashionable again)—and, all at once, as though ashamed of his expansiveness, he began, apropos of the familiar "Thought," to upbraid and reprove the present generation; in that connection, not missing the opportunity to set forth, how he would turn everything around in his own way, if the power were in his hands. "Russia," said he,—"has lagged behind Europe; she must catch up with it. People assert, that we are young—that is nonsense; and moreover, that we possess no inventive genius: X ... himself admits that we have not even invented a mouse-trap. Consequently, we are compelled, willy-nilly, to borrow from others. 'We are ill,'—says Lérmontoff,—I agree with him; but we are ill because we have only half converted ourselves into Europeans; that is where we have made our mistake, and that is what we must be cured of." ("Le cadastre,"—thought Lavrétzky).—"The best heads among us,"—he went on,—"les meilleurs têtes—have long since become convinced of this; all nations are, essentially, alike; only introduce good institutions, and there's an end of the matter. One may even conform to the existing national life; that is our business, the business of men ..." (he came near saying: "of statesmen") "who are in the service; but, in case of need, be not uneasy: the institutions will transform that same existence." Márya Dmítrievna, with emotion, backed up Pánshin. "What a clever man this is,"—she thought,—"talking in my house!" Liza said nothing, as she leaned against a window-frame; Lavrétzky also maintained silence; Márfa Timoféevna, who was playing cards in the corner with her friend, muttered something to herself. Pánshin strode up and down the room, and talked eloquently, but with a secret spite: he seemed to be scolding not the whole race, but certain individuals of his acquaintance. In the Kalítins' garden, in a large lilac-bush, dwelt a nightingale, whose first evening notes rang forth in the intervals of this eloquent harangue; the first stars lighted up in the rosy sky, above the motionless crests of the lindens. Lavrétzky rose, and began to reply to Pánshin; an argument ensued. Lavrétzky defended the youth and independence of Russia; he surrendered himself, his generation as sacrifice,—but upheld the new men, their convictions, and their desires; Pánshin retorted in a sharp and irritating way, declared that clever men must reform everything, and went so far, at last, that, forgetting his rank of Junior Gentleman of the Imperial Bedchamber, and his official career, he called Lavrétzky a "laggard conservative," he even hinted,—in a very remote way, it is true,—at his false position in society. Lavrétzky did not get angry, did not raise his voice (he remembered that Mikhalévitch also had called him a laggard—only, a Voltairian)—and calmly vanquished Pánshin on every point. He demonstrated to him the impossibility of leaps and supercilious reforms, unjustified either by a knowledge of the native land or actual faith in an ideal, even a negative ideal; he cited, as an example, his own education, and demanded, first of all, a recognition of national truth and submission to it,—that submission without which even boldness against falsehood is impossible; he did not evade, in conclusion, the reproach—merited, in his opinion—of frivolous waste of time and strength.

"All that is very fine!"—exclaimed the enraged Pánshin, at last:—"Here, you have returned to Russia,—what do you intend to do?"

"Till the soil,"—replied Lavrétzky:—"and try to till it as well as possible."

"That is very praiseworthy, there's no disputing that,"—rejoined Pánshin:—"and I have been told, that you have already had great success in that direction; but you must admit, that not every one is fitted for that sort of occupation...."

"Une nature poétique,"—began Márya Dmítrievna,—"of course, cannot till the soil ... et puis, you are called, Vladímir Nikoláitch, to do everything en grand."

This was too much even for Pánshin: he stopped short, and the conversation stopped short also. He tried to turn it on the beauty of the starry sky, on Schubert's music—but, for some reason, it would not run smoothly; he ended, by suggesting to Márya Dmítrievna, that he should play picquet with her.—"What! on such an evening?"—she replied feebly; but she ordered the cards to be brought.

Pánshin, with a crackling noise, tore open the fresh pack, while Liza and Lavrétzky, as though in pursuance of an agreement, both rose, and placed themselves beside Márfa Timoféevna. They both, suddenly, felt so very much at ease that they were even afraid to be left alone together,—and, at the same time, both felt that the embarrassment which they had experienced during the last few days had vanished, never more to return. The old woman stealthily patted Lavrétzky on the cheek, slyly screwed up her eyes, and shook her head several times, remarking in a whisper: "Thou hast got the best of the clever fellow, thanks." Everything in the room became still; the only sound was the faint crackling of the wax candles, and, now and then, the tapping of hands on the table, and an exclamation, or the reckoning of the spots,—and the song, mighty, resonant to the verge of daring, of the nightingale, poured in a broad stream through the window, in company with the dewy coolness.

XXXIV

Liza had not uttered a single word during the course of the dispute between Lavrétzky and Pánshin, but had attentively followed it, and had been entirely on Lavrétzky's side. Politics possessed very little interest for her; but the self-confident tone of the fashionable official (he had never, hitherto, so completely expressed himself) had repelled her; his scorn of Russia had wounded her. It had never entered Liza's head, that she was a patriot; but she was at her ease with Russian people; the Russian turn of mind gladdened her; without any affectation, for hours at a time, she chatted with the overseer of her mother's estate, when he came to town, and talked with him as with an equal, without any lordly condescension. Lavrétzky felt all this: he would not have undertaken to reply to Pánshin alone; he had been talking for Liza only. They said nothing to each other, even their eyes met but rarely; but both understood that they had come very close together that evening, understood that they loved and did not love the same things. On only one point did they differ; but Liza secretly hoped to bring him to God. They sat beside Márfa Timoféevna, and appeared to be watching her play; and they really were watching it,—but, in the meanwhile, their hearts had waxed great in their bosoms, and nothing escaped them: for them the nightingale was singing, the stars were shining, and the trees were softly whispering, lulled both by slumber and by the softness of the summer, and by the warmth. Lavrétzky surrendered himself wholly to the billow which was bearing him onward,—and rejoiced; but no word can express that which took place in the young girl's pure soul: it was a secret to herself; so let it remain for all others. No one knows, no one has seen, and no one ever will see, how that which is called into life and blossom pours forth and matures grain in the bosom of the earth.

The clock struck ten. Márfa Timoféevna went off to her rooms up-stairs, with Nastásya Kárpovna; Lavrétzky and Liza strolled through the room, halted in front of the open door to the garden, gazed into the dark distance, then at each other—and smiled; they would have liked, it appeared, to take each other by the hand, and talk their fill. They returned to Márya Dmítrievna and Pánshin, whose picquet had become protracted. The last "king" came to an end at length, and the hostess rose, groaning, and sighing, from the cushion-garnished arm-chair; Pánshin took his hat, kissed Márya Dmítrievna's hand, remarked that nothing now prevented other happy mortals from going to bed, or enjoying the night, but that he must sit over stupid papers until the morning dawned, bowed coldly to Liza (he had not expected that in reply to his offer of marriage, she would ask him to wait,—and therefore he was sulking at her)— and went away. Lavrétzky followed him. At the gate they parted; Pánshin aroused his coachman by poking him with the tip of his cane in the neck, seated himself in his drozhky, and drove off. Lavrétzky did not feel like going home; he walked out beyond the town, into the fields. The night was tranquil and bright, although there was no moon; Lavrétzky roamed about on the dewy grass for a long time; he came by accident upon a narrow path; he walked along it. It led him to a long fence, to a wicket-gate; he tried, without himself knowing why, to push it open: it creaked softly, and opened, as though it had been awaiting the pressure of his hand; Lavrétzky found himself in a garden, advanced a few paces along an avenue of lindens, and suddenly stopped short in amazement: he recognised the garden of the Kalítins.

He immediately stepped into a black blot of shadow which was cast by a thick hazel-bush, and stood for a long time motionless, wondering and shrugging his shoulders.

"This has not happened for nothing," he thought.

Everything was silent round about; not a sound was borne to him from the direction of the house. He cautiously advanced. Lo, at the turn in the avenue, the whole house suddenly gazed at him with its dark front; only in two of the upper windows were lights twinkling: in Liza's room, a candle was burning behind a white shade, and in Márfa Timoféevna's bedroom a shrine-lamp was glowing with a red gleam in front of the holy pictures, reflecting itself in an even halo in the golden settings; down-stairs, the door leading out on the balcony yawned broadly, as it stood wide open. Lavrétzky seated himself on a wooden bench, propped his head on his hand, and began to gaze at the door and the window. Midnight struck in the town; in the house, the small clocks shrilly rang out twelve; the watchman beat with a riffle of taps on the board. Lavrétzky thought of nothing, expected nothing; it was pleasant to him to feel himself near Liza, to sit in her garden on the bench, where she also had sat more than once.... The light disappeared in Liza's room.

"Good night, my dear girl," whispered Lavrétzky, as he continued to sit motionless, and without taking his eyes from the darkened window.

Suddenly a light appeared in one of the windows of the lower storey, passed to a second, a third.... Some one was walking through the rooms with a candle. "Can it be Liza? Impossible!"... Lavrétzky

112

half rose to his feet. A familiar figure flitted past, and Liza made her appearance in the drawing-room. In a white gown, with her hair hanging loosely on her shoulders, she softly approached a table, bent over it, set down the candle, and searched for something; then, turning her face toward the garden, she approached the open door, and, all white, light, graceful, paused on the threshold. A quiver ran through Lavrétzky's limbs.

"Liza!"—burst from his lips, in barely audible tones.

She started, and began to stare into the darkness.

"Liza!"—repeated Lavrétzky more loudly, and emerged from the shadow of the avenue.

Liza, in alarm, stretched forth her head, and staggered backward. He called her for the third time, and held out his arms toward her. She left the door, and advanced into the garden.

"Is it you?"—she said.—"Are you here?"

"It is I ... I ... listen to me,"—whispered Lavrétzky, and, grasping her hand, he led her to the bench.

She followed him without resistance; her pale face, her impassive eyes, all her movements, were expressive of unutterable amazement. Lavrétzky seated her on the bench, and himself took up his stand in front of her.

"I had no thought of coming hither,"—he began:—"I came hither by chance.... I ... I ... I love you,"—he said, with involuntary terror.

Liza slowly glanced at him; apparently, she had only that moment comprehended where she was, and that she was with him. She tried to rise, but could not, and covered her face with her hands.

"Liza,"—said Lavrétzky:—"Liza,"—he repeated, and bowed down at her feet....

Her shoulders began to quiver slightly, the fingers of her pale hands were pressed more tightly to her face.

"What is the matter with you?"—Lavrétzky uttered, and caught the sound of soft sobbing. His heart turned cold.... He understood the meaning of those tears. "Can it be that you love me?"—he whispered, and touched her knee.

"Rise," he heard her voice:—"rise, Feódor Ivánitch. What is this that you and I are doing?"

He rose, and seated himself by her side on the bench. She was no longer weeping, but was gazing attentively at him with her wet eyes.

"I am frightened: what are we doing?"—she repeated.

"I love you,"—he said again:—"I am ready to give the whole of my life to you."

113

Again she shuddered, as though something had stung her, and raised her gaze heavenward.

"All this is in God's power,"—she said.

"But do you love me, Liza? Shall we be happy?"

She dropped her eyes; he softly drew her to him, and her head sank upon his shoulder.... He turned her head a little to one side, and touched her pale lips.

Half an hour later, Lavrétzky was standing before the wicket. He found it locked, and was obliged to leap across the fence. He returned to the town, and walked through the sleeping streets. A sensation of great, of unexpected happiness filled his soul; all doubts had died within him. "Vanish, past, dark spectre," he thought: "she loves me, she will be mine." All at once, it seemed to him that in the air, over his head, wondrous, triumphant sounds rang out; the sounds rolled on still more magnificently; in a chanting, mighty flood they streamed on,—and in them, so it seemed, all his happiness was speaking and singing. He glanced around him: the sounds were floating from two upper windows of a tiny house.

"Lemm!"—cried Lavrétzky, and ran to the house.—"Lemm! Lemm!"—he repeated loudly.

The sounds died away, and the figure of the old man in his dressing-gown, with breast bare, and hair dishevelled, made its appearance at the window.

"Aha!"—he said, with dignity:—"is that you?"

"Christofór Feódoritch! what splendid music! For God's sake, let me in."

The old man, without uttering a word, with a majestic movement of the arm flung the door-key out of the window into the street. Lavrétzky briskly ran up-stairs, entered the room, and was on the point of rushing at Lemm, but the latter imperiously motioned him to a chair; he said, abruptly, in Russian: "Sit down and listen!" seated himself at the piano, gazed proudly and sternly about him, and began to play. It was long since Lavrétzky had heard anything of the sort: a sweet, passionate melody, which gripped the heart from its very first notes; it was all beaming and languishing with inspiration, with happiness, with beauty; it swelled and melted away; it touched everything which exists on earth of precious, mysterious, holy; it breathed forth deathless sadness, and floated away to die in heaven. Lavrétzky straightened himself up and stood there, cold and pale with rapture. Those sounds fairly sank into his soul, which had only just been shaken with the bliss of love; they themselves were flaming with love. "Repeat it,"—he whispered, as soon as the last chord resounded. The old man cast upon him an eagle glance, struck his breast with his hand, and saying deliberately, in his native language:—"I made that, for I am a great musician,"—he again played his wonderful composition. There was no candle in the room; the light of the rising moon fell aslant through the window; the sensitive air trembled resonantly; the pale, little room seemed a sanctuary, and the head of the old man rose high and inspired in the silvery semi-darkness. Lavrétzky approached and embraced him. At first, Lemm did not respond to his embrace, he even repulsed it with his elbow; for a long time, without moving a single limb, he continued to gaze forth, as before, sternly, almost roughly, and only bellowed a couple of times: "Aha!" At last his transfigured face grew calm, relaxed, and, in reply to Lavrétzky's warm congratulations, he first smiled a little, then fell to weeping, feebly sobbing like a child.

"This is marvellous,"—he said:—"that precisely you should now have come; but I know—I know all."

"You know all?"—ejaculated Lavrétzky, in confusion.

"You have heard me,"—returned Lemm:—"have not you understood that I know all?"

Lavrétzky could not get to sleep until the morning: all night long, he sat on his bed. And Liza did not sleep: she prayed.

XXXV

The reader knows how Lavrétzky had grown up and developed; let us say a few words about Liza's bringing up. She was ten years old when her father died; but he had paid little heed to her. Overwhelmed with business, constantly absorbed in increasing his property, splenetic, harsh, impatient, he furnished money unsparingly for teachers, tutors, clothing, and the other wants of the children; but he could not endure, as he expressed it, "to dandle the squalling brats,"—and he had no time to dandle them: he worked, toiled over his business, slept little, occasionally played cards, worked again; he compared himself to a horse harnessed to a threshing-machine. "My life has rushed by fast," he said on his deathbed, with a proud smile on his parched lips. Márya Dmítrievna, in reality, troubled herself about Liza hardly more than did the father, although she had boasted to Lavrétzky that she alone had reared her children; she had dressed Liza like a doll, in the presence of visitors had patted her on the head, and called her, to her face, a clever child and a darling—and that was all: any regular care wearied the lazy gentlewoman. During her father's lifetime, Liza had been in the hands of a governess, Mlle. Moreau, from Paris, and after his death she had passed into the charge of Márfa Timoféevna. The reader is acquainted with Márfa Timoféevna; but Mlle. Moreau was a tiny, wrinkled creature, with birdlike ways and a tiny, birdlike mind. In her youth she had led a very dissipated life, and in her riper years she had but two passions left—for dainties and for cards. When she was gorged, was not playing cards, and not chattering, her face instantly assumed an almost deathlike expression: she would sit, and gaze, and breathe, and it was evident that no thought was passing through her head. It was not even possible to call her good-natured: there are also birds which are not good-natured. Whether it was in consequence of her frivolously-spent youth, or of the Paris air, which she had breathed since her childhood,—she harboured within her a certain cheap, general scepticism, which is usually expressed by the words: "tout ça c'est des bêtises." She talked an irregular, but purely Parisian jargon, did not gossip, was not capricious,—and what more could be desired in a governess? On Liza she had little influence; all the more powerful upon her was the influence of her nurse, Agáfya Vlásievna.

The lot of this woman was remarkable. She sprang from a peasant family; at the age of sixteen, they married her to a peasant; but there was a sharp distinction between her and her sister-peasant women. For twenty years her father had been the village elder, had accumulated a good deal of money, and had petted her. She was a wonderful beauty, the most dashingly-elegant peasant maid in all the country round about, clever, a good talker, daring. Her master, Dmítry Péstoff, the father of Márya Dmítrievna, a modest, quiet man, caught sight of her one day at the threshing, talked with her, and fell passionately in love with her.

Soon afterward, she became a widow; Péstoff, although he was a married man, took her into his house, and clothed her in the style of a house-servant. Agáfya immediately accommodated herself to her new position, exactly as though she had never lived in any other way. Her skin became white, she grew plump; her arms, under their muslin sleeves, became "like fine wheat flour," like those of a cook; the samovár stood constantly on her table; she would wear nothing but velvet and silk, she slept on a feather-bed of down. This blissful life lasted for the space of five years; but Dmítry Péstoff died: his widow, a good-natured gentlewoman, desirous of sparing her husband's memory, was not willing to behave dishonourably toward her rival, the more so, as Agáfya had never forgotten herself before her; but she married her to the cow-herd, and sent her out of her sight. Three years passed. Once, on a hot summer day, the lady of the manor went to her dairy. Agáfya treated her to such splendid cold cream, bore herself so modestly, and was so neat in person, and so cheerful and satisfied with everything, that her mistress announced to her her pardon, and permitted her to come to the manor-house; and six months later, she had become so attached to her, that she promoted her to the post of housekeeper, and entrusted the entire management to her. Again Agáfya came into power, again she grew plump and white-skinned; her mistress had complete confidence in her. In this manner, five more years elapsed. Again misfortune fell upon Agáfya. Her husband, whom she had had raised to the post of footman, took to drink, began to disappear from the house, and wound up by stealing six of the family's silver spoons, and hiding them—until a convenient opportunity—in his wife's chest. This was discovered. He was again degraded to the rank of cow-herd, and a sentence of disgrace was pronounced upon Agáfya; she was not banished from the house, but she was reduced from the place of housekeeper to that of seamstress, and ordered to wear a kerchief on her head, instead of a cap. To the amazement of all, Agáfya accepted the blow which had overtaken her with humble submission. She was then over thirty years of age, all her children had died, and her husband did not long survive. The time had arrived for her to come to a sense of her position; she did so. She became very taciturn and devout, never missed a single Matins

117

service, nor a single Liturgy, and gave away all her fine clothes. Fifteen years she spent quietly, peacefully, with dignity, quarrelling with no one, yielding to every one. If any one spoke rudely to her,— she merely bowed, and returned thanks for the lesson. Her mistress had forgiven her long since, had removed the ban from her, and had given her a cap from her own head; but she herself refused to remove her kerchief, and always went about in a dark-hued gown; and after the death of her mistress, she became still more quiet and humble. A Russian easily conceives fear and affection; but it is difficult to win his respect: it is not soon given, nor to every one. Every one in the house respected Agáfya; no one even recalled her former sins, as though they had been buried in the earth, along with the old master.

When Kalítin became the husband of Márya Dmítrievna, he wished to entrust the housekeeping to Agáfya; but she declined, "because of the temptation"; he roared at her, she made him a lowly reverence, and left the room. The clever Kalítin understood people; and he also understood Agáfya, and did not forget her. On removing his residence to the town, he appointed her, with her own consent, as nurse to Liza, who had just entered her fifth year.

At first, Liza was frightened by the serious and stern face of her new nurse; but she speedily became accustomed to her, and conceived a strong affection for her. She herself was a serious child; her features recalled the clear-cut, regular face of Kalítin; only, she had not her father's eyes; hers beamed with a tranquil attention and kindness which are rare in children. She did not like to play with dolls, her laughter was neither loud nor long, she bore herself with decorum. She was not often thoughtful, and was never so without cause; after remaining silent for a time, she almost always ended by turning to some one of her elders, with a question which showed that her brain was working over a new impression. She very early ceased to lisp, and already in her fourth year she spoke with perfect distinctness. She was afraid of her father; her feeling toward her mother was undefined,—she did not fear her, neither did she fondle her; but she did not fondle Agáfya either, although she loved only her alone. Agáfya and she were never separated. It was strange to see them together. Agáfya, all in black, with a dark kerchief on her head, with a face thin and transparent as wax, yet still beautiful and expressive, would sit upright, engaged in knitting a stocking; at her feet, in a little arm-chair, sat Liza, also toiling over some sort of work, or, with her bright eyes uplifted gravely, listening to what Agáfya was relating to her, and Agáfya did not tell her fairy-stories; in a measured, even voice, she would narrate the life of the Most-pure Virgin, the lives of the hermits, the saints of God, of the holy

118

martyrs; she would tell Liza how the holy men lived in the deserts, how they worked out their salvation, endured hunger and want,—and, fearing not kings, confessed Christ; how the birds of heaven brought them food, and the wild beasts obeyed them; how on those spots where their blood fell, flowers sprang up.—"Yellow violets?"—one day asked Liza, who was very fond of flowers.... Agáfya talked gravely and meekly to Liza, as though she felt that it was not for her to utter such lofty and sacred words. Liza listened to her—and the image of the Omnipresent, Omniscient God penetrated into her soul with a certain sweet power, filled her with pure, devout awe, and Christ became for her a person close to her, almost a relative: and Agáfya taught her to pray. Sometimes she woke Liza early, at daybreak, hastily dressed her, and surreptitiously took her to Matins: Liza followed her on tiptoe, hardly breathing; the chill and semi-obscurity of the dawn, the freshness and emptiness of the streets, the very mysteriousness of these unexpected absences, the cautious return to the house, to bed,—all this mingling of the forbidden, the strange, the holy, agitated the little girl, penetrated into the very depths of her being. Agáfya never condemned anybody, and did not scold Liza for her pranks. When she was displeased over anything, she simply held her peace; and Liza understood that silence; with the swift perspicacity of a child, she also understood very well when Agáfya was displeased with other people—with Márya Dmítrievna herself, or with Kalítin. Agáfya took care of Liza for a little more than three years; she was replaced by Mlle. Moreau; but the frivolous Frenchwoman, with her harsh manners and her exclamation: "tout ça c'est des bêtises,"—could not erase from Liza's heart her beloved nurse: the seeds which had been sown had struck down roots too deep. Moreover, Agáfya, although she had ceased to have charge of Liza, remained in the house, and often saw her nursling, who confided in her as before.

But Agáfya could not get along with Márfa Timoféevna, when the latter came to live in the Kalítin house. The stern dignity of the former "peasant woman" did not please the impatient and self-willed old woman. Agáfya begged permission to go on a pilgrimage, and did not return. Dark rumours circulated, to the effect that she had withdrawn to a convent of Old Ritualists. But the traces left by her in Liza's soul were not effaced. As before, the latter went to the Liturgy as to a festival, prayed with delight, with a certain repressed and bashful enthusiasm, which secretly amazed Márya Dmítrievna not a little, although she put no constraint upon Liza, but merely endeavoured to moderate her zeal, and did not permit her to make an excessive number of prostrations: that was not lady-like manners, she said. Liza studied well,—that is to say, assiduously;

God had not endowed her with particularly brilliant capacities, with a great mind; she acquired nothing without labour. She played well on the piano; but Lemm alone knew what it cost her. She read little; she had no "words of her own," but she had thoughts of her own, and she went her own way. It was not for nothing that she resembled her father: he, also, had not been wont to ask others what he should do. Thus she grew up—quietly, at leisure; thus she attained her nineteenth year. She was very pretty, without herself being aware of the fact. An unconscious, rather awkward grace revealed itself in her every movement; her voice rang with the silvery sound of unaffected youth, the slightest sensation of pleasure evoked a winning smile on her lips, imparted a deep gleam and a certain mysterious caress to her sparkling eyes. Thoroughly imbued with the sense of duty, with the fear of wounding any one whatsoever, with a kind and gentle heart, she loved every one in general, and no one in particular; God alone she loved with rapture, timidly, tenderly. Lavrétzky was the first to break in upon her tranquil inner life.

Such was Liza.

XXXVI

At twelve o'clock on the following day, Lavrétzky set out for the Kalítins'. On the way thither, he met Pánshin, who galloped past him on horseback, with his hat pulled down to his very eyebrows. At the Kalítins', Lavrétzky was not admitted,—for the first time since he had known them. Márya Dmítrievna was "lying down,"—so the lackey announced; "they" had a headache. Neither Márfa Timoféevna nor Lizavéta Mikhaílovna was at home. Lavrétzky strolled along the garden, in anxious hope of meeting Liza, but saw no one. He returned a couple of hours later, and received the same answer, in connection with which the lackey bestowed a sidelong glance upon him. It seemed to Lavrétzky impolite to intrude himself upon them for a third time that day—and he decided to drive out to Vasílievskoe, where, without reference to this, he had business to attend to. On the way he constructed various plans, each more beautiful than the other; but in his aunt's hamlet, sadness fell upon him; he entered into conversation with Antón; the old man, as though expressly, had nothing but cheerless thoughts in his mind. He narrated to Lavrétzky, how Glafíra Petróvna, before her death, had bitten her own hand,—and, after a short pause, he added: "Every man, master—dear little father, is given to devouring himself." It was already late when Lavrétzky set out on the return journey. The sounds of the preceding day took possession of him, the image of Liza arose in his soul in all its gentle transparency; he melted at the thought that she loved him,—and drove up to his little town-house in a composed and happy frame of mind.

The first thing which struck him on entering the anteroom was the scent of patchouli, which was very repulsive to him; several tall trunks and coffers were standing there. The face of the valet who ran forth to receive him seemed to him strange. Without accounting to himself for his impressions, he crossed the threshold of the drawing-room.... From the couch there rose to greet him a lady in a black gown with flounces, and raising a batiste handkerchief to her pale face, she advanced several paces, bent her carefully-dressed head,—and fell at his feet.... Then only did he recognise her: the lady was—his wife.

It took his breath away.... He leaned against the wall.

"Theodore, do not drive me away!"—she said in French, and her voice cut his heart like a knife.

He glanced at her without comprehending, yet he immediately noticed that she had grown pale and thin.

121

"Theodore,"—she went on, from time to time raising her eyes, and cautiously wringing her wondrously-beautiful fingers, with rosy, polished nails:—"Theodore, I am to blame toward you, deeply to blame,—I will say more, I am a criminal; but do you listen to me; repentance tortures me, I have become a burden to myself, I could not longer endure my position; how many times have I meditated returning to you, but I feared your wrath;—I have decided to break every connection with the past ... puis, j'ai été si malade,—I have been so ill,"—she added, and passed her hand across her brow and her cheek,—"I have taken advantage of the rumour of my death which had got into circulation, I have abandoned everything; without halting, day and night I have hastened hither; I have hesitated, for a long time, to present myself before you, my judge— paraître devant vous, mon juge,—but, at last, I made up my mind, remembering your invariable kindness, to come to you; I learned your address in Moscow. Believe me," she continued, softly rising from the floor, and seating herself on the very edge of an armchair:—"I have often meditated death, and I would have summoned up sufficient courage to take my life—akh, life is now an intolerable burden to me!—but the thought of my daughter, of my Ádotchka, held me back; she is here, she is asleep in the adjoining room, poor child! She is weary,—you shall see her: she, at least, is not guilty toward you,—and I am so unhappy, so unhappy!"—exclaimed Mme. Lavrétzky, and burst into tears.

Lavrétzky came to himself, at last; he separated himself from the wall, and moved toward the door.

"You are going away?"—said his wife, in despair:—"oh, this is cruel!—Without saying one word to me, without even one reproach.... This scorn is killing me, this is terrible!"

Lavrétzky stopped short.

"What is it that you wish to hear from me?"—he uttered, in a toneless voice.

"Nothing, nothing,"—she caught him up with vivacity:—"I know that I have no right to demand anything;—I am not a fool, believe me;—I do not hope, I do not dare to hope for your forgiveness;—I only venture to entreat you, that you will give me directions what I am to do, where I am to live?—I will fulfil your command, whatever it may be, like a slave."

"I have no commands to give you,"—returned Lavrétzky, in the same voice:—"you know, that everything is at an end between us ... and now more than ever.—You may live where you see fit;—and if your allowance is insufficient...."

"Akh, do not utter such dreadful words,"—Varvára Pávlovna interrupted him:—"spare me, if only ... if only for the sake of that angel...." And, as she said these words, Varvára Pávlovna flew headlong into the next room, and immediately returned with a tiny, very elegantly dressed little girl in her arms. Heavy, ruddy-gold curls fell over her pretty, rosy little face, over her large, black, sleepy eyes; she smiled, and blinked at the light, and clung with her chubby hand to her mother's neck.

"Ada, vois, c'est ton père,"—said Varvára Pávlovna, pushing the curls aside from her eyes, and giving her a hearty kiss:—"prie le avec moi."

"C'est ça, papa?"—lisped the little girl, brokenly.

"Oui, mon enfant, n'est ce pas, que tu l'aimes?"

But this was too much for Lavrétzky.

"In what melodrama is it that there is precisely such a scene?"—he muttered, and left the room.

Varvára Pávlovna stood for a while rooted to the spot, slightly shrugged her shoulders, carried the little girl into the other room, undressed her, and put her to bed. Then she got a book, sat down near the lamp, waited for about an hour, and, at last, lay down on the bed herself.

"Eh bien, madame?"—inquired her maid, a Frenchwoman, whom she had brought from Paris, as she removed her corsets.

"Eh bien, Justine,"—she replied;—"he has aged greatly, but it strikes me that he is as good-natured as ever.—Give me my gloves for the night, prepare my high-necked grey gown for to-morrow; and do not forget the mutton chops for Ada.... Really, it will be difficult to obtain them here; but we must make the effort."

"À la guerre, comme à la guerre,"—responded Justine, and put out the light.

123

XXXVII

For more than two hours Lavrétzky roamed about the streets of the town. The night which he had spent in the suburbs of Paris recurred to his mind. His heart swelled to bursting within him, and in his head, which was empty, and, as it were, stunned, the same set of thoughts kept swirling,—dark, wrathful, evil thoughts. "She is alive, she is here," he whispered, with constantly augmenting amazement. He felt that he had lost Liza. Bile choked him; this blow had struck him too suddenly. How could he so lightly have believed the absurd gossip of a feuilleton, a scrap of paper? "Well, and if I had not believed it, what difference would that have made? I should not have known that Liza loves me; she herself would not have known it." He could not banish from himself the form, the voice, the glances of his wife ... and he cursed himself, cursed everything in the world.

Worn out, he arrived toward morning at Lemm's. For a long time, he could produce no effect with his knocking; at last, the old man's head, in a nightcap, made its appearance in the window, sour, wrinkled, no longer bearing the slightest resemblance to that inspiredly-morose head which, four and twenty hours previously, had gazed on Lavrétzky from the full height of its artistic majesty.

"What do you want?"—inquired Lemm:—"I cannot play every night; I have taken a decoction."—But, evidently, Lavrétzky's face was very strange: the old man made a shield for his eyes out of his hands, stared at his nocturnal visitor, and admitted him.

Lavrétzky entered the room, and sank down on a chair; the old man halted in front of him, with the skirts of his motley-hued, old dressing-gown tucked up, writhing and mumbling with his lips.

"My wife has arrived,"—said Lavrétzky, raising his head, and suddenly breaking into an involuntary laugh.

Lemm's face expressed surprise, but he did not even smile, and only wrapped himself more closely in his dressing-gown.

"You see, you do not know,"—went on Lavrétzky:—"I imagined ... I read in a newspaper, that she was no longer alive."

"O—o, you read that a short time ago?"—asked Lemm.

"Yes."

"O—o,"—repeated the old man, and elevated his eyebrows.—"And she has arrived?"

"Yes. She is now at my house; but I ... I am an unhappy man."

And again he broke into a laugh.

"You are an unhappy man,"—repeated Lemm, slowly.

"Christofór Feódoritch,"—began Lavrétzky:—"will you undertake to deliver a note?"

"H'm. May I inquire, to whom?"

"To Liza...."

"Ah,—yes, yes, I understand. Very well. But when must the note be delivered?"

"To-morrow, as early as possible."

"H'm. I can send Katrina, my cook. No, I will go myself."

"And will you bring me the answer?"

"Yes, I will."

Lemm sighed.

"Yes, my poor young friend; you really are—an unhappy man."

Lavrétzky wrote a couple of words to Liza: he informed her of his wife's arrival, begged her to appoint a meeting,—and flung himself on the narrow divan, face to the wall; and the old man lay down on the bed, and tossed about for a long time, coughing and taking sips of his decoction.

Morning came: they both rose. With strange eyes they gazed at each other. Lavrétzky wanted to kill himself at that moment. The cook, Katrina, brought them some bad coffee. The clock struck eight. Lemm put on his hat, and saying that he had a lesson to give at the Kalítins' at nine, but that he would find a decent pretext, set out. Lavrétzky again flung himself on the little couch, and again, from the depths of his soul, a sorrowful laugh welled up. He thought of how his wife had driven him out of his house; he pictured to himself Liza's position, closed his eyes, and threw his hands behind his head. At last Lemm returned, and brought him a scrap of paper, on which Liza had scrawled with pencil the following words: "We cannot see each other to-day; perhaps—to-morrow evening. Farewell." Lavrétzky quietly and abstractedly thanked Lemm, and went to his own house.

He found his wife at breakfast; Ada, all curls, in a white frock with blue ribbons, was eating a mutton chop. Varvára Pávlovna immediately rose, as soon as Lavrétzky entered the room, and approached him, with humility depicted on her face. He requested her to follow him to his study, locked the door behind him, and began to stride to and fro; she sat down, laid one hand modestly on the other, and began to watch him with her still beautiful, although slightly painted eyes.

For a long time Lavrétzky did not speak: he felt that he could not control himself; he perceived clearly, that Varvára Pávlovna was not in the least afraid of him, but was assuming the air of being on the very verge of falling into a swoon.

"Listen, madam,"—he began, at last, breathing heavily at times,

125

grinding his teeth:—"there is no necessity for our dissembling with each other; I do not believe in your repentance; and even if it were genuine, it is impossible for me to become reconciled to you, to live with you again."

Varvára Pávlovna compressed her lips and narrowed her eyes. "This is disgust,"—she thought:—"of course! I am no longer even a woman to him."

"It is impossible,"—repeated Lavrétzky, and buttoned up his coat to the throat.—"I do not know why you have taken it into your head to come hither: probably, you have no money left."

"Alas! you are insulting me,"—whispered Varvára Pávlovna.

"However that may be,—you are, unhappily, my wife, nevertheless. I cannot turn you out ... and this is what I have to propose to you. You may set out, this very day, if you like, for Lavríki, and live there; the house is good, as you know; you will receive all that is necessary, in addition to your allowance.... Do you agree?"

Varvára Pávlovna raised her embroidered handkerchief to her eyes.

"I have already told you,"—she said, her lips twitching nervously:—"that I shall agree to anything whatever you may see fit to do with me: on this occasion, nothing is left for me to do, except to ask you: will you permit me, at least, to thank you for your magnanimity?"

"No gratitude, I beg of you; it is better so,"—hastily returned Lavrétzky.—"Accordingly,"—he went on, approaching the door:—"I may count upon...."

"To-morrow I shall be at Lavríki,"—said Varvára Pávlovna, respectfully rising from her seat.—"But, Feódor Ivánitch" (she no longer called him Theodore)....

"What do you want?"

"I know that I have, as yet, in no way earned my forgiveness; may I hope, at least, in time...."

"Ekh, Varvára Pávlovna,"—Lavrétzky interrupted her:—"you are a clever woman, and as I am not a fool, I know that that is quite unnecessary for you. And I forgave you long ago; but there was always a gulf between us."

"I shall know how to submit,"—replied Varvára Pávlovna, and bowed her head. "I have not forgotten my fault; I should not be surprised to learn that you were even delighted at the news of my death,"—she added gently, pointing slightly with her hand at the copy of the newspaper which lay on the table, forgotten by Lavrétzky.

Feódor Ivánitch shuddered: the feuilleton was marked with a

126

pencil. Varvára Pávlovna gazed at him with still greater humility. She was very pretty at that moment. Her grey Paris gown gracefully clothed her willowy form, which was almost that of a girl of seventeen; her slender, delicate neck encircled with a white collar, her bosom which rose and fell evenly, her arms devoid of bracelets and rings,—her whole figure, from her shining hair to the tip of her barely revealed little boot, was so elegant....

Lavrétzky swept an angry glance over her, came near exclaiming: "Brava!" came near smiting her in the temple with his fist—and left the room. An hour later, he had already set out for Vasílievskoe, and two hours later, Varvára Pávlovna gave orders that the best carriage in town should be engaged, donned a simple straw hat with a black veil, and a modest mantle, entrusted Ada to Justine, and set out for the Kalítins: from the inquiries instituted by her servant she had learned that her husband was in the habit of going to them every day.

XXXVIII

The day of the arrival of Lavrétzky's wife in town of O*** , a cheerless day for him, was also a painful day for Liza. She had not succeeded in going down-stairs and bidding her mother "good morning," before the trampling of a horse's hoofs resounded under the window, and with secret terror she beheld Pánshin riding into the yard: "He has presented himself thus early for a definitive explanation,"—she thought—and she was not mistaken; after spending a while in the drawing-room, he suggested that she should go with him into the garden, and demanded her decision as to his fate. Liza summoned up her courage, and informed him that she could not be his wife. He listened to her to the end, as he stood with his side toward her, and his hat pulled down on his brows; courteously, but in an altered tone, he asked her: was that her last word, and had he, in any way, given her cause for such a change in her ideas? then he pressed his hand to his eyes, sighed briefly and abruptly, and removed his hand from his face.

"I have not wished to follow the beaten path,"—he said, in a dull voice,—"I have wished to find my companion after the inclination of the heart; but, evidently, that was not destined to be. Farewell, dream!"—He bowed profoundly to Liza, and returned to the house.

She hoped that he would immediately take his departure; but he went into Márya Dmítrievna's boudoir, and sat with her for about an hour. As he went away, he said to Liza: "Votre mère vous appelle; adieu à jamais ..." mounted his horse, and set off from the very porch at full gallop. Liza went in to Márya Dmítrievna, and found her in tears: Pánshin had communicated to her his misfortune.

"Why hast thou killed me? Why hast thou killed me?"—in this wise did the mortified widow begin her complaints.—"Whom else didst thou want? What! is not he a suitable husband for thee? A Junior Gentleman of the Emperor's Bedchamber! not interessant! He might marry any Maid of Honour he chose in Petersburg. And I—I had been hoping so! And hast thou changed long toward him? What has sent this cloud drifting hither—it did not come of itself! Can it be that ninny? A pretty counsellor thou hast found!

"And he, my dear one,"—pursued Márya Dmítrievna:—"how respectful, how attentive, even in his own grief! He has promised not to abandon me. Akh, I shall not survive this! Akh, I have got a deadly headache. Send Palásha to me. Thou wilt be the death of me, if thou dost not change thy mind,—dost thou hear?" And calling her an ingrate a couple of times, Márya Dmítrievna sent Liza away.

She went to her own room. But before she had time to recover her breath from her explanation with Pánshin and her mother, another thunderstorm broke over her, and this time from a quarter whence she had least expected it. Márfa Timoféevna entered her room, and immediately slammed the door behind her. The old woman's face was pale, her cap was awry, her eyes were flashing, her hands and lips were trembling. Liza was amazed: never before had she seen her sensible and reasonable aunt in such a state.

"Very fine, madam,"—began Márfa Timoféevna, in a tremulous and broken whisper: "very fine indeed! From whom hast thou learned this, my mother?... Give me water; I cannot speak."

"Calm yourself, aunty; what is the matter with you?"—said Liza, giving her a glass of water.—"Why, you yourself did not favour Mr. Pánshin."

Márfa Timoféevna set down the glass.

"I cannot drink: I shall knock out my last remaining teeth. What dost thou mean by Panshín? What has Panshín to do with it? Do thou tell me, rather, who taught thee to appoint rendezvous by night—hey? my mother?"

Liza turned pale.

"Please do not think of excusing thyself,"—continued Márfa Timoféevna.—"Schúrotchka herself saw all, and told me. I have forbidden her to chatter, but she does not lie."

"I have made no excuses, aunty,"—said Liza, in a barely audible voice.

"Ah, ah! Now, see here, my mother; didst thou appoint a meeting with him, with that old sinner, that quiet man?"

"No."

"Then how did it come about?"

"I went down-stairs, to the drawing-room, for a book; he was in the garden, and called me."

"And thou wentest? Very fine. And thou lovest him, dost thou not?"

"I do,"—replied Liza, in a tranquil voice.

"Gracious heavens! she loves him!"—Márfa Timoféevna tore off her cap.—"She loves a married man! Hey? she loves!"

"He told me,"—began Liza....

"What did he tell thee, the darling, wha-at was it?"

"He told me that his wife was dead."

Márfa Timoféevna crossed herself.—"The kingdom of heaven be hers,"—she whispered:—"she was a frivolous woman—God forgive her. So that's how it is: then he's a widower. Yes, I see that he is equal to anything. He killed off his first wife, and now he's after another. Thou art a sly one, art thou not? Only, this is what I have to say to thee, niece: in my time, when I was young, girls were severely punished for such capers. Thou must not be angry with me, my mother; only fools get angry at the truth. I have given orders that he is not to be admitted to-day. I am fond of him, but I shall never forgive him for this. A widower, forsooth! Give me some water.... But thou art my brave girl, for sending Panshín off with a long face; only, do not sit out nights with that goat's breed,—with men,—do not grieve me, an old woman! For I am not always amiable—I know how to bite, also!... A widower!"

Márfa Timoféevna departed, but Liza sat down in the corner and began to cry. She felt bitter in soul; she had not deserved such humiliation. Her love had not announced its presence by cheerfulness; this was the second time she had wept since the night before. That new, unexpected feeling had barely come to life in her heart when she had had to pay so heavily for it, when strange hands had roughly touched her private secret! She felt ashamed, and pained, and bitter: but there was neither doubt nor terror in her,—and Lavrétzky became all the dearer to her. She had hesitated as long as she did not understand herself; but after that meeting—she could hesitate no longer; she knew that she loved,—and had fallen in love honourably, not jestingly, she had become strongly attached, for her whole life; she felt that force could not break that bond.

XXXIX

Márya Dmítrievna was greatly perturbed when the arrival of
Varvára Pávlovna was announced to her; she did not even know
whether to receive her; she was afraid of offending Feódor Ivánitch.
At last, curiosity carried the day. "What of it?"—she said to herself,—
"why, she is a relative also,"—and seating herself in her arm-chair,
she said to the lackey: "Ask her in!" Several minutes elapsed; the
door opened, Varvára Pávlovna approached Márya Dmítrievna
swiftly, with barely audible footsteps, and, without giving her a
chance to rise from her chair, almost went down on her knees
before her.

"Thank you, aunty,"—she began in a touched and gentle voice,
in Russian: "thank you! I had not hoped for such condescension on
your part; you are as kind as an angel."

As she uttered these words, Varvára Pávlovna unexpectedly
took possession of one of Márya Dmítrievna's hands, and pressing it
lightly in her pale-lilac gloves, obsequiously raised it to her full, rosy
lips. Márya Dmítrievna completely lost her head, on beholding such
a beautiful, charmingly-dressed woman, almost on her knees at her
feet; she did not know what to do: she did not wish to withdraw her
hand, she wished to give her a seat, and to say something amiable to
her; she ended by rising, and kissing Varvára Pávlovna on her
smooth, fragrant brow. Varvára Pávlovna was perfectly
dumfounded by this kiss.

"Good morning,—bon jour,"—said Márya Dmítrievna:—"of
course, I had no idea, ... however, of course, I am delighted to see
you. You understand, my dear,—it is not for me to sit in judgment
between wife and husband."

"My husband is wholly in the right,"—Varvára Pávlovna
interrupted her:—"I alone am to blame."

"That is a very praiseworthy sentiment,"—returned Márya
Dmítrievna:—"very. Have you been here long? Have you seen him?
But sit down, pray."

"I arrived yesterday,"—replied Varvára Pávlovna, meekly
seating herself on a chair; "I have seen Feódor Ivánitch, I have
talked with him."

"Ah! Well, and how does he take it?"

"I was afraid that my sudden arrival would arouse his wrath,"—
went on Varvára Pávlovna:—"but he did not deprive me of his
presence."

"That is to say, he did not.... Yes, yes, I understand,"—

ejaculated Márya Dmítrievna.—"He is only rather rough in appearance, but his heart is soft."

"Feódor Ivánitch has not forgiven me; he would not listen to me.... But he was so kind as to appoint Lavríki for my place of residence."

"Ah! A very fine estate!"

"I set out thither to-morrow, in compliance with his will; but I considered it my duty to call on you first."

"I am very, very grateful to you, my dear. One must never forget one's relatives. And, do you know, I am astonished that you speak Russian so well. C'est étonnant!"

Varvára Pávlovna sighed.

"I have spent too much time abroad, Márya Dmítrievna, I know that; but my heart has always been Russian, and I have not forgotten my native land."

"Exactly so, exactly so; that is the best of all. Feódor Ivánitch, however, did not in the least expect you.... Yes; believe my experience; la patrie avant tout. Akh, please show me,—what a charming mantle that is you have on!"

"Do you like it?"—Varvára Pávlovna promptly dropped it from her shoulders.—"It is a very simple thing, from Madame Baudran."

"That is instantly perceptible. From Madame Baudran.... How charming, and what taste! I am convinced that you have brought with you a mass of the most entrancing things. I should like to look them over."

"My entire toilette is at your service, my dearest aunt. If you will permit, I can give your maid some points. I have a maid-servant from Paris,—a wonderful seamstress."

"You are very kind, my dear. But, really, I am ashamed."

"Ashamed! ..." repeated Varvára Pávlovna, reproachfully.—"If you wish to make me happy,—command me, as though I belonged to you."

Márya Dmítrievna thawed.

"Vous êtes charmante," she said.—"But why do not you take off your bonnet, your gloves?"

"What? You permit?"—asked Varvára Pávlovna, clasping her hands, as though with emotion.

"Of course; for you will dine with us, I hope. I ... I will introduce you to my daughter."—Márya Dmítrievna became slightly confused. "Well! here goes!"—she said to herself.—"She is not quite well to-day."

"Oh, ma tante, how kind you are!"—exclaimed Varvára Pávlovna, and raised her handkerchief to her eyes.

A page announced the arrival of Gedeónovsky. The old

chatterbox entered, made his bows, and smiled. Márya Dmítrievna presented him to her visitor. He came near being discomfited at first; but Varvára Pávlovna treated him with such coquettish respect, that his ears began to burn, and fibs, scandals, amiable remarks trickled out of his mouth like honey. Varvára Pávlovna listened to him with a repressed smile, and became rather talkative herself. She modestly talked about Paris, about her travels, about Baden; twice she made Márya Dmítrievna laugh, and on each occasion she heaved another little sigh, as though she were mentally reproaching herself for her ill-timed mirth; she asked permission to bring Ada; removing her gloves, she showed, with her smooth hands washed with soap à la guimauve, how and where flounces, ruches, lace, and knots of ribbon were worn; she promised to bring a phial of the new English perfume, Victoria's Essence, and rejoiced like a child when Márya Dmítrievna consented to accept it as a gift; she wept at the remembrance of the feeling she had experienced when, for the first time, she had heard the Russian bells;—"so profoundly did they stagger my very heart,"—she said.

At that moment, Liza entered.

From the morning, from the very moment when, chilled with terror, she had perused Lavrétzky's note, Liza had been preparing herself to meet his wife; she had a presentiment that she should see her, by way of punishment to her own criminal hopes, as she called them. She had made up her mind not to shun her. The sudden crisis in her fate had shaken her to the very foundations; in the course of about two hours her face had grown haggard; but she did not shed a tear. "It serves me right!"—she said to herself, with difficulty and agitation suppressing in her soul certain bitter, spiteful impulses, which alarmed even herself:—"Come, I must go down!"—she thought, as soon as she heard of Mme. Lavrétzky's arrival, and she went.... For a long time she stood outside the door of the drawing-room, before she could bring herself to open it; with the thought: "I am to blame toward her,"—she crossed the threshold, and forced herself to look at her, forced herself to smile. Varvára Pávlovna advanced to meet her as soon as she saw her, and made a slight but nevertheless respectful inclination before her.—"Allow me to introduce myself,"—she began, in an insinuating voice:—"your maman is so indulgent toward me, that I hope you will also be ... kind." The expression on Varvára Pávlovna's face, as she uttered this last word, her sly smile, her cold and at the same time soft glance, the movement of her arms and shoulders, her very gown, her whole being, aroused in Liza such a feeling of repulsion, that she could make her no answer, and with an effort she offered her hand. "This young lady despises me,"—thought Varvára Pávlovna, as she warmly pressed Liza's cold fingers, and, turning to Márya Dmítrievna, she said in an undertone: "Mais elle est délicieuse!" Liza flushed faintly, insult was audible to her in this exclamation; but she made up her mind not to trust her impressions, and seated herself by the window, at her embroidery-frame. Even there, Varvára Pávlovna did not leave her in peace: she went up to her, began to praise her taste, her art.... Liza's heart beat violently and painfully, she could hardly control herself, she could hardly sit still on her chair. It seemed to her that Varvára Pávlovna knew everything, and, secretly triumphing, was jeering at her. Fortunately for her, Gedeónovsky entered into conversation with Varvára Pávlovna, and distracted her attention. Liza bent over her embroidery-frame, and stealthily watched her. "He loved that woman,"—she said to herself. But she immediately banished from her head the thought of Lavrétzky: she was afraid of losing control over herself, she felt that her head was softly whirling. Márya Dmítrievna began to talk about music.

"I have heard, my dear,"—she began:—"that you are a wonderful performer."

"It is a long time since I have played,"—replied Varvára Pávlovna, as she seated herself, in a leisurely manner, at the piano, and ran her fingers in a dashing way over the keys.—"Would you like to have me play?"

"Pray do."

Varvára Pávlovna played a brilliant and difficult étude of Herz in a masterly style. She had a great deal of strength and execution.

"A sylph!"—exclaimed Gedeónovsky.

"Remarkable!"—assented Márya Dmítrievna.—"Well, Varvára Pávlovna, I must confess,"—she said, calling her, for the first time, by her name:—"you have amazed me; you might even give concerts. We have an old musician here, a German, an eccentric fellow, very learned; he gives Liza lessons; he will simply go out of his mind over you."

"Lizavéta Mikhaílovna is also a musician?"—inquired Varvára Pávlovna, turning her head slightly in her direction.

"Yes, she plays quite well, and loves music; but what does that signify, in comparison with you? But there is a young man here; you ought to make his acquaintance. He is—an artist in soul, and composes very prettily. He is the only one who can fully appreciate you."

"A young man?"—said Varvára Pávlovna.—"Who is he? Some poor fellow?"

"Good gracious,—he's our chief cavalier, and not among us only—et à Pétersbourg. A Junior Gentleman of the Bedchamber, received in the best society. You certainly must have heard of him,—Pánshin, Vladímir Nikoláitch. He is here on a government commission ... a future Minister, upon my word!"

"And an artist?"

"An artist in soul, and such a charming fellow. You shall see him. He has been at my house very frequently of late; I have invited him for this evening; I hope that he will come,"—added Márya Dmítrievna, with a gentle sigh and a sidelong bitter smile.

Liza understood the significance of that smile; but she cared nothing for it.

"And is he young?"—repeated Varvára Pávlovna, lightly modulating from one key to another.

"He is eight and twenty—and of the most happy personal appearance. Un jeune homme accompli, upon my word."

"A model young man, one may say,"—remarked Gedeónovsky.

Varvára Pávlovna suddenly began to play a noisy Strauss waltz, which started with such a mighty and rapid trill as made even Gedeónovsky start; in the very middle of the waltz, she abruptly changed into a mournful motif, and wound up with the aria from "Lucia": "Fra poco."... She had reflected that merry music was not compatible with her situation. The aria from "Lucia," with emphasis on the sentimental notes, greatly affected Márya Dmítrievna.

"What soul!"—she said, in a low tone, to Gedeónovsky.

"A sylph!"—repeated Gedeónovsky, and rolled his eyes heavenward.

Dinner-time arrived. Márfa Timoféevna came down-stairs when the soup was already standing on the table. She treated Varvára Pávlovna very coolly, replying with half-words to her amiabilities, and not looking at her. Varvára Pávlovna herself speedily comprehended that she could do nothing with the old woman, and ceased to address her; on the other hand, Márya Dmítrievna became more affectionate than ever with her guest: her aunt's discourtesy enraged her. However, Varvára Pávlovna was not the only person at whom Márfa Timoféevna refused to look: she never cast a glance at Liza, either, although her eyes fairly flashed. She sat like a stone image, all sallow, pale, with tightly compressed lips—and ate nothing. Liza seemed to be composed; and, as a matter of fact, all had become more tranquil in her soul; a strange insensibility, the insensibility of the man condemned to death, had come upon her. At dinner Varvára Pávlovna talked little: she seemed to have become timid once more, and spread over her face an expression of modest melancholy. Gedeónovsky alone enlivened the conversation with his tales, although he kept casting cowardly glances at Márfa Timoféevna, and a cough and tickling in the throat

135

seized upon him every time that he undertook to lie in her presence,—but she did not hinder him, she did not interrupt him. After dinner it appeared that Varvára Pávlovna was extremely fond of preference; this pleased Márya Dmítrievna to such a degree, that she even became greatly affected, and thought to herself:—"But what a fool Feódor Ivánitch must be: he was not able to appreciate such a woman!"

She sat down to play cards with her and Gedeónovsky, while Márfa Timoféevna led Liza off to her own rooms up-stairs, saying that she looked ill, that her head must be aching.

"Yes, she has a frightful headache,"—said Márya Dmítrievna, turning to Varvára Pávlovna, and rolling up her eyes.—"I myself have such sick-headaches...." Liza entered her aunt's room and dropped on a chair, exhausted. Márfa Timoféevna gazed at her for a long time, in silence, knelt down softly in front of her—and began, in the same speechless manner, to kiss her hands, in turn. Liza leaned forward, blushed, and fell to weeping, but did not raise Márfa Timoféevna, did not withdraw her hands: she felt that she had not the right to withdraw them, had not the right to prevent the old woman showing her contrition, her sympathy, asking her pardon for what had taken place on the day before; and Márfa Timoféevna could not have done with kissing those poor, pale, helpless hands—and silent tears streamed from her eyes and from Liza's eyes; and the cat Matrós purred in the wide arm-chair beside the ball of yarn and the stocking, the elongated flame of the shrine-lamp quivered gently and flickered in front of the holy picture,—in the adjoining room, behind the door, stood Nastásya Kárpovna, and also stealthily wiped her eyes, with a checked handkerchief rolled up into a ball.

XL

And, in the meantime, down-stairs in the drawing-room preference was in progress; Márya Dmítrievna won, and was in high spirits. A footman entered, and announced the arrival of Pánshin.

Márya Dmítrievna dropped her cards, and fidgeted about in her chair; Varvára Pávlovna looked at her with a half-smile, then directed her gaze to the door. Pánshin made his appearance, in a black frock-coat, with a tall English collar, buttoned up to the throat. "It was painful for me to obey, but you see I have come." That was what his freshly-shaved, unsmiling face expressed.

"Goodness, Woldemar,"—exclaimed Márya Dmítrievna:—"you always used to enter without being announced!"

Pánshin replied to Márya Dmítrievna merely with a look, bowed courteously to her, but did not kiss her hand. She introduced him to Varvára Pávlovna; he retreated a pace, bowed to her with equal courtesy, but with a shade of elegance and deference, and seated himself at the card-table. The game of preference soon came to an end. Pánshin inquired after Lizavéta Mikhaílovna, learned that she did not feel quite well, and expressed his regrets; then he entered into conversation with Varvára Pávlovna, weighing and chiselling clearly every word, in diplomatic fashion, respectfully listening to her replies to the very end. But the importance of his diplomatic tone had no effect on Varvára Pávlovna, did not communicate itself to her. Quite the contrary: she gazed into his face with merry attention, talked in a free-and-easy way, and her delicate nostrils quivered slightly, as though with suppressed laughter. Márya Dmítrievna began to extol her talent; Pánshin inclined his head as politely as his collar permitted, declared that "he was convinced of it in advance,"—and turned the conversation almost on Metternich himself. Varvára Pávlovna narrowed her velvety eyes, and saying, in a low tone: "Why, you also are an artist yourself, un confrère,"—added in a still lower tone: "Venez!"—and nodded her head in the direction of the piano. That one carelessly dropped word: "Venez!"—instantaneously, as though by magic, altered Pánshin's entire aspect. His careworn mien vanished; he smiled, became animated, unbuttoned his coat, and repeating: "What sort of an artist am I, alas! But you, I hear, are a genuine artist"—wended his way, in company with Varvára Pávlovna, to the piano.

"Make him sing his romance:—'When the moon floats,'"—exclaimed Márya Dmítrievna.

"Do you sing?"—said Varvára Pávlovna, illuminating him with a bright, swift glance.—"Sit down."

Pánshin began to decline.

"Sit down,"—she repeated, insistently tapping the back of the chair.

He sat down, coughed, pulled open his collar, and sang his romance.

"Charmant!"—said Varvára Pávlovna:—"you sing beautifully, vous avez du style,—sing it again."

She walked round the piano, and took up her stand directly opposite Pánshin. He sang his romance again, imparting a melodramatic quiver to his voice. Varvára Pávlovna gazed intently at him, with her elbows propped on the piano, and her white hands on a level with her lips. Pánshin finished.

"Charmant, charmante idée,"—said she, with the calm confidence of an expert.—"Tell me, have you written anything for the female voice, for a mezzo-soprano?"

"I hardly write anything,"—replied Pánshin;—"you see, I only do this sort of thing in the intervals between business affairs ... but do you sing?"

"Yes."

"Oh! do sing something for us,"—said Márya Dmítrievna.

Varvára Pávlovna pushed back her hair from her flushed cheeks with her hand, and shook her head.

"Our voices ought to go well together,"—she said, turning to Pánshin:—"let us sing a duet. Do you know 'Son geloso,' or 'La ci darem,' or 'Mira la bianca luna'?"

"I used to sing 'Mira la bianca luna,'"—replied Pánshin:—"but I have forgotten it long ago."

"Never mind, we will try it over in an undertone. Let me come."

Varvára Pávlovna sat down at the piano. Pánshin stood beside her. They sang the duet in an undertone, Varvára Pávlovna correcting him several times; then they sang it aloud, then they repeated it twice: "Mira la bianca lu...u...una." Varvára Pávlovna's voice had lost its freshness, but she managed it very adroitly. Pánshin was timid at first, and sang rather out of tune, but later on he warmed up, and if he did not sing faultlessly, at least he wriggled his shoulders, swayed his whole body, and elevated his hand now and then, like a genuine singer. Varvára Pávlovna played two or three little things of Thalberg's, and coquettishly "recited" a French ariette. Márya Dmítrievna no longer knew how to express her delight; several times she was on the point of sending for Liza; Gedeónovsky, also, found no words and merely rocked his head,— but all of a sudden he yawned, and barely succeeded in concealing his mouth with his hand. This yawn did not escape Varvára Pávlovna; she suddenly turned her back to the piano, said: "Assez de musique, comme ça; let us chat,"—and folded her hands. "Oui, assez de musique,"—merrily repeated Pánshin—and struck up a conversation with her,—daring, light, in the French language. "Exactly as in the best Parisian salon,"—thought Márya Dmítrievna, as she listened to their evasive and nimble speeches. Pánshin felt perfectly contented; his eyes sparkled, he smiled; at first, he passed his hand over his face, contracted his brows, and sighed spasmodically when he chanced to meet the glances of Márya Dmítrievna; but later on, he entirely forgot her, and surrendered himself completely to the enjoyment of the half-fashionable, half-artistic chatter. Varvára Pávlovna showed herself to be a great philosopher: she had an answer ready for everything, she did not hesitate over anything, she doubted nothing; it could be seen that she had talked much and often with clever persons of various sorts. All her thoughts, all her feelings, circled about Paris. Pánshin turned the conversation on literature: it appeared that she, as well as he, read only French books: Georges Sand excited her indignation; Balzac she admired, although he fatigued her; in Sue and Scribe she discerned great experts of the heart; she adored Dumas and Féval; in her soul she preferred Paul de Kock to the whole of them, but, of course, she did not even mention his name. To tell the truth, literature did not interest her greatly. Varvára Pávlovna very artfully avoided everything which could even distantly recall her position; there was not a hint about love in her remarks: on the contrary, they were rather distinguished by severity toward the impulses of passion, by disenchantment, by meekness. Pánshin retorted; she disagreed with him ... but, strange to say!—at the very time when words of condemnation, often harsh, were issuing from her lips, the sound of those words caressed and enervated, and her eyes said ... precisely what those lovely eyes said, it would be difficult to state; but their speech was not severe, not clear, yet sweet. Pánshin endeavoured to understand their mysterious significance, endeavoured to talk with his own eyes, but he was conscious that he was not at all successful; he recognised the fact that Varvára Pávlovna, in her quality of a genuine foreign lioness, stood above him, and therefore he was not in full control of himself. Varvára Pávlovna had a habit, while talking, of lightly touching the sleeve of her interlocutor; these momentary touches greatly agitated Vladímir Nikoláitch. Varvára Pávlovna possessed the art of getting on easily with every one; two hours had not elapsed before it seemed to Pánshin that he had known her always, and Liza, that same Liza, whom he loved, nevertheless, to whom he had offered his hand on the preceding day,—vanished as in a mist. Tea was served; the conversation became still more unconstrained. Márya Dmítrievna rang for her page, and ordered him to tell Liza to come down-stairs if her head felt better. Pánshin, on hearing Liza's name, set to talking about self-sacrifice, about who was the more capable of sacrifice—man or woman? Márya Dmítrievna immediately became agitated, began to assert that woman is the more capable, declared that she would prove it in two words, got entangled, and wound up by a decidedly infelicitous comparison. Varvára Pávlovna picked up a music-book, half-concealed herself with it, and leaning over in the direction of Pánshin, nibbling at a biscuit, with a calm smile on her lips and in her glance, she remarked, in an undertone: "Elle n'a pas inventé la poudre, la bonne dame." Pánshin was somewhat alarmed and amazed at Varvára Pávlovna's audacity; but he did not understand how much scorn for him, himself, was concealed in that unexpected sally, and, forgetting the affection and the devotion of Márya Dmítrievna, forgetting the dinners wherewith she had fed him, the money which she had lent him,—he, with the same little smile, the same tone, replied (unlucky wight!): "Je crois bien,"—and not even: "Je crois bien," but:—"Je crois ben!"

Varvára Pávlovna cast a friendly glance at him, and rose. Liza had entered; in vain had Márfa Timoféevna sought to hold her back: she had made up her mind to endure the trial to the end. Varvára Pávlovna advanced to meet her, in company with Pánshin, on whose face the former diplomatic expression had again made its appearance.

"How is your health?"—he asked Liza.

"I feel better now, thank you,"—she replied.

"We have been having a little music here; it is a pity that you did not hear Varvára Pávlovna. She sings superbly, un artiste consommée."

"Come here, ma chérie,"—rang out Márya Dmítrievna's voice.

Varvára Pávlovna instantly, with the submissiveness of a little child, went up to her, and seated herself on a small tabouret at her feet. Márya Dmítrievna had called her for the purpose of leaving her daughter alone with Pánshin, if only for a moment: she still secretly cherished the hope that the girl would come to her senses. Moreover, a thought had occurred to her, to which she desired to give immediate expression.

"Do you know,"—she whispered to Varvára Pávlovna:—"I want to make an effort to reconcile you with your husband: I do not guarantee success, but I will try. You know that he has great respect for me."

Varvára Pávlovna slowly raised her eyes to Márya Dmítrievna, and clasped her hands prettily.

"You would be my saviour, ma tante,"—she said, in a mournful voice:—"I do not know how to thank you for all your affection; but I am too guilty toward Feódor Ivánitch; he cannot forgive me."

"But is it possible that you ... really ..." began Márya Dmítrievna, with curiosity.

"Do not ask me,"—Varvára Pávlovna interrupted her, and dropped her eyes.—"I was young, giddy.... However, I do not wish to defend myself."

"Well, nevertheless, why not make the effort? Do not despair,"—returned Márya Dmítrievna, and was on the point of patting her on the shoulder, but glanced at her face—and grew timid. "She is a modest, modest creature,"—she thought,—"and exactly like a young girl still."

"Are you ill?"—Pánshin was saying, meanwhile, to Liza.

"Yes, I am not very well."

"I understand you,"—he said, after a rather prolonged silence.— "Yes, I understand you."

"How so?"

"I understand you,"—significantly repeated Pánshin, who simply did not know what to say.

Liza became confused, and then said to herself: "So be it!" Pánshin assumed a mysterious air, and fell silent, gazing severely to one side.

"But the clock has struck eleven, I think,"—remarked Márya Dmítrievna.

The guests understood the hint, and began to take their leave. Varvára Pávlovna was made to promise that she would come to dinner on the morrow, and bring Ada; Gedeónovsky, who had almost fallen asleep as he sat in one corner, offered to escort her home. Pánshin solemnly saluted every one, and at the steps, as he put Varvára Pávlovna into her carriage, he pressed her hand and shouted after her: "Au revoir!" Gedeónovsky seated himself by her side; all the way home, she amused herself by placing the tip of her foot on his foot, as though by accident; he became confused, and paid her compliments; she giggled and made eyes at him when the light from a street-lantern fell on the carriage. The waltz which she had herself played, rang in her head, and excited her; wherever she happened to find herself, all she had to do was to imagine to herself lights, a ball-room, the swift whirling to the sounds of music—and her soul went fairly aflame, her eyes darkened strangely, a smile hovered over her lips, something gracefully-bacchic was disseminated all over her body. On arriving at home, Varvára

Pávlovna sprang lightly from the carriage,—only fashionable lionesses know how to spring out in that way,—turned to Gedeónovsky, and suddenly burst into a ringing laugh, straight in his face.

"A charming person,"—thought the State Councillor, as he wended his way homeward to his lodgings, where his servant was awaiting him with a bottle of eau de Cologne:—"it is well that I am a staid man ... only, what was she laughing at?"

Márfa Timoféevna sat all night long by Liza's pillow.

XLI

Lavrétzky spent a day and a half at Vasílievskoe, and during nearly the whole of that time he wandered about the neighbourhood. He could not remain long in one place: anguish gnawed him; he experienced all the torture of incessant, impetuous, and impotent impulses. He recalled the feeling which had taken possession of his soul on the day following his arrival in the country; he recalled his intentions at that time, and waxed very angry with himself. What could have torn him away from that which he recognised as his duty, the sole task of his future? The thirst for happiness—once more, the thirst for happiness!—"Obviously, Mikhalévitch is right," he thought. "Thou hast wished once more to taste of happiness in life,"—he said to himself,—"thou hast forgotten what a luxury, what an unmerited mercy it is when it has visited a man even once. It was not complete, thou wilt say? But put forth thy claims to complete, genuine happiness! Look about thee: who of those around thee is blissful, who enjoys himself? Yonder, a peasant is driving to the reaping; perchance, he is satisfied with his lot.... What of that? Wouldst thou change with him? Remember thy mother: how insignificantly small were her demands, and what lot fell to her share? Thou hast, evidently, only been bragging before Pánshin, when thou saidst to him, that thou hadst come to Russia in order to till the earth; thou hast come in order to run after the girls in thine old age. The news of thy freedom came, and thou didst discard everything, thou didst forget everything, thou didst run like a little boy after a butterfly."... Liza's image uninterruptedly presented itself before his thoughts; with an effort he drove it away, as he did also another importunate image, other imperturbably-crafty, beautiful, and detested features. Old Antón noticed that his master was not himself; after heaving several sighs outside the door, and several more on the threshold, he made up his mind to approach him, and advised him to drink something warm. Lavrétzky shouted at him, ordered him to leave the room, but afterward begged his pardon; but this caused Antón to grow still more disconsolate. Lavrétzky could not sit in the drawing-room; he felt as though his great-grandfather Andréi were gazing scornfully from the canvas at his puny descendant.—"Ekh, look out for thyself! thou art sailing in shoal water!" his lips, pursed up on one side, seemed to be saying. "Can it be,"—he thought,—"that I shall not be able to conquer myself,—that I shall give in to this—nonsense?" (The severely-wounded in war always call their wounds "nonsense."

If a man could not deceive himself,—he could not live on the earth.) "Am I really a miserable little boy? Well, yes: I have beheld close by, I have almost held in my hand, the possibility of happiness for my whole life—it has suddenly vanished; and in a lottery, if you turn the wheel just a little further, a poor man might become a rich one. If it was not to be, it was not to be,—and that's the end of the matter. I'll set to work, with clenched teeth, and I will command myself to hold my tongue; luckily, it is not the first time I have had to take myself in hand. And why did I run away, why am I sitting here, with my head thrust into a bush, like an ostrich? To be afraid to look catastrophe in the face—is nonsense!—Antón!"—he called loudly,— "order the tarantás to be harnessed up immediately. Yes,"—he meditated once more,—"I must command myself to hold my tongue, I must keep a tight rein on myself."...

With such arguments did Lavrétzky strive to alleviate his grief; but it was great and powerful; and even Apraxyéya, who had outlived not so much her mind as every feeling, even Apraxyéya shook her head, and sorrowfully followed him with her eyes, when he seated himself in the tarantás, in order to drive to the town. The horses galloped off; he sat motionless and upright, and stared impassively ahead along the road.

XLII

Liza had written to Lavrétzky on the day before, that he was to come to their house in the evening; but he first went up to his own quarters. He did not find either his wife or his daughter at home; from the servants he learned that she had gone with her to the Kalítins'. This news both startled and enraged him. "Evidently, Varvára Pávlovna is determined not to give me a chance to live,"— he thought, with the excitement of wrath in his heart. He began to stride to and fro, incessantly thrusting aside with his feet and hands the child's toys, the books, and the feminine appurtenances which came in his way; he summoned Justine, and ordered her to remove all that "rubbish."—"Oui, monsieur,"—said she, with a grimace, and began to put the room in order, gracefully bending, and giving Lavrétzky to understand, by every movement, that she regarded him as an unlicked bear. With hatred he watched her worn but still "piquant," sneering, Parisian face, her white cuffs, her silken apron, and light cap. He sent her away, at last, and after long wavering (Varvára Pávlovna still did not return) he made up his mind to betake himself to the Kalítins',—not to Márya Dmítrievna—(not, on any account, would he have entered her drawing-room, that drawing-room where his wife was), but to Márfa Timoféevna; he remembered that a rear staircase from the maids' entrance led straight to her rooms. This is what Lavrétzky did. Chance favoured him: in the yard he met Schúrotchka; she conducted him to Márfa Timoféevna. He found her, contrary to her wont, alone; she was sitting in a corner, with hair uncovered, bowed over, with her hands clasped in her lap. On perceiving Lavrétzky, the old woman was greatly alarmed, rose briskly to her feet, and began to walk hither and yon in the room, as though in search of her cap.

"Ah, here thou art, here thou art,"—she began, avoiding his gaze, and bustling about—"well, how do you do? Come, what now? What is to be done? Where wert thou yesterday? Well, she has come,—well, yes. Well, we must just ... somehow or other."

Lavrétzky dropped into a chair.

"Come, sit down, sit down,"—went on the old woman.—"Thou hast come straight up-stairs. Well, yes, of course. What? thou art come to look at me? Thanks."

The old woman was silent for a while; Lavrétzky did not know what to say to her; but she understood him.

"Liza ... yes, Liza was here just now,"—went on Márfa Timoféevna, tying and untying the cords of her reticule. "She is not

145

quite well. Schúrotchka, where art thou? Come hither, my mother, why canst thou not sit still? And I have a headache. It must be from that—from the singing and from the music."

"From what singing, aunty?"

"Why, of course, they keep singing—what do you call it?—duets. And always in Italian: tchi-tchi, and tcha-tcha, regular magpies. They begin to drag the notes out, and it's just like tugging at your soul. Pánshin and that wife of yours. And all that has come about so quickly; already they are on the footing of relatives, they do not stand on ceremony. However, I will say this much: even a dog seeks a refuge; no harm will come to her, so long as people don't turn her out."

"Nevertheless, I must confess that I did not expect this,"—replied Lavrétzky:—"it must have required great boldness."

"No, my dear soul, that is not boldness; it is calculation. The Lord be with her—I want nothing to do with her! They tell me that thou art sending her to Lavríki,—is it true?"

"Yes, I am placing that estate at the disposal of Varvára Pávlovna."

"Has she asked for money?"

"Not yet."

"Well, it will not be long before she does. But I have only just taken a good look at thee. Art thou well?"

"Yes."

"Schúrotchka,"—suddenly cried Márfa Timoféevna:—"go, and tell Lizavéta Mikhaílovna—that is to say, no, ask her ... she's downstairs, isn't she?"

"Yes, ma'am."

"Well, yes; then ask her: 'Where did she put my book?' She knows."

"I obey, ma'am."

Again the old woman began to bustle about, and to open the drawers of her commode. Lavrétzky sat motionless on his chair.

Suddenly light footsteps became audible on the stairs—and Liza entered. Lavrétzky rose to his feet, and bowed; Liza halted by the door.

"Liza, Lízotchka,"—said Márfa Timoféevna hastily;—"where is my book, where didst thou put my book?"

"What book, aunty?"

"Why, my book; good heavens! However, I did not call thee.... Well, it makes no difference. What are you doing there—downstairs? See here, Feódor Ivánitch has come.—How is thy head?"

"It is all right."

"Thou art always saying: 'It is all right.' What's going on with you down-stairs,—music again?"

"No—they are playing cards."

"Yes, of course, she is up to everything. Schúrotchka, I perceive that thou wishest to have a run in the garden. Go along."

"Why, no, Márfa Timoféevna...."

"Don't argue, if you please. Go! Nastásya Kárpovna has gone into the garden alone: stay with her. Respect the old woman."— Schúrotchka left the room.—"Why, where is my cap? Really, now, where has it got to?"

"Pray let me look for it,"—said Liza.

"Sit down, sit down; my own legs haven't given out yet. I must have left it yonder, in my bedroom."

And, casting a sidelong glance at Lavrétzky, Márfa Timoféevna left the room. She was on the point of leaving the door open, but suddenly turned round toward it, and shut it.

Liza leaned against the back of her chair, and gently lifted her hands to her face; Lavrétzky remained standing, as he was.

"This is how we were to meet again,"—he said, at last.

Liza took her hands from her face.

"Yes,"—she said dully:—"we were promptly punished."

"Punished?"—said Lavrétzky. "But what were you punished for?"

Liza raised her eyes to him. They expressed neither grief nor anxiety: they looked smaller and dimmer. Her face was pale; her slightly parted lips had also grown pale.

Lavrétzky's heart shuddered with pity and with love.

"You wrote to me: 'All is at an end,'"—he whispered:—"Yes, all is at an end—before it has begun."

"We must forget all that,"—said Liza:—"I am glad that you came; I wanted to write to you, but it is better thus. Only, we must make use, as promptly as possible, of these minutes. It remains for both of us to do our duty. You, Feódor Ivánitch, ought to become reconciled to your wife."

"Liza!"

"I implore you to do it; in that way alone can we expiate ... everything which has taken place. Think it over—and you will not refuse me."

"Liza, for God's sake,—you are demanding the impossible. I am ready to do everything you command; but become reconciled to her now!... I agree to everything, I have forgotten everything; but I cannot force my heart to.... Have mercy, this is cruel!"

"I do not require from you ... what you think; do not live with her, if you cannot; but become reconciled,"—replied Liza, and again

147

raised her hand to her eyes.—"Remember your little daughter; do this for me."

"Very well,"—said Lavrétzky, through his teeth:—"I will do it; let us assume that thereby I am fulfilling my duty. Well, and you—in what does your duty consist?"

"I know what it is."

Lavrétzky suddenly started.

"Surely, you are not preparing to marry Pánshin?"—he asked.

Liza smiled almost imperceptibly.

"Oh, no!"—she said.

"Akh, Liza, Liza!"—cried Lavrétzky:—"how happy we might have been!"

Again Liza glanced at him.

"Now you see yourself, Feódor Ivánitch, that happiness does not depend upon us, but upon God."

"Yes, because you...."

The door of the adjoining room opened swiftly, and Márfa Timoféevna entered, with her cap in her hand.

"I have found it at last,"—she said, taking up her stand between Lavrétzky and Liza.—"I had mislaid it myself. That's what it is to be old, alack! However, youth is no better. Well, and art thou going to Lavríki thyself, with thy wife?"—she added, addressing Feódor Ivánitch.

"With her, to Lavríki?—I do not know,"—he said, after a pause.

"Thou art not going down-stairs?"

"Not to-day."

"Well, very good, as it pleases thee; but I think thou shouldst go down-stairs, Liza. Akh, gracious goodness!—and I have forgotten to give the bullfinch his food. Just wait, I'll be back directly...."

And Márfa Timoféevna ran out of the room, without putting on her cap.

Lavrétzky went quickly up to Liza.

"Liza,"—he began in a beseeching voice:—"we are parting forever, my heart is breaking,—give me your hand in farewell."

Liza raised her head. Her weary, almost extinct gaze rested on him....

"No,"—she said, and drew back the hand which she had already put forward—"no. Lavrétzky"—(she called him thus, for the first time)—"I will not give you my hand. To what end? Go away, I entreat you. You know that I love you,"—she added, with an effort:—"but no ... no."

And she raised her handkerchief to her eyes.

The door creaked.... The handkerchief slipped off Liza's knees. Lavrétzky caught it before it fell to the floor, hastily thrust it into his side pocket, and, turning round, his eyes met those of Márfa Timoféevna.

"Lízotchka, I think thy mother is calling thee,"—remarked the old woman.

Liza immediately rose, and left the room.

Márfa Timoféevna sat down again in her corner. Lavrétzky began to take leave of her.

"Fédya,"—she suddenly said.

"What, aunty?"

"Art thou an honourable man?"

"What?"

"I ask thee: art thou an honourable man?"

"I hope so."

"H'm. But give me thy word of honour that thou art an honourable man."

"Certainly.—But why?"

"I know why. Yes, and thou also, my benefactor, if thou wilt think it over well,—for thou art not stupid,—wilt understand thyself why I ask this of thee. And now, farewell, my dear. Thanks for thy visit; and remember the word that has been spoken, Fédya, and kiss me. Okh, my soul, it is hard for thee, I know: but then, life is not easy for any one. That is why I used to envy the flies; here, I thought, is something that finds life good; but once, in the night, I heard a fly grieving in the claws of a spider,—no, I thought, a thundercloud hangs over them also. What is to be done, Fédya? but remember thy word, nevertheless.—Go."

Lavrétzky emerged from the back entrance, and was already approaching the gate ... when a lackey overtook him.

"Márya Dmítrievna ordered me to ask you to be so good as to come to her,"—he announced to Lavrétzky.

"Say to her, my good fellow, that I cannot at present ..." began Feódor Ivánitch.

"She ordered me to entreat you urgently,"—went on the lackey:—"she ordered me to say, that she is at home."

"But have the visitors gone?"—asked Lavrétzky.

"Yes, sir,"—returned the lackey, and grinned.

Lavrétzky shrugged his shoulders, and followed him.

XLIII

Márya Dmítrievna was sitting alone, in her boudoir, in a sofa-chair, and sniffing eau de Cologne; a glass of orange-flower water was standing beside her, on a small table. She was excited, and seemed to be timorous.

Lavrétzky entered.

"You wished to see me,"—he said, saluting her coldly.

"Yes,"—returned Márya Dmítrievna, and drank a little of the water. "I heard that you went straight up-stairs to aunty; I gave orders that you should be requested to come to me: I must have a talk with you. Sit down, if you please."—Márya Dmítrievna took breath.—"You know,"—she went on:—"that your wife has arrived?"

"That fact is known to me,"—said Lavrétzky.

"Well, yes,—that is, I meant to say, she came to me, and I received her; that is what I wish to have an explanation about with you now, Feódor Ivánitch. I, thank God, have won universal respect, I may say, and I would not do anything improper for all the world. Although I foresaw that it would be disagreeable to you, still, I could not make up my mind to refuse her, Feódor Ivánitch; she is my relative—through you: put yourself in my place—what right had I to turn her out of my house?—You agree with me?"

"There is no necessity for your agitating yourself, Márya Dmítrievna,"—returned Lavrétzky: "you have behaved very well indeed; I am not in the least angry. I have not the slightest intention of depriving Varvára Pávlovna of the right to see her acquaintances; I only refrained from entering your apartments to-day because I wished to avoid meeting her,—that was all."

"Akh, how delighted I am to hear that from you, Feódor Ivánitch,"—exclaimed Márya Dmítrievna:—"however, I always expected this from your noble sentiments. But that I should feel agitated, is not wonderful: I am a woman and a mother. And your wife ... of course, I cannot judge between her and you—I told her so myself; but she is such an amiable lady, that she cannot cause anything but pleasure."

Lavrétzky laughed, and played with his hat.

"And this is what I wished to say to you, Feódor Ivánitch,"—went on Márya Dmítrievna, moving a little nearer to him:—"if you had only seen how modestly, how respectfully she behaves!—Really, it is touching. But if you had heard how she speaks of you! 'I am wholly culpable with regard to him,' she says; 'I did not know how to appreciate him,' she says; 'he is an angel,' she says, 'not a man.'

Truly, she did say that, 'an angel.' She is so penitent.... I never beheld such penitence, I give you my word!"

"Well, Márya Dmítrievna,"—said Lavrétzky:—"permit me to ask you a question: I am told that Varvára Pávlovna has been singing for you; did she sing during her repentance—or how?"...

"Akh, aren't you ashamed to talk like that! She sang and played merely with the object of giving me pleasure, because I begged, almost commanded her to do so. I perceive that she is distressed— so distressed, I wonder how I can divert her. And I had heard that she had such a fine talent.—Upon my word, Feódor Ivánitch, she is a completely crushed, overwhelmed woman—ask Sergyéi Petróvitch if she is not, tout à fait,—what have you to say to that?"

Lavrétzky simply shrugged his shoulders.

"And then, what a little angel that Ada of yours is, what a darling!—How pretty she is, how clever! how well she talks French; and she understands Russian—she called me tyótenka [aunty]. And do you know, as for being shy, like nearly all children of her age,— there is no shyness about her. She is awfully like you, Feódor Ivánitch. Her eyes, her brows ... well, she's you all over again, your perfect image. I am not very fond of such small children, I must confess; but I have simply lost my heart to your little daughter."

"Márya Dmítrievna,"—exclaimed Lavrétzky, suddenly:—"allow me to ask you why you are pleased to say all this to me?"

"Why?"—again Márya Dmítrievna sniffed at her eau de Cologne, and sipped her water:—"I say it, Feódor Ivánitch, because ... you see, I am a relative, I take the closest interest in you.... I know that you have the very kindest of hearts. Hearken to me, mon cousin,—I am a woman of experience, and I am not talking at random: forgive, forgive your wife."—Márya Dmítrievna's eyes suddenly filled with tears.—"Reflect: youth, inexperience ... well, perhaps, a bad example—she had not the sort of a mother who might have put her on the right road. Forgive her, Feódor Ivánitch; she has been sufficiently punished."

Tears trickled down Márya Dmítrievna's cheeks; she did not wipe them away: she loved to weep. Lavrétzky sat as on hot coals. "My God,"—he thought,—"what sort of torture, what sort of a day has fallen to my lot!"

"You do not answer,"—began Márya Dmítrievna again:—"what am I to understand by that?—is it possible that you can be so cruel? No, I will not believe that. I feel that my words have convinced you. Feódor Ivánitch, God will reward you for your kindness of heart, and you will now receive your wife from my hands...."

Lavrétzky involuntarily rose from his chair; Márya Dmítrievna also rose, and stepping briskly behind a screen, led forth Varvára

Pávlovna. Pale, half-fainting, with eyes cast down, she seemed to have renounced every thought, every impulse of her own—to have placed herself wholly in the hands of Márya Dmítrievna.

Lavrétzky retreated a pace.

"You were here?"—he exclaimed.

"Do not blame her,"—said Márya Dmítrievna, hastily;—"she did not wish to remain on any account whatever, but I ordered her to stay, and placed her there behind the screen. She assured me that it would only make you more angry; but I would not listen to her; I know you better than she does. Receive your wife from my hands; go, Várya, be not afraid, fall at your husband's feet" (she tugged at her hand)—"and my blessing on you!...."

"Wait, Márya Dmítrievna,"—Lavrétzky interrupted her, in a dull, but quivering voice:—"you are, probably, fond of sentimental scenes," (Lavrétzky was not mistaken: Márya Dmítrievna had retained from her boarding-school days a passion for a certain theatricalness); "they amuse you; but others suffer from them. However, I will not discuss the matter with you; in this scene you are not the principal actor. What do you want of me, madam?"—he added, addressing his wife. "Have not I done for you all that I could? Do not retort, that you have not plotted this meeting; I shall not believe you,—and you know that I cannot believe you. What, then, do you want? You are clever,—you never do anything without an object. You must understand that I am not capable of living with you as I used to live; not because I am angry with you, but because I have become a different man. I told you that on the day after your return, and you yourself, at that moment, acquiesced with me in your own soul. But you wish to reinstate yourself in public opinion; it is not enough for you to live in my house, you want to live under one roof with me,—is not that the truth?"

"I want you to forgive me,"—said Varvára Pávlovna, without raising her eyes.

"She wants you to forgive her,"—repeated Márya Dmítrievna.

"And not for my own sake, but for Ada's,"—whispered Varvára Pávlovna.

"Not for her sake, but for Ada's,"—repeated Márya Dmítrievna.

"Very good. You wish that?"—ejaculated Lavrétzky, with an effort. "As you like, I agree to that."

Varvára Pávlovna cast a swift glance at him, and Márya Dmítrievna cried out:—"Well, God be praised"—and again tugged at Varvára Pávlovna's hand. "Now receive from me...."

"Wait, I tell you,"—Lavrétzky interrupted her. "I consent to live with you, Varvára Pávlovna,"—he continued:—"That is to say, I will take you to Lavríki, and I will live with you as long as my strength holds out, and then I shall go away,—and return now and then. You see, I do not wish to deceive you; but do not demand anything more. You yourself would smile, were I to comply with the desire of your respected relative, and press you to my heart, and assure you that ... there had been no past, that the felled tree could burst into blossom once more. But I perceive that I must submit. You will not understand that word; ... it matters not. I repeat, I will live with you ... or, no, I cannot promise that ... I will join you, I will regard you again as my wife...."

"But give her your hand on that, at least,"—said Márya Dmítrievna, whose tears were long since dried up.

"Up to the present moment, I have not deceived Varvára Pávlovna,"—returned Lavrétzky;—"she will believe me as it is. I will take her to Lavríki;—and recollect, Varvára Pávlovna: our compact will be regarded as broken just as soon as you leave that place. And now, permit me to withdraw."

He bowed to both ladies, and hastily quitted the room.

"You are not taking her with you,"—called Márya Dmítrievna after him.... "Let him alone,"—Varvára Pávlovna whispered to her, and immediately threw her arms round her, began to utter thanks, to kiss her hands, and to call her her saviour.

Márya Dmítrievna accepted her caresses with condescension; but in her secret soul she was pleased neither with Lavrétzky nor with Varvára Pávlovna, nor with the whole scene which she had planned. There had turned out to be very little sentimentality; Varvára Pávlovna, in her opinion, should have flung herself at her husband's feet.

"How was it that you did not understand me?"—she commented:—"why, I told you: 'fall at his feet.'"

"It was better thus, dear aunty; do not disturb yourself—everything is all right,"—insisted Varvára Pávlovna.

"Well, and he is as cold as ice,"—remarked Márya Dmítrievna. "Even if you did not weep, why, I fairly overflowed before him. He means to shut you up in Lavríki. The idea,—and you cannot even come to see me! All men are unfeeling,"—she said, in conclusion, and shook her head significantly.

"On the other hand, women know how to value kindness and magnanimity,"—said Varvára Pávlovna, and softly dropping on her knees before Márya Dmítrievna, she embraced the latter's corpulent form with her arms, and pressed her face against her. That face wore a quiet smile, but Márya Dmítrievna's tears were flowing again.

And Lavrétzky went home, locked himself up in his valet's room, flung himself on the divan, and lay there until the morning.

XLIV

The next day was Sunday. The chiming of the bells for the early Liturgy did not awaken Lavrétzky—he had not closed an eye all night long—but it did remind him of another Sunday, when, at the wish of Liza, he had gone to church. He hastily rose; a certain secret voice told him that he would see her there again to-day. He noiselessly quitted the house, ordered Varvára Pávlovna to be informed that he would return to dinner, and with great strides wended his way thither, whither the monotonously-mournful chiming summoned him. He arrived early: there was hardly any one in the church; a chanter in the choir was reading the Hours; his voice, occasionally broken by a cough, boomed on in measured cadence, now rising, now falling. Lavrétzky took up his stand not far from the entrance. The prayerfully inclined arrived one by one, paused, crossed themselves, bowed on all sides;[13] their footsteps resounded in the emptiness and silence, distinctly re-echoing from the arches overhead. A decrepit little old woman, in an ancient hooded cloak, knelt down beside Lavrétzky, and began to pray assiduously; her yellow, toothless, wrinkled face expressed intense emotion; her red eyes gazed fixedly upward at the holy picture on the ikonostásis; her bony hand kept incessantly emerging from under her cloak, and slowly but vigorously made a great, sweeping sign of the cross. A peasant, with a thick beard and a surly face, tousled and dishevelled, entered the church, went down at once on both knees, and immediately set to crossing himself, hastily flinging back his head and shaking it after every prostration. Such bitter woe was depicted on his countenance, and in all his movements, that Lavrétzky made up his mind to approach and ask him what was the matter. The peasant started back timidly and roughly, and looked at him.... "My son is dead,"—he said, in hasty accents—and again began to prostrate himself to the floor. "What can take the place, for them, of the consolation of the church?"—Lavrétzky thought,—and tried to pray himself; but his heart had grown heavy and hard, and his thoughts were far away. He was still expecting Liza—but Liza did not come. The church began to fill with people; still she did not come. The Liturgy began, the deacon had already read the Gospel,

---

[13] That is—they figuratively begged the pardon of all whom they might have offended, before entering on the Church service. The officiating priest does the same.—Translator.

the bell had pealed for the hymn "Worthy";[14] Lavrétzky moved a little,—and suddenly caught sight of Liza. She had arrived before him, but he had not descried her; crowded into the space between the wall and the choir, she neither glanced around nor moved. Lavrétzky did not take his eyes from her until the very end of the Liturgy: he was bidding her farewell. The congregation began to disperse, but she still stood on; she seemed to be awaiting Lavrétzky's departure. At last, she crossed herself for the last time, and went away, without looking round; she had only a maid with her. Lavrétzky followed her out of the church, and overtook her in the street; she was walking very rapidly, with her head bowed and her veil lowered over her face.

"Good morning, Lizavéta Mikhaílovna,"—said he, loudly, with forced ease:—"may I accompany you?"

She said nothing; he walked along by her side.

"Are you satisfied with me?"—he asked her, lowering his voice.—"You have heard what took place last night?"

"Yes, yes,"—she said in a whisper:—"you did well."

And she walked on faster than ever.

"You are satisfied?"

Liza only nodded her head.

"Feódor Ivánitch,"—she began, in a composed, but weak voice:—"I have wanted to ask you: do not come to our house again; go away as speedily as possible; we can see each other later on,—sometime, a year hence. But now, do this for me; comply with my request, for God's sake."

"I am ready to obey you in all things, Lizavéta Mikhaílovna; but is it possible that we are to part thus? will you not say a single word to me?"

"Feódor Ivánitch, here you are now, walking by my side. But you are already far away from me. And not you alone, but also...."

"Finish, I entreat you!"—exclaimed Lavrétzky:—"what is it that you mean to say?"

"You will hear, perhaps ... but whatever happens, forget ... no, do not forget me,—remember me."

"I forget you!..."

"Enough; farewell. Do not follow me."

"Liza ..."—Lavrétzky was beginning.

---

[14] "Worthy and right is it, to bow down to the Father, and to the Son, and to the Holy Spirit, to the Trinity, consubstantial and indivisible"—at a very solemn point, and quite late in the Liturgy.—Translator.

"Farewell, farewell!"—she repeated, dropped her veil still lower, and advanced almost at a run.

Lavrétzky gazed after her, and dropping his head, went back down the street. He hit upon Lemm, who was also walking along, with his hat pulled down on his nose, and staring at the ground under his feet.

They stared at each other in silence.

"Well, what have you to say?"—said Lavrétzky at last.

"What have I to say?"—returned Lemm surlily:—"I have nothing to say. Everything is dead, and we are dead. (Alles ist todt und wir sind todt.) You are going to the right, I think?"

"Yes."

"Then I go to the left. Good-bye."

On the following morning, Feódor Ivánitch and his wife set out for Lavríki. She drove in front, in the carriage, with Ada and Justine; he came behind, in his tarantás. The pretty little girl never quitted the carriage-window during the whole journey; she was surprised at everything: at the peasants, the peasant women, the wells, the shaft-arches, the carriage-bells, at the multitude of jackdaws; Justine shared her surprise. Varvára Pávlovna laughed at their comments and exclamations.... She was in high spirits; before their departure from the town of O*** she had had an explanation with her husband.

"I understand your position,"—she had said to him,—and he, from the expression of her clever eyes, was able to conclude that she did fully understand his position,—"but you must do me the justice, at least, to say that I am easy to live with; I shall not obtrude myself upon you, embarrass you; I wanted to assure Ada's future. I need nothing further."

"Yes, and you have attained your object,"—said Feódor Ivánitch.

"My sole idea now is to shut myself up in the wilds; I shall forever remember your good deed in my prayers...."

"Faugh!... enough of that,"—he interrupted her.

"And I shall know how to respect your independence, and your repose,"—she completed her phrase, which she had prepared in advance.

Lavrétzky had made her a low bow. Varvára Pávlovna understood that her husband, in his soul, was grateful to her.

On the second day, toward the evening, they reached Lavríki; a week later, Lavrétzky set off for Moscow, leaving his wife five thousand rubles for her expenses—and the day after Lavrétzky's departure, Pánshin, whom Varvára Pávlovna had begged not to forget her in her isolation, made his appearance. She gave him the warmest sort of a welcome, and until late into the night the lofty rooms of the house and the very garden rang with the sounds of music, singing, and merry French speeches. Pánshin visited Varvára Pávlovna for three days; when he took leave of her, and warmly pressed her beautiful hands, he promised to return very soon—and he kept his promise.

XLV

Liza had a separate little room, on the second story of her mother's house, small, clean, bright, with a white bed, pots of flowers in the corners and in front of the holy pictures, with a tiny writing-table, a case of books, and a crucifix on the wall. This little chamber was called the nursery; Liza had been born in it. On returning to it from church, where she had seen Lavrétzky, she put everything in order, even more carefully than usual, wiped the dust off everything, looked over and tied up with ribbons her note-books and the letters of her friends, locked all the drawers, watered the plants, and touched every flower with her hand. She did all this without haste, without noise, with a certain touched and tranquil solicitude on her face. She halted, at last, in the middle of the room, slowly looked around her, and stepping up to the table over which hung the crucifix, she knelt down, laid her head on her clasped hands, and remained motionless.

Márfa Timoféevna entered, and found her in this position. Liza did not notice her entrance. The old woman went outside the door, on tiptoe, and gave vent to several loud coughs. Liza rose quickly to her feet, and wiped her eyes, in which glittered clear tears which had not fallen.

"I see that thou hast been arranging thy little cell again,"—said Márfa Timoféevna, and bent low over a pot containing a young rose-bush:—"what a splendid perfume it has!"

Liza gazed thoughtfully at her aunt.

"What a word you have uttered!"—she whispered.

"What sort of a word, what word?"—interposed the old woman, vivaciously;—"what dost thou mean?—This is dreadful,"—she said, suddenly tearing off her cap, and seating herself on Liza's bed:— "this is beyond my strength! today is the fourth day that I seem to be seething in a kettle; I can no longer pretend that I notice nothing,—I cannot see thee growing pale, withering away, weeping,—I cannot, I cannot!"

"Why, what is the matter with you, aunty?"—said Liza:—"I am all right...."

"All right?"—exclaimed Márfa Timoféevna:—"tell that to others, but not to me! All right! But who was it that was on her knees just now? whose eyelashes are still wet with tears? All right! Why, look at thyself, what hast thou done to thy face, what has become of thine eyes?—All right! As though I did not know all!"

"It will pass off, aunty; give me time."

"It will pass off, but when? O Lord God, my Master! is it possible that thou didst love him so? why, he is an old man, Lízotchka. Well, I do not dispute that he is a good man, he does not bite; but what does that signify? we are all good people: the world is large, there will always be plenty of that sort."

"I tell you, that it will all pass off, it is all over already."

"Listen, Lízotchka, to what I have to say to thee,"—said Márfa Timoféevna, suddenly, making Liza sit down beside her on the bed, and adjusting now her hair, now her kerchief.—"It only seems to you, while it is fresh, that your grief is beyond remedy. Ekh, my darling, for death alone there is no remedy! Only say to thyself: 'I won't give in—so there now!' and afterward thou wilt be amazed thyself—how soon, how well, it will pass off. Only have patience."

"Aunty,"—replied Liza:—"it is already past, all is over already."

"Past—over—forsooth! Why, even thy little nose has grown pointed, and thou sayest: 'It is over—it is over!'"

"Yes, it is over, aunty, if you will only help me,"—cried Liza, with sudden animation, and threw herself on Márfa Timoféevna's neck.—"Dear aunty, be my friend, help me; do not be angry, understand me."

"Why, what is this, what is this, my mother? Don't frighten me, please; I shall scream in another minute; don't look at me like that: tell me quickly what thou meanest?"

"I ... I want ..." Liza hid her face in Márfa Timoféevna's bosom.... "I want to enter a convent,"—she said, in a dull tone.

The old woman fairly leaped on the bed.

"Cross thyself, my mother, Lízotchka; come to thy senses: God be with thee, what dost thou mean?"—she stammered at last: "lie down, my darling, sleep a little: this comes from lack of sleep, my dear."

Liza raised her head, her cheeks were burning.

"No, aunty,"—she articulated, "do not speak like that. I have made up my mind, I have prayed, I have asked counsel of God; all is ended, my life with you is ended. Such a lesson is not in vain; and it is not the first time I have thought of this. Happiness was not suited to me; even when I cherished hopes of happiness, my heart was always heavy. I know everything, my own sins and the sins of others, and how papa acquired his wealth; I know everything. All that must be atoned for by prayer—atoned for by prayer. I am sorry for all of you—I am sorry for mamma, for Lyénotchka; but there is no help for it; I feel that I cannot live here; I have already taken leave of everything, I have made my reverence to everything in the house for the last time; something is calling me hence; I am weary; I

159

want to shut myself up forever. Do not hold me back, do not dissuade me; help me, or I will go away alone."

Márfa Timoféevna listened in terror to her niece.

"She is ill, she is raving,"—she thought:—"I must send for a doctor; but for which? Gedeónovsky was praising some one the other day; he's always lying,—but, perhaps, he told the truth that time." But when she became convinced that Liza was not ill, and was not raving, when to all her objections Liza steadfastly made one and the same reply, Márfa Timoféevna became seriously frightened and grieved.—"But thou dost not know, my darling,"—she began to try to prevail upon her;—"what sort of a life they lead in convents! Why, my own one, they will feed thee with green hemp-oil; they will put on thee coarse, awfully coarse linen; they will make thee go about cold; thou canst not endure all that, Lízotchka. All that is the traces of Agáfya in thee; it was she who led thee astray. Why, she began by living her life, living a gay life; do thou live thy life also. Let me, at least, die in peace, and then do what thou wilt. And who ever heard of any one going into a convent, all on account of such a goat's beard—the Lord forgive me!—on account of a man? Come, if thy heart is so heavy, go away on a journey, pray to a saint, have a prayer-service said, but don't put the black cowl on thy head, my dear little father, my dear little mother...."

And Márfa Timoféevna began to weep bitterly.

Liza comforted her, wiped away her tears, but remained inflexible. In her despair, Márfa Timoféevna tried to resort to threats: she would tell Liza's mother everything; but even that was of no avail. Only as a concession to the old woman's urgent entreaties, did Liza consent to defer the fulfilment of her intention for six months; in return, Márfa Timoféevna was compelled to give her her word that she would help her, and obtain the permission of Márya Dmítrievna if, at the end of six months, she had not changed her mind.

With the advent of the first cold weather, Varvára Pávlovna, despite her promise to shut herself up in the depths of the country, after providing herself with money, removed to Petersburg, where she hired a modest but pretty apartment, which had been found for her by Pánshin, who had quitted the Government of O*** before her. During the latter part of his sojourn in O*** he had completely fallen out of favour with Márya Dmítrievna; he had suddenly ceased to call upon her and hardly ever quitted Lavríki. Varvára Pávlovna had enslaved him, precisely that,—enslaved him; no other word will express her unlimited, irrevocable, irresponsible power over him.

Lavrétzky passed the winter in Moscow, but in the spring of the following year the news reached him that Liza had entered the B*** convent, in one of the most remote corners of Russia.

EPILOGUE

Eight years have passed. Spring has come again.... But first, let us say a few words about the fate of Mikhalévitch, Pánshin, Mme. Lavrétzky—and take our leave of them. Mikhalévitch, after long peregrinations, has finally hit upon his real vocation: he has obtained the post of head inspector in a government institution. He is very well satisfied with his lot, and his pupils "adore" him, although they mimic him. Pánshin has advanced greatly in rank, and already has a directorship in view; he walks with his back somewhat bent: it must be the cross of the Order of Vladímir, which has been conferred upon him, that drags him forward. The official in him has, decidedly, carried the day over the artist; his still youthful face has turned quite yellow, his hair has grown thin, and he no longer sings or draws, but secretly occupies himself with literature: he has written a little comedy, in the nature of "a proverb,"—and, as every one who writes nowadays "shows up" some one or something, he has shown up in it a coquette, and he reads it surreptitiously to two or three ladies who are favourably disposed toward him. But he has not married, although many fine opportunities of so doing have presented themselves: for this Varvára Pávlovna is responsible. As for her, she lives uninterruptedly in Paris, as of yore: Feódor Ivánitch has given her a bill of exchange on himself, and bought himself free from her,— from the possibility of a second, unexpected invasion. She has grown old and fat, but it is still pretty and elegant. Every person has his own ideal: Varvára Pávlovna has found hers—in the dramatic productions of Dumas fils. She assiduously frequents the theatre where consumptive and sentimental ladies of the frail class are put on the stage; to be Mme. Doche seems to her the very apex of human felicity; one day, she declared that she desired no better lot for her daughter. It is to be hoped that fate will deliver Mademoiselle Ada from such felicity: from a rosy, plump child, she has turned into a weak-chested, pale-faced young girl; her nerves are already deranged. The number of Varvára Pávlovna's admirers has decreased; but they have not transferred their allegiance: she will, in all probability, retain several of them to the end of her life. The most ardent of them, of late, has been a certain Zakurdálo-Skubýrnikoff, one of the retired dandies of the Guards, a man of eight and thirty, of remarkably robust build. The Frenchmen who frequent Mme. Lavrétzky's salon call him "le gros taureau de l'Ukraïne"; Varvára Pávlovna never invites him to her fashionable evening gatherings, but he enjoys her favour in the fullest measure.

So ... eight years have passed. Again the sky is breathing forth the beaming happiness of spring; again it is smiling upon the earth and upon men; again, beneath its caress, everything has burst into blossom, into love and song. The town of O*** has undergone very little change in the course of those eight years; but Márya Dmítrievna's house seems to have grown young: its recently painted walls shine as in welcome, and the panes of the open windows are crimsoning and glittering in the rays of the setting sun. Through these windows, out upon the street, are wafted the sounds of ringing young voices, of incessant laughter; the whole house seems bubbling with life, and overflowing the brim with merriment. The mistress of the house herself has long since gone to her grave: Márya Dmítrievna died two years after Liza's profession as a nun; and Márfa Timoféevna did not long survive her niece; they rest side by side in the town cemetery. Nastásya Kárpovna, also, is dead; the faithful old woman went, every week, for the space of several years, to pray over the ashes of her friend.... Her time came, and her bones also were laid in the damp earth. But Márya Dmítrievna's house has not passed into the hands of strangers, has not left her family; the nest has not been destroyed: Lyénotchka, who has become a stately, beautiful young girl, and her betrothed, a fair-haired officer of hussars; Márya Dmítrievna's son, who has just been married in Petersburg, and has come with his young wife to spend the spring in O***; his wife's sister, an Institute-girl of sixteen, with brilliantly scarlet cheeks and clear eyes; Schúrotchka, who has also grown up and become pretty—these are the young folks who are making the walls of the Kalítin house re-echo with laughter and chatter. Everything about it has been changed, everything has been brought into accord with the new inhabitants. Beardless young house-servants, who grin and jest, have taken the places of the former sedate old servitors; where overgrown Róska was wont to stroll, two setters are chasing madly about, and leaping over the divans; the stable has been filled with clean-limbed amblers, high-spirited shaft-horses, fiery trace-horses[15] with braided manes, and riding-horses from the Don; the hours for breakfast, dinner, and supper have become mixed up and confused; according to the expression of the neighbours, "an unprecedented state of affairs" has been established.

On the evening of which we are speaking, the inhabitants of the Kalítin house (the oldest of them, Lyénotchka's betrothed, was only four and twenty) were engaged in a far from complicated, but,

---

[15] The trotter as shaft-horse, and the galloping side-horses of a troïka.— Translator.

judging from their vigorous laughter, a very amusing game: they were running through the rooms, and catching each other; the dogs, also, were running and barking, and the canaries which hung in cages in front of the windows vied with each other in singing at the tops of their voices, increasing the uproar of ringing volleys of noise with their furious chirping. While this deafening diversion was at its very height, a mud-stained tarantás drove up to the gate, and a man of forty-five, clad in travelling garb, descended from it, and stopped short in amazement. He stood motionless for some time, swept an attentive glance over the house, passed through the gate into the yard, and slowly ascended the steps. There was no one in the anteroom to receive him; but the door of the "hall" flew wide open; through it, all flushed, bounced Schúrotchka, and instantly, in pursuit of her, with ringing laughter, rushed the whole youthful band. She came to a sudden halt and fell silent at the sight of the stranger; but the clear eyes fastened upon him were as caressing as ever, the fresh faces did not cease to smile. Márya Dmítrievna's son stepped up to the visitor, and courteously asked him what he wished.

"I am Lavrétzky,"—said the visitor.

A vigorous shout rang out in response—and not because all these young people were so extremely delighted at the arrival of the distant, almost forgotten relative, but simply because they were ready to make an uproar and rejoice on every convenient opportunity. They immediately surrounded Lavrétzky: Lyénotchka, in the quality of an old acquaintance, was the first to introduce herself, and to assure him that, in another moment, she certainly would have recognised him, and then she presented all the rest of the company, calling each one of them, including her betrothed, by his pet name. The whole throng moved through the dining-room to the drawing-room. The hangings in both rooms were different, but the furniture remained the same; Lavrétzky recognised the piano; even the same embroidery-frame was standing in the window, in the same position—and almost with the same unfinished bit of embroidery as eight years previously. They made him sit down in a comfortable easy-chair; all seated themselves decorously around him. Questions, exclamations, stories showered down without cessation.

"But it is a long time since we have seen you,"—remarked Lyénotchka, ingenuously:—"and we have not seen Varvára Pávlovna either."

"I should think so!"—interposed her brother, hurriedly. "I carried thee off to Petersburg, but Feódor Ivánitch lived in the country all the time."

163

"Yes, and mamma has died since, you know."

"And Márfa Timoféevna,"—said Schúrotchka.

"And Nastásya Kárpovna,"—rejoined Lyénotchka.—"And M'sieu Lemm...."

"What? And is Lemm dead also?"—asked Lavrétzky.

"Yes,"—replied young Kalítin:—"he went away from here to Odessa—they say that some one decoyed him thither; and there he died."

"You do not know—whether he left any music behind him?"

"I don't know,—it is hardly probable."

All fell silent, and exchanged glances. A cloud of sadness had descended upon all the young faces.

"And Matróska is alive,"—suddenly remarked Lyénotchka.

"And Gedeónovsky is alive,"—added her brother.

At the name of Gedeónovsky a vigorous peal of laughter rang out in unison.

"Yes, he is alive, and lies just as he always did,"—went on Márya Dmítrievna's son:—"and just imagine, that naughty child there" (and he pointed at his wife's sister, the Institute-girl) "put pepper in his snuff-box yesterday."

"How he did sneeze!" exclaimed Lyénotehka:—and again a peal of irrepressible laughter rang out.

"We received news of Liza recently,"—said young Kalítin,—and again everything grew still round about:—"things are well with her,—her health is now improving somewhat."

"Is she still in the same convent?"—asked Lavrétzky, not without an effort.

"Yes, still in the same place."

"Does she write to you?"

"No, never; the news reaches us through other people."—A sudden, profound silence ensued. "The angel of silence has flown past," all said to themselves.

"Would not you like to go into the garden?"—Kalítin turned to Lavrétzky:—"it is very pretty now, although we have rather neglected it."

Lavrétzky went out into the garden, and the first thing that struck his eyes was the bench on which he had once spent with Liza a few happy moments, never to be repeated; it had grown black and crooked; but he recognised it, and his soul was seized by that feeling which has no peer in sweetness and in sorrow,—the feeling of living grief for vanished youth, for happiness which it once possessed. In company with the young people, he strolled through the alleys: the linden-trees had not grown much older and taller during the last eight years, but their shade had become more dense; on the other hand, all the shrubs had sprung upward, the raspberry-bushes had waxed strong, the hazel copse had become entirely impenetrable, and everywhere there was an odour of thickets, forest, grass, and lilacs.

"What a good place this would be to play at puss-in-the-corner,"—suddenly cried Lyénotchka, as they entered a small, verdant glade, hemmed in by lindens:—"by the way, there are five of us."

"And hast thou forgotten Feódor Ivánitch?"—her brother observed to her.... "Or art thou not reckoning in thyself?"

Lyénotchka blushed faintly.

"But is it possible that Feódor Ivánitch, at his age, can..."—she began.

"Please play,"—interposed Lavrétzky, hastily:—"pay no heed to me. It will be all the more agreeable to me if I know that I am not embarrassing you. And there is no need for you to bother about me; we old fellows have occupations of which you, as yet, know nothing, and which no diversion can replace: memories."

The young people listened to Lavrétzky with courteous and almost mocking respect,—exactly as though their teacher were reading them a lesson,—and suddenly all of them flew away from him, and ran over the glade; four of them took up their stand near the trees, one stood in the centre,—and the fun began.

But Lavrétzky returned to the house, went into the dining-room, approached the piano, and touched one of the keys: a faint, but pure sound rang out, and secretly trembled in his heart: with that note began that inspired melody wherewith, long ago, on that same blissful night, Lemm, the dead Lemm, had led him to such raptures. Then Lavrétzky passed into the drawing-room, and did not emerge from it for a long time: in that room, where he had so often seen Liza, her image rose up before him more vividly than ever; it seemed to him, that he felt around him the traces of her presence; but his grief for her was exhausting and not light: there was in it none of the tranquillity which death inspires. Liza was still living somewhere, dully, far away; he thought of her as among the living, but did not recognise the young girl whom he had once loved in that pale spectre swathed in the conventual garment, surrounded by smoky clouds of incense. Lavrétzky would not have recognised himself, had he been able to contemplate himself as he mentally contemplated Liza. In the course of those eight years the crisis had, at last, been effected in his life; that crisis which many do not experience, but without which it is not possible to remain an honourable man to the end: he had really ceased to think of his own happiness, of selfish aims. He had calmed down, and—why should the truth be concealed?—he had aged, not alone in face and body, he had aged in soul; to preserve the heart youthful to old age, as some say, is difficult, and almost absurd: he may feel content who has not lost faith in good, steadfastness of will, desire for activity.... Lavrétzky had a right to feel satisfied: he had become a really fine agriculturist, he had really learned to till the soil, and he had toiled not for himself alone; in so far as he had been able, he had freed from care and established on a firm foundation the existence of his serfs.

Lavrétzky emerged from the house into the garden: he seated himself on the familiar bench—and in that dear spot, in the face of the house, where he had, on the last occasion, stretched out his hands in vain to the fatal cup in which seethes and sparkles the wine of delight,—he, a solitary, homeless wanderer,—to the sounds of the merry cries of the younger generation which had already superseded him,—took a survey of his life. His heart was sad, but not heavy and not very sorrowful: he had nothing which he had need to regret or be ashamed of. "Play on, make merry, grow on, young forces,"—he thought, and there was no bitterness in his meditations:—"life lies before you, and it will be easier for you to live: you will not be compelled, as we have been, to seek your road, to struggle, to fall, and to rise to your feet again amid the gloom; we have given ourselves great trouble, that we might remain whole,— and how many of us have failed in that!—but you must do deeds, work,—and the blessing of old fellows like me be upon you. But all that remains for me, after to-day, after these emotions, is to make my final reverence to you, and, although with sadness, yet without envy, without any dark feelings, to say, in view of the end, in view of God who is awaiting me: 'Long live solitary old age! Burn thyself out, useless life!'"

Lavrétzky rose softly, and softly went away; no one noticed him, no one detained him; the merry cries resounded more loudly than ever in the garden behind the green, dense wall of lofty lindens. He seated himself in his tarantás, and ordered the coachman to drive home, and not to press the horses hard.

"And the end?" perchance some dissatisfied reader will say. "And what became of Lavrétzky? of Liza?" But what can one say about people who are still alive, but who have already departed from the earthly arena,—why revert to them? They say that Lavrétzky paid a visit to that distant convent where Liza had hidden herself— and saw her. In going from one choir to the other, she passed close to him—passed with the even, hurriedly-submissive gait of a nun— and did not cast a glance at him; only the lashes of the eye which was turned toward him trembled almost imperceptibly, and her

166

haggard face was bowed a little lower than usual—and the fingers of her clasped hands, interlaced with her rosary, were pressed more tightly to one another. What did they both think,—what did they both feel? Who knows? Who shall say? There are moments in life, there are feelings ... we can only indicate them,—and pass by.

www.ingramcontent.com/pod-product-compliance
Lightning Source LLC
Chambersburg PA
CBHW011506170626
46812CB00008B/2988